Dark Lava
A Lei Crime Novel

Dark Lava

A Lei Crime Novel

By

Toby Neal

Chapter 1

Anger is cruel and fury overwhelming,
but who can stand before jealousy?
Proverbs 27:4

The worst things always seem to happen at night, even in Hawaii. Lieutenant Michael Stevens stood in front of the defaced rock wall, hands on hips as he surveyed the damage. A chipped hole gaped raw as a torn-out tooth where the petroglyph, a rare rock art carving, should have been.

"I keep watch on the *heiau*." The witness, sturdy as a fireplug, glared up at Stevens from under the ledge of an overhanging brow. "I live across da street. I come check 'em every day, pick up trash, li'dat. Last night I hear something, like—one motor. I was sleeping, but I wake up 'cause it goes on. Then I see a light ovah here." He spoke in agitated pidgin, hands waving.

"What's your name, sir?" Stevens dug a spiral notebook out of his back jeans pocket, along with a stub of pencil tied to it with twine. He knew it was old-school. Many officers were using PDAs and tablets these days—but he liked the ease and confidentiality of his chicken-scratch code.

"Manuel Okapa. Our family, we keep watch on the *heiau*. This—so shame this!" Okapa spat beside their feet in disgust. "I like kill whoever did this!"

Stevens waited a beat. He caught Okapa's eye, shiny and hard as a polished *kukui* nut. "Sure you want to say that to a cop?" Stevens asked.

Okapa spat again in answer, unfazed. "I wish I brought my hunting rifle over here and blew 'em away. But the light go out, and the noise stop. I thought someone was maybe dropping off something. Sometimes the poor families that no can afford the dumps, they drop their broken-kine rubbish here. They know I take 'em away."

Stevens noted Okapa's threats and disclosure of a gun in his notebook for future reference. He turned a bit to take in the scene. The *heiau*, a site sacred to Hawaiian culture, was situated on a promontory overlooking the ocean, separated from Okapa's dilapidated cottage by the busy two-lane Hana Highway. Even this early, a steady stream of rental cars swished by them, on their way to experience the lush, waterfall-marked Road to Hana.

"What kind of trash do they leave? Appliances?"

"Yeah, li'dat." Okapa squatted down in front of the wound in the rock. His stubby brown fingers traced the hole, tender and reverent. "I heard this kine thing was happening on Oahu but nevah thought we get 'em over here."

"Looks like it was taken out with some sort of hand-held jackhammer," Stevens said, squatting beside the man. Okapa's touching of the rock's surface would have disrupted any fingerprints, but it was too late now. He took out his smartphone and shot several pictures of the defaced stone, inadvertently catching one of Okapa's hands, gentle on the rock's wound. "Did you see anything else missing? Disturbed?"

"Come. We go look." Okapa stood up, and Stevens glanced back at the blue-and-white Maui Police Department cruiser parked close to them, his Bronco just behind it off the busy highway. One of his new trainees, Brandon Mahoe, had responded to the defacement call and had immediately contacted Stevens as his superior to come investigate. Mahoe was Maui born and raised, and he'd immediately appreciated that the stealing of a petroglyph was more than ordinary property damage. The young man, hands on his duty belt, looked questioningly at Stevens.

"Stay here and don't let anyone pull over," Stevens said. "Find something to cover the damage for now— some branches or something. We don't want to attract attention to this yet."

Stevens's mind was already racing ahead to the press coverage this would draw, potentially connecting this crime with a string of looted *heiaus* on Oahu. The pressure would be on MPD as soon as the community caught wind of this outrage.

He followed Okapa's squat form, feeling overly tall as he towered beside the shorter man. He'd found his height sometimes provoked defensive reactions in smaller local people, and his wife's partner and friend, Pono Kaihale, had given him a frank talk on how to interact with the locals more effectively. "Don't stand too close and look down at them—better to stand side by side. Not a lot of eye contact, because that's seen as challenging. Be prepared to disclose some personal information about who you are, where you're from, and try to find some common connecting place, family or history. Tell 'em you're married to a Hawaii girl if they give you a hard time."

As if reading these thoughts, Okapa tossed over his shoulder, "How long you been here?"

"Two years, Maui. Big Island and Kauai before that," Stevens replied. *"Maui no ka oi.* Maui is the best."

Okapa's gapped teeth showed in a brief smile. "As how."

Apparently he'd hit the right note, because Okapa's shoulders relaxed a bit. Every island had its pride, Stevens had discovered.

They followed a tiny path through waist-high vegetation. Thick bunchy grass, ti leaf, and several hala trees, their umbrella-like structures providing pools of shade. "I used to cut da plants back, keep it nice here. But then I see the tourists always pulling over to the side, trampling in here with their cameras. So I let 'em grow, and less come here. Only the hula *halaus* come out for dance. This is one dance *heiau*."

"Oh. I didn't know there were different kinds. Anything you can tell me would be helpful."

"Yeah. Get some for worship da gods, like the big one in Wailuku. This one for dance. *Halau* is one small-kine school with a *kumu,* teacher. That *kumu* leads and trains dancers in the group. This place was used to teach and worship with hula by the *halaus*."

They reached a wide area, ringed by red, green, and striped varieties of ti leaf growing taller than Stevens had ever seen. The layout was an open area of flat stones ringed by a wall of stacked ones. He'd noticed Hawaii's monuments were simple, made of materials naturally occurring, and without the oral traditions of the people and the movement to reclaim the culture, much history would have been lost and the *heiaus* themselves swallowed back into the land.

Beyond the large, rough circle of stones, the cobalt ocean glittered in the distance, hala trees surrounding the edge of the cliff and bracketing the view with their Dr. Seuss–like silhouettes. Stevens thought the hala and ti plants must have been placed there deliberately because he knew Hawaiians wove the long, fibrous hala leaves into basketry and matting and made dance costumes with ti.

"Auwe!" Okapa cried, pointing. On the far side of the *heiau* were three large stone slabs, and the one in the middle had a raw, chipped-out crater. "They took the other one!"

Stevens followed the distraught guardian, thumbing the camera icon on his phone. He held up a hand to stop Okapa as the man bent to touch the stone.

"Let me dust this one for prints." Stevens unhooked his radio from his belt. "Mahoe, bring my kit from the Bronco. Over."

"Ten-four," Mahoe said.

"Tell me who knows about this place," Stevens said, hanging the radio back on his belt and taking pictures of the stones and the surrounding area.

Okapa's rage was evident. He muttered under his breath as he stomped across the stones, ripping out weeds in the dance area. He looked up with a fierce frown.

"Everyone. Because of that damn book."

"What book?"

"Maui's Secrets. One stupid *haole* wen' collect all our

sacred places and put 'em in that book. Now everybody can buy it and find whatever. I like beef that guy myself."

Stevens narrowed his eyes. "Where can I find a copy?"

Okapa spat. "ABC Store. Anywhere get 'em. I like burn all those books."

Stevens wrote down the title just as Mahoe burst into view at a trot, carrying Stevens's crime kit. The young man's square, earnest face blanched at the sight of the second desecration. *"Auwe!"* he cried.

Stevens looked down from Mahoe's dismay, mentally filing that expression away. Maybe his wife, Lei, could help him learn how to say it right. The exclamation seemed to capture a wealth of grief and outrage.

"I need to dust for prints and photograph this area," he told Mahoe. "You can watch me work the first rock, and then I'll have you do the other two. We need to pay special attention to the tool marks. Who knows? Maybe whoever it was didn't wear gloves. Mr. Okapa, why don't you stand in one place and look carefully all around. You can't tramp around, disturbing the site, but if you could just look for anything out of place, that would be a help."

Okapa folded his arms, still muttering under his breath, but began looking carefully around the *heiau*.

Stevens flipped the clasps of his metal crime kit and opened it, exposing tools and supplies. He snapped on gloves and handed a pair to Mahoe, gesturing the young man over. He leaned in close to whisper to him.

"Remember. At a scene, you try to maintain the three Cs: care, custody, and control. Okapa could touch, move, or destroy something by walking around, but giving him something to do that doesn't contaminate the scene is also important. It keeps him engaged with us positively." Mahoe nodded. Stevens went on, pointing to the canisters of powder nested in foam. "This is probably just review from training, but when choosing powder, you want to pick a color that will contrast with whatever you're dusting. These stones are a dark gray. Which one do you think I should use?" he asked Mahoe, testing.

"White."

"Good." Stevens lifted the soft-bristled brush, dipped it in the powder, and twisted it to load the brush. Then he spun the powder in gentle twirling motions over the rock face.

This was not the porous black lava stone that much of the *heiau* was made of; these three stones were the much harder bluestone often quarried for decorative rock walls. The surface held the powder well, the face of the rock gently sloping and weathered by the elements.

"Mr. Okapa, what did the petroglyph here depict?" Stevens called as the *heiau*'s guardian stared around, still glowering.

"Was a dancer with one rainbow on top." Okapa gestured, demonstrating the way the stick figure stone carving would have been drawn. "That one at the front marked the *heiau*. It had three dancers."

"Why do you think someone would steal these?" Stevens asked, still spreading the powder until it covered the entire rock face.

"I've been watching the news about the other defacements on Oahu." Mahoe was the one to answer. "They think some underground collector is hiring people to take them."

"How much would something like this be worth?" Stevens took out his bulb blower, squeezing gently to blow the powder off the rough surface.

"There are not that many early Hawaiian artifacts, period," Mahoe said. "Every petroglyph is priceless and can't be replaced."

"As why it so bad this wen' happen," Okapa said. "'Cause this *heiau* only had two. And these were good ones. We were so proud of them."

Stevens blew more air on the rock, and white powder drifted down onto the red dirt soil beneath like misplaced snow.

"I think I see something. A partial," Stevens pointed out to Mahoe. "It's over on the side. Maybe there were two people digging out the carving, or one of them rested his hand on the side of the rock for leverage."

Already they could see there was nothing on the face of the rock. Stevens handed the brush and powder to Mahoe and let the young man dust the sides and top of the stone and the ones on either side of it.

Several prints picked up, all around the edges of the defaced rock. Stevens squinted at the prints, held his hand up. "I think whoever was using the drill or tool grabbed on to the rock for support. These prints look smeared because of the pressure, but I'll try the gel tape and see if we can lift some and get a good impression."

He unrolled gel tape and pressed it lightly over the print, pulling away carefully. He did several and then set the tape in a plastic case to photograph with a scanner back at the station.

"Let's see you do one." He handed the roll of tape to Mahoe. "I'm going to take photos of the tool marks." They worked quietly side by side as Stevens set the ruler against the rock face and shot photos of the tool marks, then mixed up a batch of rubber dental putty, spreading it into the scars on the rock. It hardened in moments, and Stevens peeled it up, sliding it into an evidence bag as Mahoe finished taking his impressions.

"Eh, Lieutenant!"

Stevens looked up at Okapa's shout, toward the gesturing man. Okapa was pointing at a hole in the ground on the other side of a lantana bush.

"They took a stone from here. Was one oval stone brought up from the ocean."

Stevens joined him. "How do you know what stone it was?"

Okapa just fixed him with a belligerent stare. "I know every rock in this place."

Stevens took out his smartphone and shot a picture of the hole. "How big was it?"

"Big enough to need two people to carry it."

Stevens made a note on his spiral pad. His eyes roamed the area, and he spotted a gleam of something in the grass. He squatted, found a beer can. Using the tips of his gloved hands, he picked it up by the rim and put it in an evidence bag. "Mahoe, get the camera and shoot the area. Follow a grid pattern—remember your training." Mahoe hurried to follow directions.

"You think they wen' drink the beer here?" Okapa said, his bushy brows drawing together. "Drinking beer while they stealing our sacred carvings! I like kill 'em! Pro'lly was one stupid *haole* with no respect. No Hawaiian would do this!"

Stevens looked up at Okapa. He could feel the other man's rage, and he stood deliberately, uncoiling to his own full height, without breaking eye contact. "You want to be careful about what you say, Mr. Okapa. It's just a beer can. We don't know anything about it."

Okapa whirled and stomped off through the underbrush toward the road.

Mahoe rejoined Stevens. "I took off everything I could find." The young man had packed up the crime kit too. Stevens glanced at the carefully stowed evidence collected. "Good job. What can you tell me about our volatile friend here?"

A flush stained Mahoe's neck. "He one *kupuna*—an elder. He…"

Stevens could see the struggle the young man had in disclosing anything negative about a respected man in his culture. He remembered something from Pono's cultural tips and looked away from Mahoe, turning to align his body with the officer's, standing side by side. He addressed his remarks out over the *heiau*. "I'm worried about Mr. Okapa. I don't think some half-cocked vigilante justice is going to help the situation. I don't like the idea of Okapa having a gun."

"I know." Mahoe blew out a breath, and Stevens could sense his relief that a superior officer wasn't suspecting the respected *kupuna*. "I'm worried about him, too. He has a reputation for anger—that's why his wife left—but this *heiau* is his life. I think he'll cool down. I'll talk to him."

"Good." Stevens moved out toward the narrow,

overgrown path. "As terrible as this is, the last thing we need is some kind of violent racially-motivated outburst when we haven't even identified a suspect." He paused. "Speaking of—what is this scene telling you? I want to hear what you've been able to assess from it."

Mahoe swiveled, hands on hips, imitating Stevens's stance. "I think there were at least two in the crew. They had proper tools, came prepared. They knew exactly what they wanted, from what I can tell, and they worked fast, according to Mr. Okapa, which means they probably came ahead of time during the day to case where the artifacts were."

"Very good." Stevens clapped the young man on the shoulder and set off down the narrow, overgrown path with Mahoe following. "Further, I think they were professionals in removal technique. I could see very little waste or fracture on the rock faces, and believe it or not, those hand jacks are hard to operate. So my sense is that these are pros procuring something for a buyer, which means they're probably connected with the Oahu desecrations."

"We have to stop this," Mahoe muttered. "Whatever it takes."

They emerged beside the cruiser and the Bronco. Okapa had already crossed the now-busy highway, and Stevens could see him glowering at them from a chair on the front porch of his weathered, tin-roofed cottage.

"Why don't you go take his official statement?" Stevens said. "Give him a chance to tell the tale and cool down."

"Yes, sir." Mahoe looked both ways and trotted across the road, already taking out his notebook.

Stevens beeped open the Bronco and stowed the crime kit and evidence bags in the back. Getting into the SUV, he looked over at the tableau across the street. Mahoe was seated beside Okapa, one hand on the older man's shoulder, head down, listening, as the older man gesticulated.

Turning the key, Stevens hoped this was the last he was going to see of Okapa.

Haiku Station was a small, former dry-goods store across a potholed parking lot from a large Quonset-style former pineapple-packing plant that had been converted into a shopping center. Stevens had a small crew under his command—one other detective, four patrol officers, and Mahoe, a new recruit.

Stevens felt good about how Mahoe was coming along. The benefits of nurturing talent had been drummed into him by his first commanding officer in Los Angeles, along with the fact that all the training in the world couldn't make up for a recruit without the "gut instinct" for police work.

Stevens lifted a hand briefly to the watch officer on duty as he passed through the open room where his team's desks were situated, heading for the back room where his office was located. He hadn't seen his wife since yesterday—Lei was at a daylong training in a wilderness area, learning ordnance retrieval, and he missed her.

He supposed that was the word to apply to a feeling like a limb had been amputated, like something vital was gone. He wondered how he was going to deal with it when she left for California in a few weeks for a two-week multi-agency intensive training on explosive devices.

He logged into his e-mail and frowned at one from his ex-wife, Anchara. He hadn't seen her since the day she left him. They kept in touch via e-mail, but she didn't communicate often.

Dear Michael, I have something I need to tell you. Something I should have told you a long time ago. Can we meet in the next week or so? It's better done in person. In friendship, Anchara.

She always ended her e-mails that way—"in friendship." Anchara had always been unknowable to him, walled off, even when he'd tried his best to break down her emotional and physical barriers. When they'd started out, he'd been determined to really make it work, determined to get over Lei once and for all, and they'd been attracted to each other. In bed she had a feral quality, wide brown eyes opaque, her body flexible and tireless. Still, no matter what he tried, his best efforts failed to bring her satisfaction.

Not that she'd ever let on. Still, he knew, and it ate at him. He'd felt the weight of his mistake in marrying her like an anvil on his chest every time they had sex. They'd talked about it once, afterward.

"Why can't you come?" he'd finally asked, playing with one of the black satin ribbons of her hair, the sweat of their effort drying in the light Maui breeze.

"I did." She widened those huge eyes, batted them at him. "I'm sure the neighbors agree."

"You pretended to."

That shadow that was always there, separating them, appeared again. It contained both her past as a sex slave on a cruise ship and Lei, who'd always hold his heart.

"I want to," she whispered. "But I don't know if I can. With anyone."

Stevens had been trying hard to keep his mind off Lei and give the marriage a real shot, but Anchara had moved ahead with the divorce without his knowledge the minute her green card for United States residency was imminent.

Stevens decided not to respond to her e-mail today. Whatever it was could wait. He had no great eagerness to see her again—Lei was the woman he missed.

He phoned Lei even as he twirled the dial on the

evidence locker in the corner of his office.

"Hey." Her slightly husky voice conjured her instantly before him—tilted brown eyes sleepy, curls disordered, that slender body he was always hungry for, warm in their bed. "You woke me up—I just got home and we were up most of the night."

"Wish I was there waking you up some other way." He stacked the bag with the beer can and the labeled plastic boxes holding the gel tape on the shelf and picked up the clipboard dangling from a string to log in the items.

"Me too." He heard Lei yawn, pictured her olive-skinned, toned arms stretching, her small round breasts distending the thin sleep tee as her body arched. He felt himself respond to the rustle of her tiny movements in a way that wasn't appropriate for work, and he gritted his teeth. "So when are you going to be home?" she asked.

"Usual time. Got called out early—a *heiau* desecration." He sketched a few details—as a fellow officer, she often helped with his cases, and he hers.

"That sucks so bad." Lei yawned again. "I'm too fuzzy to make sense. I'm going to turn the phone off and try to get some sleep."

"I'll see you later. I love you," he said. He'd said it to her every day since their wedding a month ago.

"I love you, too. Come home soon. I'll keep the bed warm." She clicked off.

Lei Texeira. Smart, intuitive, neurotic as hell. Scary brave—and as necessary to him as breathing.

Stevens set the phone down, trying not to think of her under the silky sheets in that skimpy tank top, or that he was doing his best to get her pregnant. Trying not to think about the spooky threat that had come against them on their honeymoon, always somewhere on his mind. Well, she'd have the alarm on, and their Rottweiler, Keiki, on the bed with her...

A knock at the doorjamb. He looked up, irritated. "Yes?"

Mahoe came in and shut the door. "I gotta tell you something, sir."

Chapter 2

L ei turned the phone off and set it on the bedside table.
Keiki, monitoring the whole exchange, set her big
square head back on her paws, brown eyes on her mistress.

"It's okay, girl." Lei patted the bed beside her. "I know
you don't like it when we aren't both here."

Keiki crawled up beside her, and Lei scratched
behind the dog's silky triangle ears, her fingertips playing
with the brown eyebrow patches above the Rottweiler's
expressive eyes.

She shut her eyes as she tried to fall back asleep, but
memories played, of the improvised explosive device
detection exercises she and her partner, Abe Torufu, had
participated in at the back of a remote valley.

They'd been going full bore for twenty-four hours,
tracking mock explosive devices hidden in various
sections of the wilderness area, learning to spot mines,
pipe bombs, even the crude gas-fueled Molotov-cocktail-
style explosive threats they were likely to encounter on
the job. The one-day intensive had been put together with
Homeland Security, the fire department, army reservists,

and police officers as part of a joint task force training with personnel from all over the islands. The trainers had turned them loose in teams with their detection and disarming equipment, and the team who found and disabled the most devices won.

She and Torufu hadn't won.

Lei frowned, remembering the moment the imitation IED they'd discovered, a crude pipe bomb rigged with nails, had "exploded," a click that activated pulsing red beacons on the chest badges they wore. It had been both humiliating and scary to even be "virtually" blown to bits. She decided the less Stevens knew about her new duties, the better.

Stevens. She draped an arm over her eyes, smiling a little at their conversation, at the timbre of his voice, which told her how much he wanted her. He'd said he'd tell her he loved her every day after they were married, and he had. Her body woke up a little, remembering his touch, wishing he was with her.

Lei wondered how long their passion would last now that they'd married. Their relationship was already more deep and layered than she had ever known could exist, intensified by the fact that they'd decided to start a family. That decision seemed to have added poignancy to their lovemaking.

Why had she been so afraid of getting married? She couldn't remember now. Maybe that's how it would be when she was a mother—her fears would be drowned in the actual experience, something it was impossible to anticipate.

But how would this affect her bomb squad training? She was pretty sure, if she did get pregnant, she'd be suspended from duties. She was afraid to ask her commanding officer, Captain Omura.

It was better not to think about all that right now. She rolled over and put her pillow over her head.

Lei eventually woke in the afternoon to Keiki's persistent licking of her protruding foot. She sat up and groaned at the pain from a million tiny bruises and muscle exertions caused by the last twenty-four hours spent climbing and crawling through brush. "Okay, girl, I'll let you out."

She got up and walked through the modest little house, yawning. She scooped frizzing curls off of her forehead, combing them into place with her fingers as she deactivated the alarm and unlocked the dog door that led into the backyard. Keiki trotted out to do her business.

Lei went into the kitchen and over to the coffeemaker. She spotted a note protruding from under the unit. *Just push the button. It's all tanked up for you. In case I don't see you today—I love you.* Stevens had signed the bold, block-printed note with a smiley face.

Lei folded the note into a little triangle, an old habit,

and slid it into her pocket, smiling. She pushed the coffeemaker button, and the unit gurgled to life.

Time for her daily call to her Aunty Rosario, ill with pancreatic cancer. Lei went back to the bedroom, picked up the cell phone, and pressed a speed-dial button worn from use.

"Hey, Sweets." Her aunt's voice was rough. "How's your day going?"

"Hi, Aunty. It's just starting. I was catching up on some sleep from a training exercise. How about you?"

Her aunty had refused treatment for the cancer. She'd gone downhill slower than the doctors had predicted, but some days she was weak and in pain and spent the day in bed. When Rosario was feeling better, she went to work as usual at the Hawaiian Food Place, her restaurant in San Rafael, California.

"Still kicking," Rosario said. "Tell me about that training you were going to. It has to be more interesting than hearing about me lying around in bed here and how many ounces of food I was able to keep down."

"Well, I can't tell you much. It's classified. But I've been getting a workout." Lei looked ruefully down at the scratches on her hands from wires and vegetation; she examined the bruises on her arms and legs, too. "Just another day with Maui Police Department."

She was enjoying learning the different kinds of

triggers, timers, and explosives. Torufu was patient with her mechanical ineptitude, and his large, mellow presence calmed her in those tense minutes when confronted with whatever unknown apparatus they were working on.

So far they hadn't actually worked together on a threat in the field; Torufu went alone on calls for now. He'd volunteered to redo all the training with her so he could "learn to work with a partner," but she knew it was so that he could see how well she did in the line of duty with so much at stake.

"How's my dad?" Lei asked. Rosario's main caregiver was her brother, Lei's father, Wayne Texeira.

"He's right here. Why don't you say hi?" Rosario handed the phone to Lei's father, and his familiar voice brought a smile to her face.

"Hey, Sweets."

"It's funny how you guys keep calling me that. You know I'm not that sweet."

"That's why we like it." They both laughed. They'd had that conversation before. Repeating it built little rituals in a relationship that had lost a lot of time due to Wayne's lengthy incarceration for drug dealing and manslaughter.

"I've been praying for something," Wayne said. Her father had got his minister's license just before Lei's wedding, and he'd been the one to officiate at the beachside ceremony. "Praying I'm going to be a grandpa soon."

"Dad," Lei said in a warning voice. She put her fingers on her forehead, pressed. Her dilemma with the bomb squad lurked at the back of her eyeballs.

"We don't have that much time," Wayne whispered. She could tell he was walking away to where her aunt couldn't hear him speaking. "She's taking a bad turn again, honey. That news would do so much for her. I know she'd try to hang on to see the baby."

Lei pressed harder on her eyes, her stomach knotting. "I'm not doing anything to stop it," she whispered. "But it hasn't happened."

A long silence. "Well, it's the working on it that's the fun part," her father said with fake cheer.

"Please, let's not talk about this," Lei said. "I'm worried about Aunty enough, and it will seriously mess me up at work. I'll tell you if there's any news—but I don't want to have this conversation again, Dad." Her words came out more forcefully than she'd meant them to.

"I'm so rude. I'm sorry," Wayne said, his voice contrite. "I'll shut up about it. Now, what's with this bomb squad thing? Did you volunteer for this? Doesn't seem like something Stevens would like his new bride doing."

"It's none of his business what job I'm doing," Lei

flared, feeling heat fan the back of her neck. Her dad
was pushing all her buttons today. "I was assigned to
the squad, but it's always a voluntary position. I could
decline, but I happen to think it's a challenging and
important role."

"Of course it is," Wayne said, the contrition replaced
by a hard note. "It's just that you're always getting hurt on
the job. I can't imagine…" His voice faltered.

"You know what, Dad? It's none of anybody's
business, and the baby thing too. Put Aunty back on,
please."

Lei rubbed the rough white gold medallion at her
throat as her dad silently handed the phone back to Aunty
Rosario.

"Did I hear your father say you're on the bomb squad
now?" Rosario's voice was thready with alarm, and the
knot in Lei's stomach twisted. She had been keeping that
from Aunty, hoping she'd never have to know.

"Just doing some cross-training so I'm more prepared
for any kind of emergency," Lei fibbed. "Boring stuff.
How's Aunty Momi doing?" She was able to deflect any
further questions from her aunt, but she hung up feeling
agitated.

What she needed was a run. She got into running
clothes and was on the narrow, winding jungle road with
its grassy shoulders, Keiki on a leash beside her, in a

matter of minutes.

Moving, sweating, the metronome of her steps calming her heartbeat, she was able to push worries about the job, irritation at her dad, and ever-present grief about Aunty Rosario to the back of her mind and just be in her body.

"Come, sit." Stevens gestured to the two hard plastic chairs in front of his desk. Mahoe advanced into the office and sat down. "I stashed the evidence we collected in my temporary safe, but I'd like to process it with you as soon as I get a little caught up with the duty roster and such. How did your talk with Okapa go?"

"That's the thing." The young officer slid into one of the chairs and rubbed his big hands up and down his navy-clad thighs. "He's really fired up. Said there's a group forming to guard the *heiaus*—and they're going to be armed."

Stevens sat back in his office chair and swiveled a little as he steepled his fingers. "Is Okapa in charge of it?"

"Fortunately, no. It was already underway in response to what's been happening on Oahu, and Okapa had already volunteered for it, but someone in Kahului is in charge."

"Well, there's nothing wrong with citizens forming a sort of 'neighborhood watch' for something like that," Stevens said. "But they should be armed with cell phones to call for help."

"I wen' tell him dat." Mahoe blew out a breath, irritated into pidgin. "But he no like listen."

"Did you get any other names? Contact info of the people pulling this together?"

"He wouldn't tell me nothing. Got all stubborn."

"Okay. Thanks for talking with him." Stevens projected the calm authority that he knew the young man needed by leaning forward, giving good eye contact, and lowering his jaw. "Why don't you get started working on the evidence we collected this morning?" He turned, unlocked the safe, and handed Mahoe the various marked evidence bags. "Start with scanning the fingerprints and running them against anyone in the system."

"Yes, sir." Mahoe rose quickly and took the evidence bags. Stevens felt a twinge of worry that the green young officer might mess something up with the print processing—it would be better if he monitored everything, but he had to get his reports in. "In fact, why don't you get Ferreira to help you." Joshua Ferreira was their only detective at the moment, a barrel-chested old pro. "Pick his brain about Okapa and his vigilante group while you're at it. He knows everyone around here."

Stevens could see relief in Mahoe's widened eyes. He could tell the young man wanted his boss to trust him and give him responsibility, but not too much too soon. "Yes, sir." Mahoe left with the evidence bags.

Stevens picked up the phone and called Kahului Station. "Captain Omura, please." As he asked for the island's commanding officer, his mind filled with a picture of the tiny Japanese powerhouse who'd earned the nickname Steel Butterfly by fighting her way to the top of a male-dominated workplace through sheer excellence at police work.

"Lieutenant. What's up?" Omura's voice was brisk. He could almost see her behind an immaculate desk, the phone against her sleek bobbed hair, her eyes on her computer, and shiny red nails tapping the keyboard.

"I won't keep you long, sir, but I wanted to apprise you immediately that we've had a pretty bad *heiau* desecration. I'm concerned it's going to happen again, and that it might be connected to the incidents on Oahu." He outlined the situation briefly.

"Get all the info into the case file and send it to me immediately. I think I'll want to include this in the daily island-wide briefing."

"Speaking of island-wide, there's some sort of vigilante group forming." He brought her up to date on the intel Mahoe had gathered. "The Hawaiian community is going to be up in arms about this, and we need to have a response planned."

"Let's see if we can organize a team that knows where

these sites are, and get some extra manpower to cover
them. Even better that we get proactive immediately
and show support for the group. If we work with them,
get involved with them, it's less likely someone will go
off half-cocked and beat up a tourist wandering onto a
heiau," Omura said. They coordinated some more details,
including a teleconference later in the afternoon with the
detectives on the Oahu case, and Omura wrapped up the
call. "Hope Lei gets some sleep today. They worked 'em
hard in that training exercise in Iao Valley. She and Torufu
didn't do too well."

"What do you mean?" Stevens ran a hand through
his hair, immediately agitated at the mention of Lei's
bomb squad duties—her recklessness on cases had caused
him loss of sleep and temper many times. He'd loudly
opposed her change in duties, to no avail. "What does it
mean they didn't do too well? That sounds ominous."

Omura snorted a laugh. "I'll leave that to your wife
to describe. When I assigned her to IED, I knew you
wouldn't like it. Fortunately, that's not my concern." She
hung up briskly.

Stevens hung up more slowly. He'd been put in his
place, reminded who was boss, and that both he and Lei
answered to Omura.

That didn't mean he had to like it.

Chapter 3

Stevens was barely done putting the case file with photos and notes together for Omura when his phone rang again. He picked it up automatically, still typing. "Lieutenant Stevens."

"Aloha, Michael. This is Wendy Watanabe from KHIN 2 News. How are you today?" The TV reporter's voice was bright and cheery. She dressed and acted like a perky parakeet, he thought, until she got you where she wanted you—then she was pure tiger. He and Lei had learned the hard way to respect Watanabe's skills at pursuing a story.

"Lieutenant Stevens," he said gruffly, correcting her overly familiar use of his name. Might as well establish a tone. He looked around to see whom he could dress down later for not running interference on the call, but the watch officer was away from his desk, which explained how she'd gotten through.

"Okay. Lieutenant Stevens, then. That tells me you're not happy about having me call to ask about the recent *heiau* desecration in Haiku?"

"Ask your questions." Stevens's voice was cold. His modus operandi with reporters was to volunteer nothing unless he had to.

"I'm taping you, for the record. Tell me about the destruction you found this morning at the *heiau*."

"I don't hear a question there."

"All right, then." Watanabe's cheery tone was giving way to annoyance. "We have had a report that two petroglyphs were chiseled out of a sacred dance *heiau* on the Road to Hana. Can you confirm?"

Stevens shut his eyes, put his finger and thumb against the bridge of his nose and squeezed. It was a matter of public record, anyway, but the news going out wasn't going to allow them much time to get their special team in place, let alone follow up on any trace he'd collected this morning. Stevens softened his tone. "Listen. Wendy. Can you hold off on this story until the ten o'clock news at least? We're trying to move fast and hard on this to protect the *heiaus*. If you run this right away, I'm concerned our leads will get leaked and the community will overreact."

A long pause. Stevens could almost hear Watanabe's clever brain working. "Tit for tat," the reporter said. "What can you give me to boost the story?"

"Well," Stevens hedged.

"Seriously, Michael? You want me to sit on this

without giving me something?"

"Okay, I will." He paused, drew a breath, and blew it out. "Another reason we're concerned is that the job appears to be done by pros. That infers it's connected to the Oahu cases."

Watanabe snorted, a sound like a kitten sneezing. "That's obvious. Give me something more. Like a person of interest you're looking for."

"Too soon for that, though I do have a nugget for you. Who gave you the tip about the *heiau?*"

"I can't reveal my sources."

"We're at an impasse, then." Stevens went back to hard.

"Okay. I don't have a name, but the call came in an older man's voice. Rough pidgin."

Okapa.

"Thanks. For that, and for holding off, here's another reason we're worried about press coverage inflaming the public—there's a vigilante group forming to protect the *heiaus.* We're worried that citizens taking the law into their own hands could backfire." Stevens spoke carefully, aware he was being recorded and might well be quoted on TV.

"That's a good lead," Watanabe said, her voice going perky again. "What's the police response to a vigilante group?"

"Island-wide, as a department, we hope to work with the citizens' group to protect Maui's most sacred places."

"Nice sound bite for tonight's ten o'clock report," Watanabe said, her tone acid.

"Thanks for your cooperation with the Maui Police Department." Stevens's tone matched hers. He hung up.

An hour later, Stevens pulled his older Bronco up to the locked gate of his and Lei's little cottage in Haiku. Keiki, their Rottweiler, trotted back and forth in front of the gate, whining an eager greeting. He put the SUV in neutral and got out, opening the gate and giving Keiki an ear rub. "Eat anybody today, girl?" The dog licked his hand in answer, and he pointed to the porch. She turned and trotted up onto the worn wooden steps, turning to plunk her cropped behind on the top step and watching as he pulled the truck in and locked the gate behind it.

A hassle, to have the fence and gate, but they'd been attacked in their home more than once. Making that a little harder was never a bad idea.

Stevens's energy was sapped by the long day: processing the evidence from the *heiau* (prints not in the system), departmental meeting in Kahului organizing the *heiau* protection task force, and a long conference call with Detective Marcus Kamuela and the other HPD staff on Oahu already working on the desecrations on their sister island.

As he came up the steps, the light inside the kitchen outlined the slender figure of his wife. She was stirring something on the stove, her tousled curls gilded by the overhead light. The sight brought a draft of energy back into him.

He was usually the one home first, cooking. "I'm marking this on the calendar," Stevens said, walking across the room to take her in his arms from behind, rubbing his cheek on the crown of her head. "Lei Texeira cooking. I might have a heart attack."

She elbowed him in the sternum even as she snuggled against him. "I can work a can opener. Got some chili going. And cornbread. Aunty gave me the recipe over the phone."

"This I gotta taste."

She pointed down. "You're still wearing your shoes. And your gun." But she turned in his arms to kiss him, and that kiss promised more later.

Stevens went back to the front door, unlaced the lightweight hiking boots he wore for work. Sometimes, even after years in Hawaii, he forgot the customs that people here kept as a matter of course, like not wearing shoes in the house.

"Did you get enough sleep?" he asked, unstrapping his shoulder holster while heading for the back bedroom. He hung his weapon, still holstered, from the headboard of their king-sized bed. Lei's was slung across her side. Married law enforcement, sleeping under their guns. There was something endearing about it—or maybe he just liked being married. He went back into the kitchen.

"I did get enough sleep. Technically." Lei yawned, still stirring. "I'm sore, though. They worked us hard for a solid twenty-four hours." She tapped the spoon on the side of the pan, then opened the oven. "This is just about ready."

He cracked the top on a Longboard Lager and sat down at the little table. "I hear you and Torufu didn't win the competition."

"Who told you that?" She bent at the waist, looking at him over her shoulder. She looked unbelievably sexy with that ass, covered by a pair of worn jeans, pointed at him and a potholder in her hand. He tried to remember what he'd been saying.

"Never mind." He didn't want to get into it now, ruin the mood. "What can I do to help get this food on the table?"

The chili was edible and the cornbread truly delicious, slathered in butter and kiawe honey from a local apiary.

"I could get to like this." Stevens tilted his chair back on two legs, rolled the Longboard Lager bottle back and forth across his belly, eyes on his wife. He winked when he caught her eye. "Come here. I think you deserve a reward."

Lei laughed as she cleared the table. "I think *you* deserve the reward. This is the first time I've been home to make dinner since we got married."

"Yeah. And I mentioned I could get used to it."

She plucked the bottle out of his fingers, set it on the table, and straddled him on the chair. He never got tired of looking at her triangular face. Her brown, tilted eyes were where her half-Japanese heritage showed, bracketed by level brows. Those freckles he loved and she hated, tiny cinnamon dots across her nose. A big lush mouth, full of sass and sensuality. Curling hair, a-frizz at the moment, a halo the color of fallen leaves around her well-shaped skull.

Stevens knew exactly what that skull looked like, from when she'd shaved her head for a case. He didn't know any woman but Lei who would do that.

Stevens circled her lithe body with his arms, squeezing her hard, because he could never resist doing that, as if he could crush her close enough that they'd merge into one person. He buried his face in Lei's neck and inhaled her scent, feeling his hunger intensify. Her hands stroked through his hair, slid along his shoulders as he held her even closer, and he heard her whisper, "I love you so much it scares me."

"I know. Me too." His words were muffled against her

skin, which tasted a little like salty coconut as he nibbled her neck. "Let's go to bed." He stood up with her in his arms and took her there.

He settled Lei on the bed, and when she reached up to undo his shirt, he caught her hands, stretching her arms above her head and holding her wrists in one of his. "Close your eyes," he whispered into the curls beside the curve of her ear. "Just feel everything."

Lei smiled and shut her eyes obediently. She relaxed beneath him, her arms going soft. Her utter trust, something that had taken so long to win, brought a surge of powerful feeling flashing over him. He kissed that mouth, that luscious, expressive mouth, until it opened beneath his and gave up all its secrets.

He took her clothes off, lifting her shirt over her head but leaving it around her wrists, a mock restraint, as he loosened her jeans and shimmied them off her long runner's legs. He took a moment to enjoy looking at her body, trim and toned. The skin of her stomach was a subtle ivory the texture of silk, contrasting with her tanned arms and legs. Her small breasts were tender, pert rounds. That ass he adored was temporarily hidden, but knowing it was there, and that he'd get to it in due time, increased his desire.

She wasn't vain. She didn't know how beautiful she was. It was one more thing he loved about her. He leaned over and licked the tiny bowl of her navel, and she giggled.

Lei. Giggling.

He wished he could stop time, trap this memory in amber so that he could take it out and savor it again later. He tickled her just a little, causing her to gasp, and he turned it to kisses and she sighed, all the while leaving her hands where he'd put them, her eyes shut.

"You're perfect," he said, and watched her smile again, the smile of a child on Christmas morning, full of hope and excitement, her lips trembling a little as she made herself wait for him. For whatever he would do to her. That smile made him want to dive into her, cast aside control—but he had something more interesting in mind.

He tore his own clothing off in a few utilitarian gestures and lay down beside her. He used his lips and tongue and fingers to explore and awaken every inch of her body, beginning with the scars of old pain on her wrists, white lines that reminded him of lacy spiderwebs.

Her past. Her story. But not painful any longer. Those scars were dear to him, because they were part of her. He kissed and laved them with his tongue, nibbled them with his teeth, and she moaned.

He wanted to make sure she *felt* how beautiful she was, in every way he could show her, with his hands and lips and body. It went on a good long while.

In the end, they fell together into the deep sleep that

only follows ecstasy.

"You told me to get you up for the ten o'clock news."
Lei shook him awake. "I hate to wake you for someone
like Wendy Watanabe."

"I gotta see what she says about my case." Stevens
stood up from the bed, still naked, and Lei handed him
the pair of old LAPD sweats he slept in. He sucked in his
belly, conscious of her eyes on him as he pulled them on.

Lei gave him a little punch in the shoulder. "Not bad,
old man," she said. "Think I'll keep you."

"Hey. I can still wear you out." He tried to smack her
butt, but she darted ahead of him, laughing, into the living
room, where Wendy Watanabe dominated the screen in a
bright fuchsia suit.

Stevens sat on the couch, reaching for Lei and pulling
her against his side as he focused on the diminutive
reporter. "Maui's finest are hard at work on a case that
looks like an extension of the looting that has plagued
Oahu's sacred places."

Stevens frowned as they rolled clips of the looted
Oahu sites, feeling his stomach churn at how extensive
this case looked to be.

Wendy reappeared, and he noticed her lipstick was the
exact color as her suit, an annoying detail. He focused on
her words as a series of photos, dramatically enhanced,

showed the desecration of the hula *heiau* here on Maui.
"Someone has extracted these petroglyphs quickly and
professionally. Mr. Okapa, guardian of the *heiau*, is here
to tell us what went on in the early hours of this morning."

Okapa's rugged face filled the screen, his long gray
hair whipping in a breeze off the cliffs. He'd worn a cloth
kihei robe printed in traditional patterns, and a polished
kukui nut lei encircled his neck. He looked almost regal as
he recounted the story Stevens had heard from him earlier.
"I goin' tell you straight, anyone come here again going
get it!" Okapa finished his tale with a threatening wave of
a carved staff.

"Well, Mr. Okapa, we appreciate your passion." The
reporter covering the story for Maui held a microphone to
Okapa's mouth. "Tell us about the citizens' group you are
a part of."

"All these folks who care about the *heiaus*, we getting
together one watch patrol, da Heiau Hui." Okapa held up
a T-shirt in forest green with a graphic of a petroglyph
warrior on it, spear raised. "You see this shirt? We going
wear 'em, and we going camp out in shifts at the sacred
places. And we going get that book banned!"

"What book is that, Mr. Okapa?"

"*Maui's Secrets*. We get one grant for buy all the
copies. We going burn 'em. Then we goin' picket the
stores that carry 'em."

"Whoa," Stevens breathed. "Shit."

"Yeah," Lei said beside him. He felt the tension in her body, too. "This could turn ugly pretty easily."

"This case could become a lightning rod for resentment," Stevens said.

"Lightning rod?" Lei turned, reaching into his lap with a grin. "I think that's a good name for my friend here." She was trying to lighten the atmosphere, but it wasn't working. He removed her hand.

"Funny. And this isn't. I gotta call Omura."

Meanwhile, Wendy Watanabe had moved on to other disasters as Stevens speed-dialed Omura's cell.

"I wonder if you're calling me because you just watched the news," Omura said in lieu of a greeting.

"Exactly. Okapa was complaining about this *Maui's Secrets* book when I interviewed him, but this is the first I've heard about some sort of backlash against it."

"I think we need to get some more detectives on this case, but I already don't have enough manpower. Let's call Oahu again tomorrow and see if we can pool our resources, maybe get that book pulled from the shelves temporarily as a sign of goodwill."

"Goodwill toward who? The Heiau Hui? My guess is, whoever's targeting the *heiaus* already has the artifacts they want mapped out. Taking down the book is closing the barn door after the horse is gone."

"Still. It might placate people like Okapa, who blame the book for exposure."

"Okay, you're the boss. Did you want me to try to contact the publisher?"

"Wasn't that what I said?"

Stevens blew out a breath. "Yes, sir."

Stevens hung up. He felt wired with worry and annoyed by Omura's directive. It could give this vigilante group a message that they had more power than they should, and he worried about where that could go, not to mention dealing with the book publisher's response. He doubted they'd want to pull the profitable book for revision.

MPD needed eyes and ears in the Hui, to monitor it. His old war horse detective Joshua Ferreira was way too well-known. So was Pono, and any of the other detectives he could think of. Even though Okapa knew Mahoe was a police officer, perhaps Brandon could pretend sympathy for the cause enough to believably join.

Stevens got up to wash the dishes for something to do. Lei came up behind him this time, reaching around his waist to put her hands into the dishwater with his. She played with his fingers until they twined together in the warm, soapy water, distracting him. He closed his eyes, savoring the feeling of her pressed against his back, the solidity of her presence.

After so long, she was finally his.

"I'm sorry you're stressed," she said, muffled against his back. She kissed his shoulder blade, nibbled his spine.

"I'm really worried about this case. Nobody's died yet, but I have a bad feeling. Okapa's threats are the tip of the iceberg. Why don't you talk to Pono about what the Hawaiian community is saying? He's always got his finger on the pulse of things."

"All right." She pulled her hands out of the suds, shook them, and wiped them playfully all over his front. "But let's go back to bed soon."

He finished the dishes, listening to her one-sided conversation with her ex-partner, a burly Hawaiian with the truest "spirit of aloha" Stevens had ever met—a man he was now proud to call a friend.

Thinking of Pono reminded him of his brother, Jared. Jared had come to their wedding last month and had been looking to transfer to the Maui Fire Department.

"Thanks for leaving me to deal with Mom, bro," Jared had said the day before the wedding. Their mother hadn't shown—she'd gone on a bender the day before—and Stevens figured it was just as well. She probably would have made a scene at the wedding. But Jared, he felt bad about. His younger brother's face was chiseled lean and his blue eyes had a hollow clarity that spoke of long days and sleepless nights.

"I just had to get out," Stevens said, referring to his move to Hawaii four years before. "I didn't want to watch Mom drink herself to death."

"Well, I don't either. This job is killing me, and summer's coming." Summer in LA. *Fire season.* Stevens felt for his brother and had said he'd ask around about openings on Maui, and that meant Pono.

"Ask Pono about jobs in the fire department for Jared," Stevens said, drying his hands on the dish towel. "Bro wants out from LA as soon as possible."

Lei passed this on, covered the receiver with her hand. "He says he'll e-mail you a link tomorrow. Kahului Station is down a position."

"I knew he'd know something. Good."

Stevens went to the bathroom and brushed his teeth. His eyes fell on the white terry robe he'd appropriated from their cruise-ship honeymoon. That reminded him of the shrouds. Someone had paid for two linen shrouds, given them to him and Lei's family in a double threat, accompanied by a cryptic note that read, *There are plenty of these to go around.* He'd had them, and the box they came in, tested for trace and fingerprints.

Nothing useful had been found. Two twenty-foot lengths of bleached linen haunted him.

As they'd been meant to. Someone was still out there who wanted them dead.

He went back to bed, and it wasn't long before Lei and Keiki joined him. He didn't fall asleep until Lei was pressed against him, her curly hair tickling his cheek.

Chapter 4

Lei wound her hair into a bun and stabbed it with bobby pins at the stoplight as she drove into Kahului for work the next morning. Enough bobby pins would hold it a few hours, at least. She put in her Bluetooth and called Aunty Rosario, chatting until she pulled up in front of the barracks-like MPD building in the heart of Kahului, Maui's biggest town.

Torufu was already at their cubicle when she hurried in, slopping hot coffee from the dispenser in the break room on her hand.

"Mrs. Stevens," he said, wiggling a toothpick up and down between Chiclet-sized teeth. "Mrs. Stevens" was his nickname for her, though she'd kept her maiden name legally. "We have training review at oh nine hundred."

"Yippee. Can't wait to revisit the fun of how we blew ourselves up," Lei said, realizing she'd never finished talking with Michael about her bomb tech training. Just as well. He wouldn't have liked the story, and it probably would have led to one of those variations-on-a-theme fights they had about safety.

She took off the backpack she carried in lieu of a purse and draped it over her chair. They still had regular cases, and as usual, she was backed up on her e-mail.

At the review meeting, she and Torufu sat with the other participants in the training and listened to the statistics on how many IEDs had been located (eighty-nine percent), successfully deactivated (sixty-two percent), and how many "fatalities" (eight).

"What this tells us, people, is that we need more of these trainings," the coordinator, a burly bomb expert from Homeland Security, said. "We have another one scheduled in six months." A suppressed groan circulated the room.

Lei squeezed the web of flesh between her thumb and forefinger, deflecting the feeling of failure she'd struggled with on and off throughout her career. And now she was on one of the most pressure-intense teams on the force, where failure could mean death—not just for herself, but for anyone in the area of an explosive.

Once again doubt assaulted her. Was she right for the bomb squad? Did she have the calm under pressure necessary? She still didn't know, and the further she got in the training, the harder it would be to pull out if she realized she couldn't cut it.

Lei set her hands in her lap, and they brushed her abdomen. Maybe last night was the night she got pregnant. She shut her eyes for a second, transported by memory to those incredibly tender and passionate moments in Stevens's arms. She hadn't realized how getting married and the decision to start a family would change something between them that couldn't be put into words.

It wasn't like it hadn't already been good. But now there was something almost sacred between them.

She still felt edgy, like something would happen to snatch their happiness away. Getting the shroud receipt on their honeymoon and the news about Aunty's cancer hadn't helped that feeling. But when she and Stevens reconnected in Honolulu during her brief stint in the FBI, she'd decided to live as if she was going to have *more*. More happiness and everything else that came with the risk of fully living—including heartbreak, if that was what came, too.

More. For better or worse, richer or poorer, in sickness and in health.

"Lei. We're up." Torufu squeezed her arm, his hand massive as a baseball mitt.

Lei rose and followed Torufu to the side conference room, where instructors were debriefing each of the teams. They sat in molded-plastic seats in front of a kidney-shaped Formica table with their two instructors, each equipped with clipboards and blank expressions.

"So, your team placed eighth out of eleven teams,"

Master-Sergeant Kent said, flipping pages. He had the buzz-cut, grizzled look of a career soldier. "Not very reassuring for Maui Police Department."

Lei pressed the web of her hand but didn't respond. Neither did Torufu.

"You located four IEDs in your section. Six were in the section, so that wasn't the worst. The two of you earned points for your search technique and for good communication and teamwork doing the search. But you weren't able to deactivate one of your IEDs, which is an automatic fail." He flipped the papers he'd been consulting shut. "So. Tell us where that deactivation went wrong. We have video to help." One of the staff people wheeled a TV set over so they could watch their humiliation all over again—apparently, they'd put small video cams over each of the places where the IEDs were hidden.

Lei was glad she hadn't known that at the time.

The video was a little jerky and grainy, but it showed them clearly: Torufu, head down as he scanned the ground, looming over Lei as she swung the hand-held metal detector with GPS they'd been allowed for tracking the IEDs.

"Here," Lei said, in the video, pointing to something just off the trail. There was no audio, but she knew what she'd said. They approached the site, and Kent froze the action with a remote.

"See how you're going straight in? We gave you an ultraviolet detection light. Some of these IEDs are wired with motion sensors, and it would have been good to use it."

Lei had her spiral notepad out, and she made a note for form's sake. Truth was, they'd counted on the IEDs being fairly crude, as this exercise was supposed to help with identifying the type of homemade explosives they had a greater chance of encountering. The competition had been timed. They'd cut a corner, and it had cost them.

She watched, feeling herself stiffen in remembered shock as the IED "exploded." She was grateful the camera, not wired for audio, missed the expletives both she and Torufu had let fly.

"So." Lieutenant Guttierez from the Oahu Police Department, lean and dark as a whippet, picked up the thread of critique. "Why do you think the device detonated?"

Neither of them answered until finally Lei said, "It was on a motion sensor. We set it off when we approached it. There was no time to deactivate it."

"Bingo." There was a long moment of silence. Lei shut her eyes, remembering the moment the device had gone off. Thank God there had been only one device with a motion-sensor trigger mechanism; they'd neglected to use the laser detector at all.

"Did you identify what type of device it was? Why don't you answer this one, Lieutenant Texeira," Gutierrez said.

"It appeared to be a pipe bomb. Had a clock timer trigger mechanism. Sergeant Torufu engaged with the device. I was handing him tools…" Lei's voice trailed off. She wasn't sure how to proceed. Torufu had been working, and she'd just been providing backup, listening to Torufu's muttered commentary under his breath. That had been their version of teamwork on projects up until now, and it suited them.

"That's what we're most concerned with in reviewing your tape," Guttierez said. "Texeira, you seem to have an eye for identifying and finding devices, but it's Torufu here who has the skills—sometimes—for deactivating them. Torufu, were you aware of the guidelines of the training, that Texeira was supposed to work on fifty percent of discovered devices?"

"Yes," Torufu said. He shrugged massive shoulders. "She has an eye. I've been doing it longer. I thought we did pretty well, considering she's hardly had any training."

"Be that as it may," Master-Sergeant Kent said. "You were given some guidelines and didn't follow them. That was actually impacting your low score more than failing on this particular IED. But remember—even though there was a timer on this training, in real life haste is never worth it. Take all the time you need, and use all the risk-reducing technology you can when locating a device."

"Having a device 'explode' is an important part of training. It keeps you alert to the very real possibility of being blown to kingdom come," Guttierez concluded. Lei and Torufu exchanged a rueful glance.

"Texeira, we're sending over a selection of trigger mechanisms to your station. Take some time every day to work on them. You need more hands-on practice recognizing and deactivating the many kinds of devices," Kent continued. "Have you read your electronics manual?"

"Yes, sir," Lei said.

"Well, read it again. And, Torufu, if you're going to work with a partner, you need to treat her like one. Give her a job to do, then get out of the way and let her do it. Many times, being small is going to be an advantage," Lieutenant Guttierez said. "Often devices are hidden in small spaces, making them both harder to find and harder to neutralize. If you two get in that situation and Texeira isn't ready, you'll both be singing with the angels before you know it."

Torufu clapped her on the shoulder as they left, making her stagger. "It's all you from here on out with the wire snips and screwdriver, Mrs. Stevens," he said. "I got no great love of angel choirs."

"Oh, great," Lei said, her throat tight, and she touched the pendant at her throat.

Stevens had gone straight in to Kahului Station in the morning to speak to Omura. She'd gathered four detectives for the response team. Stevens looked around at the circle of concerned faces: Veterans all, they would not be able to infiltrate the Heiau Hui without being identified.

"I think we should have a man inside the vigilante group," Stevens said, when they'd been through preliminary briefing. "I'm looking at my new recruit, Brandon Mahoe. He's formed a nice connection with our witness Manuel Okapa, the *heiau* guardian. If Okapa won't buy bringing him into the Hui, maybe he can at least use Okapa or someone close to the group as a confidential informant."

"I agree we need someone on the inside," Gerry Bunuelos, a little rat terrier of a man with a quick smile, spoke up. "I'm just worried if Mahoe's unseasoned, he won't handle the pressure well."

"Does anyone have a better idea? We need someone not widely known as a police officer, but with Hawaiian community connections," Omura said. "Is that an oxymoron?"

"Yes," Pono Kaihale said, and Stevens snorted a laugh. It was true—to be Hawaiian was to be connected with your community, your family, your *ohana*.

Omura inclined her head. "Ask your officer. Inform him of the risks. We don't know enough about this group to assess how dangerous they are, though I hope to have a better idea after this afternoon. I've got a meeting set up on Skype with the Heiau Hui leader on Oahu and a man here in Maui who's supposedly in charge. I asked for the conversation so I could offer to supplement their efforts with foot patrols and quick police response to alarm calls. Stevens, I'd like you there as lead on this case."

Stevens inclined his head in agreement and held up his battered notepad. "Wanted to tell you the response of the publisher of *Maui's Secrets* to my request to pull the book down: It was a four-letter word, followed by, 'This is a free country with free speech.'"

"Too bad," Gerry said, frowning. "I don't know what that book has to do with the case, though."

"Nothing, that I can tell," Stevens said. "But Okapa said the Hui blames the book for exposing the sacred sites and making them vulnerable to looting, so the group has, according to Okapa on the news last night, decided to focus on pulling down the book as a way to protect the *heiaus* long-term."

"This could get ugly, fast," Gerry said, echoing Lei's comment last night. Simmering below the paradise surface, a current of resentment against outsiders occasionally erupted into race- or class-oriented violence or property damage, as had happened last year with the Smiley Bandit case and the brief but deadly anarchy movement that it had sparked.

"It's on us to keep it from going that way," Omura said briskly. "Stevens, meet me back here in three hours for the conference call with the Hui, and let me know what your young man says about going undercover."

Chapter 5

Back at Haiku Station, Stevens fired up a second pot of coffee to give himself time to think of how to approach Brandon Mahoe. What he was doing was essentially asking a young, green recruit to spy on his people. It was for a good reason—to keep everyone in the movement safe and to keep the community safe. But still, it was a lot to ask and he knew it.

On the other hand, it could turn out to be a group of retirees walking around with walkie-talkies, not the militant or vengeful dynamic he was worried about.

He sat, sipped a fresh cup of coffee, and let his mind wander for a moment to Lei, to the incredible night they'd had. He was tired this morning, but in a good way. Maybe last night was the night she got pregnant. He didn't want to keep wondering that but couldn't seem to help it.

Mahoe was knocking on the doorframe, interrupting his thoughts. "You sent for me, sir?"

Stevens pulled himself together and set the coffee mug aside. "Come in and shut the door, please. I have a special assignment I need to discuss with you."

Mahoe sat on the chair in front of Stevens's desk, the door shut behind him. Stevens spotted a tiny patch of toilet paper adhered to a shaving nick on the handsome young man's square jaw. His dark navy uniform was neat and pressed, and he sat attentively, his head up with unconscious pride. Stevens steeled himself for what he was about to ask.

"Brandon." Stevens took out Mahoe's file and opened it. Very thin, because there wasn't much more than his application to the police academy and proof of graduation only a few months before. "May I call you Brandon?"

"Yes, sir."

"We have an assignment I want to talk to you about. Remember Mr. Okapa?"

"Who could forget, sir? I saw him on the news last night."

"Well, you seemed to have made a bit of a connection with him, though my guess is he's a tough old bird for anyone to get to know. So kudos on how you handled him yesterday."

"He's my mama's cousin, two times removed, so I call him Uncle Manuel. That always helps."

Stevens couldn't help grinning. He tried a little pidgin. "As how, brah."

Now Mahoe grinned. "You get 'em, boss."

"Okay. All joking aside." Stevens leaned forward

as he made eye contact with the young man. "We need someone on the inside of the Heiau Hui to keep us informed on the mood and activities of the group. I wonder if you'd consider volunteering for this assignment."

Mahoe sat back, the eager light fading from his eyes. "Sir. You're asking me to be a snitch."

Stevens kept eye contact, though it was almost painful. "That's not how I'd put it. You would be helping the group, keeping them safe, keeping them from getting in trouble with the law. Helping us help them. Captain Omura has agreed we need someone on the inside so we can coordinate our efforts. She approved me asking you."

Mahoe's jaw bunched and his eyes narrowed. "Why me?"

"Because you're new and relatively unknown as a police officer. Most of our detectives are easily recognized and well connected with family and friends on the island, which can be a good thing most of the time but not when going undercover. You won't deny being a police officer, since Okapa already knows that—but you'll join the Hui to participate with them not as a police officer but as a Hawaiian passionate to protect the sites and artifacts."

"I am passionate about that," Mahoe said. "But if they find out I'm reporting to you, it will ruin my reputation. Trust will be broken."

"So that's why we have to be very careful. We don't even know if the group is going to be a problem, so maybe there's no need for all this concern. In which case, you can be just another volunteer to help guard the sites. No big deal." Stevens outlined some safety and communication measures for them to follow, including a burner phone where he could call or text Stevens directly and a rendezvous point for check-ins.

"You'll report to me only, well outside any contact within the station, where you'll go on reduced shifts to allow you time to work with the Hui. Why don't you think about it, let me know tomorrow? I'll have a little more of a temperature check about the attitude of the Hui after today's teleconference with Captain Omura."

"Okay." Mahoe stood, straightened his uniform, smoothing the brass buttons and adjusting his duty belt. He rubbed his chin and dislodged the toilet paper. He already looked older to Stevens, with this weighty decision before him. "Yes, sir. I'll let you know tomorrow."

"And no talking to anyone about this, no matter what you decide," Stevens said. "This conversation can't go any further than this office."

Mahoe frowned, looking offended. "Of course, sir." He stepped out and closed the door. Stevens sighed, his shoulders slumping. What he disliked most about being a commanding officer was sending men and women into danger.

He remembered his first assignment undercover in LA. He'd joined a white supremacist gang, trying to identify the main management and drug distribution channels of the gang. He'd ridden a Harley and done some things he'd rather not remember, and in the end had barely escaped with his life. He'd grown up more in a year on that detail than he had in his entire twenty-five before, and looking down, remembered the knife fight that had left a scar across his side as a souvenir. Even now, nine years later, it itched as a reminder.

He rubbed the tiny purple tattoo on the inside of his forearm—a heart surrounding LEI that he'd had done on Kaua`i after drinking too much with Lei's partner, Jack Jenkins, back when it seemed they'd never be together. He often found himself touching it, a superstitious gesture, when he was troubled.

As he was now.

He got up and gathered his materials to head back into Kahului for the teleconference with Omura.

On the road to Kahului, his cell rang on the seat beside him—a distinct ringtone he hadn't heard in a year: a bit of birdsong that had reminded him of Anchara Mookjai, his ex-wife.

She never called. It was part of the unspoken agreement they had. Feeling the pang of guilt and regret that accompanied that ringtone, Stevens violated the Maui ban on cell phones and picked up while driving. "Hello?"

"Michael?" Anchara called him Michael, never Stevens or Mike. She said his name in a distinct way, two syllables, Mee-kull, and when she said it, he realized he'd missed her voice, missed the sound of his name on her tongue.

The guilt got worse and made his voice harsh when he said, "Why are you calling me?"

"I'm in trouble." Her soft voice snagged on the words as if she were suppressing tears. "I have to see you."

He thought of Lei, of how she'd feel about him spending time, any time, with Anchara. It hadn't been nearly long enough since the whole fiasco of his relationship to Anchara unwound. "That's not a good idea."

"I know, and I wouldn't ask it if I didn't have to. When can I see you?"

"What's going on?"

"I have to see you in person to tell you."

Stevens shook his head, remembered she couldn't see him do that. "I am going into a meeting—I can't."

"After, then."

A beat passed. Anchara wouldn't call him if she wasn't desperate. She'd always tried hard to be independent, overcoming her start in the United States as a sex slave from Thailand, the language and culture barriers, the abuse of her past. Whatever happened, she deserved his help—for the fact that he hadn't been able to love her as she deserved, as much as anything else.

"All right. I'll call you after the meeting." Stevens hung up and dropped the phone back on the seat, wishing he hadn't answered it.

Chapter 6

The conference room at Kahului Station was a utilitarian space: a long Formica table surrounded by chairs and walls with whiteboards on them, a circular plaster Maui Police Department logo on the far back wall. Captain Omura, looking perfect in a brass-buttoned uniform over a skirt that made the most of her figure, gestured Stevens in when he arrived.

He shut the conference room door, still feeling distracted by the phone call from Anchara. What could the emergency be? And how could getting involved do any good? He had to hear her out. He owed her that, but he wasn't looking forward to it.

Omura pushed a button and the computer console emerged from a slot on the table. Stevens sat beside her so they'd both be visible in the Skype camera window.

"How is Lei holding up after yesterday's training?" Omura asked, her fingers flying over the keyboard as she opened her notes on the computer.

"Fine, but sore. We never got around to talking about how she did on the exercises." He frowned, realizing that he'd forgotten to get the story out of his wife.

"Well, we have bigger fish to fry here. I found this guy that's supposedly in charge of the Hui on Maui through one of Gerry Bunuelos's confidential informants. I don't actually know how reliable that intel is; what I'm hoping is that we can get talking to him and then pipe in the Hui leadership from Oahu and show support for them while making it clear we're in charge of the investigation."

"Sounds good, sir."

"What did your recruit say about being our 'inside man'?"

"He's thinking it over. He wasn't sure if he should be offended I asked him, I could tell. It helped to mention your name."

"Well, sweeten the pot a bit. Tell him you'll recommend a step level raise if he takes that on."

"With your okay, I will."

"Ready?" Omura had the man's profile up on the monitor. Charles Awapuhi had a scowling profile picture in which he sported a shaved head embellished with tribal tattoos across his scalp.

"When you are."

Omura initiated the video call, the call icon pulsing on the screen. Awapuhi accepted the call, and suddenly the man's visage filled the screen. The tattoos on his skull were so intricate it looked like he wore a cap. His thick brows were drawn together in a frown.

"Hello, Mr. Awapuhi. I'm Captain C. J. Omura, and this is Lieutenant Michael Stevens of the Maui Police Department. Thanks for assisting us in the investigation into the desecration of the *heiau* in Haiku."

"I nevah said was I going to assist notting," Awapuhi said. "I only talking because I like know what MPD is going do to protect the *heiaus*."

Stevens leaned forward so he was more visible in the camera. "Can you describe your role in the Heiau Hui, Mr. Awapuhi?"

"Helping the *ohana* come together on Maui," Awapuhi said. "You the *haole* who wen' talk with Manuel Okapa?"

"I am," Stevens said. He didn't like the way Awapuhi spat the word *haole.* "I'm the commander of Haiku Station and we responded to the initial call."

"What you doing to find out who wen' do this thing?"

"We are processing evidence collected at the scene. We are coordinating with Oahu's task force to combine with any evidence they are able to share with us in case the desecrations are related."

"In case?" Awapuhi snorted. "We know they are. And what are you doing to help get rid of that book that has exposed the *heiaus'* locations?"

"We are in touch with the publisher and working on it," Stevens said, keeping his voice conciliatory with an effort. It wasn't the place or time to tell Awapuhi the publisher's response had been profanity.

Awapuhi sat back, appearing somewhat mollified. "Well, we are putting together shifts of volunteers that will be covering our list of identified sacred sites so they have a human presence during the night, since that's when most of the sites on Oahu were raided."

"How many volunteers do you have so far? And what kind of measures are you taking if anyone appearing to be bent on crime is spotted?" Omura asked.

"Not answering that," Awapuhi replied, with a return of his initial truculence.

Omura forged on. "Can we get a list of the sites, with GPS coordinates? Since you're focusing on nighttime, we could focus on day, send foot and car patrols."

"I checked with the leadership of Heiau Hui on Oahu, and we aren't willing to release the names and locations of the sites to you," Awapuhi said.

Omura's brows snapped together in irritation. "I don't know how you expect us to assist you without even the locations of the sites so we can send officers out to monitor them."

"We don't need MPD's help; nor do we want it. When you get that book taken down, we'll talk further."

"And we can slap you with an obstruction of justice charge," Stevens snapped, tired of the attitude.

"We'll handle our own justice. Go ahead." Awapuhi cut the connection, an abrupt severing. Stevens noticed that, as the conversation progressed, Awapuhi had dropped the thick pidgin he'd started with—the man was more educated than he'd been letting on.

Omura turned to him, still frowning. "That didn't go how I'd have liked. I'll put Gerry on a full background workup on Awapuhi. I can tell he never intended to tell us anything or share the location of the sites. This makes Mahoe's involvement, or someone else we can put on the inside, even more important."

"Agree," Stevens said. "Can we get the sites' location some other way? I don't think we should have to prove anything by getting the book taken down—and that's not going to be an easy fight, anyway."

"Awapuhi's trying to throw his weight around. I think appearing to cooperate will just make him more aggressive, so I agree with you. We can subpoena the sites from them, but I'd rather get them some other way. Maybe we can tap a Hawaiiana professor from University of Hawaii or something. I'll bring it up at the staff debrief and see what intel we can come up with. In the meantime, let's get ahold of Oahu's team and find out how they're doing with the Hui." Omura selected another icon and made contact. Minutes later, Detective Marcus Kamuela's good-looking face filled the screen, distorted by the angle. "Captain Omura. I'm on my phone out in the field. How can I assist you?"

"Hey, Marcus." Stevens inserted his head into the frame.

Kamuela grinned. "The happy honeymooner! Back on the job, I see."

"Couple of weeks now. Missed you at the wedding."

"Heavy case. Couldn't get away." Kamuela was dating Marcella Scott, Lei's best friend, and ongoing promises that they'd all get together and "do something" had been continually deferred by work.

"Nuff chitchat, boys." Omura reinserted herself into the main camera frame. "Detective Kamuela, I'm calling about the Heiau Hui. Just tried to conference with their supposed main coordinator on Maui, Charles Awapuhi, and he was not cooperative. Wouldn't even share the locations they are guarding so we could coordinate support. What have your relations been like with them?"

"Rocky." Marcus sat down, and a cement block wall appeared behind him as the camera phone stabilized. "We have our own list of sites one of our Hawaiiana experts with the Bishop Museum helped us put together, but coordinating efforts? No. The group has all but accused us of being behind the looting. The detail working the case all keep our shields in plain view at all times, or we're liable to get our heads blown off." He gestured to his shield, hanging from his neck by a beaded chain, so it appeared square in the middle of his muscular chest.

"So they're armed doing their patrols?"

"You got it. Everything from baseball bats to a shotgun. We've required review of permits for all guns, but so far they've had them. Some of the sites are on private land, and the owners have been complaining to us about these, and I quote, 'trigger-happy thugs' tromping around on their property—but many are too intimidated to protest or are supporting the Hui's efforts. Basically, we're all waiting for some idiot tourist's head to get blown off because they were at the wrong place at the wrong time."

A pause as Omura and Stevens exchanged glances. It seemed as if Oahu was just a more complicated picture of what they were seeing on Maui.

"Any breaks in the case? If we could shut this thing down, the Hui problem would dry up," Omura said. "We have to be careful not to lose sight of the real culprits here."

"Of course." Marcus's wide nostrils flared a bit at the suggestion. "We have a lead, actually. We think it's a crew of professional art thieves. Interpol and the FBI are both involved now because these thieves are wanted in connection with theft of everything from rare old masters paintings to one of the rocks from Stonehenge."

"So what we need to do is find who's actually creating

demand for these artifacts," Stevens said.

"Yes. Hawaiiana has always been a relatively small, unknown collectible area. Most of the best pieces are in the Bishop Museum and other museums—there are some private collections, but genuine Hawaiian artifacts are really so rare that those collections have ended up donated in most cases," Omura said. "I've been studying up on this a bit now that it's landed on our doorstep."

"I will keep you informed of anything new that turns up on our end," Kamuela said. "Anything else, Captain?"

"Just this—the Hui is targeting the *Maui's Secrets* book because it lists the locations of the *heiaus*. Do you have anything like that on Oahu?" Omura tapped her ballpoint on the tablet she'd opened to make notes on.

"We have an *Oahu's Secrets* book, too, but for some reason the *heiaus* weren't listed in that one, so that hasn't been a problem here."

"Well, the Hui won't even cooperate with us enough to share the locations, so I'm planning to pick up a copy of the book on my way home," Stevens said. "Pretty sad we're reduced to helping protect them by finding them in that book."

"You could find a Hawaiiana expert, one of the *kupuna* who'd be willing to share the locations. My mom lives on Maui; I'll give her a call and ask her for someone?" Marcus raised his brows in question.

Stevens glanced at Omura; she inclined her head in agreement. "Sounds good, Marcus. Can you contact her and have her call me on my personal cell?"

"Can do. She's pretty connected; I'm sure she knows the locations of some of them herself."

They ended the connection.

"Let me know the minute you hear from Kamuela's mother, or get a lead on the *heiau* locations," Omura said. "I'm asking for volunteers to pick up extra shifts for our guard detail. I'm not confident we can actually catch these thieves in the act, but we need to make every effort."

"Will do. I plan to pick up a copy of *Maui's Secrets* on the way back to the station, in any case. Find out what all the buzz is about," Stevens said.

Half an hour later, Stevens pressed down Anchara's speed-dial button on his way out of the nearby ABC Store, a copy of the brightly colored *Maui's Secrets* book tucked under his arm.

"Michael." If possible, Anchara's voice sounded even more strained when she answered the phone. "I'm at the Valley Isle Motel, room 256. Please come quickly."

The hairs on the back of his neck prickled with alarm. The C-grade motel in the middle of Kahului was a known haunt for hookers and trysts. Meeting her there wasn't a good idea at any time of day. "No. Meet me at Marco's." He named the nearby Italian-themed restaurant they used to breakfast at regularly.

"I can't. I'm—injured."

He'd unconsciously pressed harder on the accelerator. "Call nine-one-one."

"Michael, please." He could tell she was crying. "I just need you to come." And she hung up.

Stevens was only two blocks away.

"Sonofabitch," he muttered, considering his options even as he headed to the motel. He could call an ambulance and saddle Anchara with an expense she could hardly afford that might not be merited. He could call Lei, preemptively tell her he was meeting Anchara and that she had some undisclosed problem—but on the other hand, what if the problem had to do with him and was something better off handled alone? He should get there, assess first, and make his calls after.

"Sonofabitch," he said again, even as he pulled into the parking lot. The main building was pale aqua with crudely painted humpback whale murals frolicking along a two-story structure. Two threadbare palms held down the cracked asphalt parking lot.

He parked the Bronco in one of the stalls and got his emergency first-aid kit from under the seat, feeling his heartbeat accelerate as he remembered the last time he'd seen his ex-wife. They'd made love early in the morning before work. He'd been back in touch with Lei because of one of her FBI cases, and he'd been distracted ever since, feeling trapped, trying to hide it, and eaten with regret. Anchara had come in with a cup of coffee for him, rubbed his shoulders, and seduced him. He'd let her.

When he'd returned to their pretty house in Wailuku Heights later that day, Anchara was gone. She'd left a letter on the nightstand—a letter that set him free, later followed by the divorce papers.

Stevens stepped away from the Bronco, locked it, and looked up at the second floor of the motel.

Room 256 looked like all the rest, closed with the drapes pulled—the kind of room cheap affairs and lonely old man suicides happened in. He took the exterior stairs on the side of the building at a jog, his rubber-soled work boots ringing on the metal treads.

One of those rubber mats impressed with ALOHA marked the door's entrance. He knocked.

"Anchara?"

No answer. No footsteps. Maybe she was in the bathroom.

Stevens pounded, his anxiety spiking. "Anchara!"

He tried the handle, and it turned.

He pushed the door open, his weapon in one hand and the first-aid kit in the other.

The metallic reek of fresh blood hit him at the same

time as a tableau so visually horrific he couldn't process it.

Anchara was still alive. Her face was so pale he didn't recognize her for a second, those huge brown eyes glassy and staring. Her mouth was moving, but no sound came out. One hand reached toward him, fingers trembling. The mountain of her naked, distended pregnant belly looked like an island in a sea of blood.

Chapter 7

Answering a threat call, Lei and Torufu pulled up at a police barrier made of sawhorses blocking off the road. They'd got the report of a possible bomb in a parked car at the Maui Mall. The busy downtown area had been immediately evacuated, causing a ruckus with traffic and a sense of anxiety and pressure that squeezed Lei's chest like a steel band.

They jumped out of the explosive ordnance disposal van, already in full gear. Lei opened the back of the vehicle, and Torufu lowered the corrugated metal ramp to deploy the surveillance and deactivation device, a small, heavy robot on six wheels capable of going in any direction. The witness reporting the explosive was escorted over to them by two burly officers.

"I'm sure it's safe," the young man babbled. "I was bringing it in to the station myself when I hit a bump and thought it might go off. It's something from my uncle's collection—a missile shell or something. I don't even know if it's live."

Lei, already boiling in the heavy fire- and flak-proof suit, gave the young man a once-over. He had the soft belly and pallid complexion of a video gamer, and his eyes were so wide that white showed entirely around the irises.

"Describe the explosive."

"I-it's like a giant bullet. Pointed on one end, f-flat on the other. M-made out of metal. G-green," the man stuttered.

Torufu had the robot, nicknamed Whiz-Bang, lined up. Using the remote control, he steered the device down the metal ramp into the parking lot. "Sounds like a missile of some sort," Torufu said. "What's the origin?"

"My uncle collected World War II memorabilia. I inherited it, all in a storage locker. Today I finally went to sort it out, see if there was anything worth selling. I found the shell in a box. I thought I'd take it to the police station, give it to you folks—but then when I hit that bump, I thought I better just stop where I was and let you deal with it." He seemed to be calming down, his speech flowing better. Lei resisted an impulse to pat him on the arm.

"I wish you'd called us from the storage locker," Lei said, gesturing to the snarled traffic and evacuated mall.

"It is what it is," Torufu said. "Texeira, let's get a look at what we've got. Officers, hold that man until we can verify his story."

Lei squatted with Torufu in the back of the van as

her partner steered Whiz-Bang. She'd never driven the device, which had a large and unwieldy-looking hand-held control panel.

"Never directly approach a possible reported explosive if you can help it," Torufu said. "Use the robot or an optical lead."

"I know," Lei said with a touch of impatience. She felt herself getting hotter by the minute in the protective coverall, and the interior of the van was already an oven.

"And don't believe witnesses. At least sixty percent of the time, the person who reports a bomb is the one who set it."

"You told me that already," Lei said.

Torufu shrugged. The heat and pressure were making both of them irritable. The red Ford Focus containing the device was directly ahead. Lei put her large, heavy helmet on, looking out through the faceplate and activating the built-in interior communication unit. "Comm check."

"Whiz-Bang on the move. Let's get this mall back to normal." Torufu's voice sounded tinny and distorted in the hollow of the helmet.

Lei crouched beside him in the van as he pushed the lever steering the robot forward, and the little tank-like vehicle picked up speed. Torufu stopped it at the red Ford. "We need to check for wires and trip lines first. Witness said the explosive was in the backseat, right?"

"I don't think he said." Lei felt like her voice was echoing in her own ears—her breathing, and the heavy thud of her heart, were amplified inside the protective gear.

She wondered where Stevens was at this minute, and hoped it was somewhere more comfortable than here, in this claustrophobic suit, the eyes of the entire town and the news media on them. No, she definitely didn't like this aspect of the job.

"Deploying visual," Torufu said.

"Roger that," Lei acknowledged.

"Observe and we'll discuss later." Torufu held the control panel lower so she could watch him flick a switch and take hold of a small joystick. Looking over at Whiz-Bang, she saw a telescoping sight, like a periscope, rise up out of the top of the robot. When it got to the height of the car window, Torufu pushed a button and a flexible head, somewhat like a headlamp, lifted up into position, close to the window but not touching it. He activated the camera and a bright spotlight beneath it. Suddenly, the digital screen in front of them was filled with a grainy image of the car.

Torufu moved the joystick. "No trip wires, motion detectors, or pressure plates visible." Lei could see all around the door handles, inside the windows. Inside the car, Big Gulp cups, McDonalds bags, sandy towels, and other detritus filled the screen.

"Where's the missile?" Lei hissed. She felt a trickle of sweat beading along her spine and traveling down into the waistband of the Lycra shorts she wore under the coverall.

"I'm looking."

They ended up having to reposition the robot and peer into the front seat, where the large artillery shell, still in its wooden box surrounded by shavings, rested. "Looks like the witness's story checks out," Lei said.

"We can put this in the containment chamber. Let's get Whiz-Bang back to the van and prep the containment vessel. You drive him back." Torufu handed her the controller. Lei smiled at Torufu's paternal tone.

The control panel was heavier than it looked, and Lei felt her muscles tense as she held her arms at a ninety-degree angle. Her hands, covered in heavy gauntlets, were clumsy at the controls, but with Torufu directing, she managed to get the robot turned around and headed back to the van in a relatively straight line, its camera stowed. Torufu took over to steer the robot back up the ramp and park it in the vehicle. They each took off their helmets. Lei's hair was plastered to her head with sweat, and the beads of moisture on her spine had become a trickle.

"What now, partner?" she asked.

"Prep the transport container." They climbed out of the van's roasting-hot interior, and Lei felt a wave of dizziness as she and Torufu rolled the bombproof containment safe down the ramp. Torufu was talking to the army on his headset. Lei glanced over at her backpack, slung over the back of the seat, and could see it vibrating as her phone went off—but with her hands gloved, there was no way to answer it.

Torufu ended his call. "They'll take it in at the armory. An ordnance specialist is on their way over to assist."

"Do we need to wait for them? I'm feeling pretty dizzy," Lei said, crumpling suddenly to lean on the bumper of the van.

"Hydrate." Torufu reached back into the van to a flat of water bottles on the metal floor. He tossed her one, twisted the top off his, and guzzled. Lei drank as fast as she could. Torufu tossed his empty bottle back into the van. "No, we won't wait. Let's get the device out of the car and contained so the mall can reopen."

The two of them put their helmets back on and pushed the heavy containment safe across the parking lot. Lei was grateful for Torufu's brawn as they finally reached the car with the extremely heavy metal container. Working carefully, they opened the door and, careful not to jostle the missile, lowered it, wooden box and all, into the safe and closed the lid, latching it.

"This safe is rated to contain the equivalent of two hundred pounds of dynamite going off," Torufu said. "I think we should be fine."

Several officers helped push the heavy safe up the ramp and clamp it down in the van. Lei drank another bottle of water, sitting in the driver's seat, as Torufu secured the container and finalized the plans to hand off the missile to the army.

Lei checked her phone—Stevens had called but had not left a message. She'd get back to him when she could get out of the heavy gear and have a conversation.

Torufu got in beside her. "To the armory, stat. I can't wait to get out of this gear."

"You're telling me. Turn up the AC," Lei said, putting the van in gear. "Can't say I enjoyed that."

Torufu frowned. "That was about as easy as these calls get."

Lei said nothing, stewing in doubts and sweat in the bombproof suit.

Stevens slid his phone back into his pocket. Lei still wasn't picking up. He sat on the top step of the building's exterior staircase as personnel came and went from the room.

Someone touched his shoulder. "Mike." It was Gerry Bunuelos, a crease between his brows as he looked at Stevens. "You're covered with blood, man."

Stevens looked down at his hands—they were soaked. So were his shirt, his pants, and his shoes. A violent wave of nausea overcame him, and he turned to the side to vomit over the railing. Bunuelos patted his shoulder. "I need to get your statement. Let's go to the station for that."

Stevens wiped his mouth on the shoulder of his shirt, hoping it was clean. "Yeah."

"Let's go."

Stevens barely registered that Gerry put him in the back of the police cruiser for the short ride to the station, but he began to come out of the fog of shock when the crime-scene tech wouldn't let him wash. Instead, eyes flat and expression concealed behind a paper mask like he was diseased, she swabbed samples of blood off of the various areas on his body, pulled a hair sample and photographed him from all directions.

He had to stop her to vomit again, into a nearby trash can, and he wasn't even surprised by then when she scooped a sample of that unspeakable muck into a plastic container.

"Change into these clothes," she said, handing him a neatly folded stack of scrubs marked MAUI DEPARTMENT OF CORRECTIONS. "I need your clothing."

"I didn't do anything but try to administer first aid. And it was too late," he said to the woman. Knowing it was useless. Knowing there was nothing he could say that would shortcut this horror—or end the horror that now lived in his memories. Knowing that this crime tech and her judgment of him was only the beginning.

Finally, somewhat washed and changed, Stevens took his phone out of his pocket, removed his belt, his weapon, creds, wallet, and badge.

"I need to process all of that," the tech said, and with the numbness that had fallen over him, he watched her bag it all.

He was obviously the prime suspect in his pregnant ex-wife's murder.

Of course he was. He'd think the same, arriving at the bloodbath of that room, seeing a man unresponsive with shock standing there, covered in blood.

Gerry and Pono appeared together in the doorway. "Do you want to call counsel or your union rep?" Pono asked, his bass voice serious.

"Yes, I believe I will," Stevens said. The tech held his bloodstained phone while Stevens scrolled through the contacts and contacted his lawyer. They put him in an interview room to wait, and he sat down on the hard chair, crossed his arms, and lay his head down on them.

He wished he could cry, release even a fraction of the grief and horror that felt locked inside his throat. As many crime scenes as he'd seen, as much blood as he'd waded through, both in the army and the LAPD, it still shocked him that so much blood could be contained in such a tiny woman.

The thought made him want to vomit again.

His lawyer, Shawn Shimoda, finally arrived along with his union rep, Cal Bendes. Captain Omura, her lips pale and pinched together, followed them in, a notebook and pen in her hand.

"I have recused Bunuelos and Kaihale from this case against their wishes," she said. "They're too close to you. I'm putting McGregor and Chun on the case going forward."

Stevens nodded. Looking at his hands, he spotted a rime of blood under his nail. He wondered if it was hers, or from the baby.

"Did the baby live?" he asked.

"We're not sure yet." Omura flicked on the recording equipment. Gone was the easy camaraderie of their working relationship from that morning. When she sat down, her eyes were expressionless, her face almost immobile. "Why don't you tell us what happened today."

"Anchara called me." Stevens picked at the blood under his nail. He needed to get it off him, every bit of it. "She called me and told me she needed to see me, right before we had our Skype meeting with the Hui leader. She said she was in trouble. I told her I'd call her after the meeting." He got the bit of blood out, flicked it away, and ran both hands through his hair. He felt a suspicious stickiness. He resisted the urge to rip out his hair in handfuls. Instead, he placed his hands on the table to control them. "Anchara asked me to meet her at the motel. I said no; let's meet at Marco's. She said she was injured, I had to meet her there." He raised his eyes to Omura's. "I was worried about how meeting her at the motel would look. I knew Lei wouldn't like it, and that motel doesn't have a good reputation. I was only two blocks from the place by then, though, and decided to see what was up before I called anyone else. I went to the door, knocked. She didn't answer. I was alarmed. I pounded and called a second time. I tried the knob—it opened, and she was there, naked. There was blood everywhere." He stopped. Swallowed. Glanced at the mirrored interview window. He knew Pono and Gerry and half the station would be watching, if they'd been allowed to.

"Go on," Omura prompted.

"I approached the bed. At first I thought she was having the baby and hemorrhaging, but when I approached, I saw she'd been stabbed." He ran a hand through his hair again, tried to tame the tremble in his voice. "She was bleeding out from wounds to the chest."

"Had you known she was pregnant?"

Shimoda stirred beside Stevens. "You don't have to answer that," the lawyer said.

Stevens turned to him. "I want to answer. The answer's no. I heard from Lei that Anchara attended our wedding a month ago, but she sat in the far back by herself. She must have slipped out before anyone noticed, to hide the pregnancy. I haven't seen her since the day she left me."

"So how long ago was that?"

"I'm not sure." His mind couldn't compute the months. "I want to tell you what happened next."

"Okay then." Omura's voice was gentle. He reminded himself to be cautious—today she was neither his friend nor his chief.

"I approached the bed. She was still alive, trying to speak. 'The baby. The baby,' she said." He swallowed again. "I was calling nine-one-one. I ran to the bathroom and got a stack of towels. The knife she'd been stabbed with was lying beside the bed. I didn't touch it. I put towels and pressure on the wound to slow down the bleeding. 'Take the baby,' she said. 'Use the knife and take the baby.'" Stevens felt that violent nausea again, and he put his head down until it passed. "I told her no. I said hang on; help was coming. She passed out. I did CPR on her, chest compressions, rotary breathing." He shut his eyes against the memory of her breasts, unfamiliarly round and full, leaking the thin yellowish milk newborns needed as he'd done the chest compressions. "The paramedics finally got there. They moved her out and took her to the hospital. I heard from Pono that they performed an emergency C-section when they determined she was dead."

"Where were you when this went on?"

"I just stood there, after they left. There wasn't anything I could do really. I don't know if the baby was alive. Pono had gotten there by then. He can tell you."

"Is it your baby?" Omura's question was soft but had all the sting of a lash as it sawed across his consciousness.

He shook his head, buried his face in his hands. "I don't know. I don't think so. I don't see how."

"When was the last time you had relations with Anchara Mookjai? Sexual relations?"

"The morning she left, like I said."

"And when was that?"

"I don't know. I can't think. But if you want to do a paternity test on the baby, I consent."

"Stop. You're not thinking clearly," Shimoda said, holding up a hand. "You don't have to agree to this."

"I do. She was my wife!" He pounded his chest with each word. "I didn't love her, but she was my wife, and if that's my child, I will do right by him as best I can!"

"If you insist, but it's against my advice," Shimoda said. Omura made a note that Stevens consented to the paternity test and pushed it over to him. Stevens signed it.

"So then what happened?" Omura went on.

"I tried to call Lei. I tried and tried. She didn't pick up. I went outside when the crime techs arrived to help process the scene."

"All right. Let's get a timeline of events." Omura looked down at her pad. "Let's use your wedding to Lei as a starting point, since we all know that date, and work back from there." After rehashing various events, they established that there was a physical possibility the child was Stevens's.

"Anchara and I only stayed in touch with e-mail. She never called, and I didn't see her after the day she left. She very clearly wanted to move on from the marriage," Stevens said.

"So did you ever abuse her?" Omura slid it in like a knife between his ribs.

"You're kidding, right?" He pinned Omura with a hard gaze. "She'd been a sex slave. She'd been abused in ways I can't imagine. I married her to help her, not hurt her more."

"And yet that's what you did," Omura said. "You just told us you didn't love Anchara. You hurt her when you married another woman, the woman you loved all along."

A long pause. Stevens couldn't think of what to say. It was the ugly truth, if not all of it.

"I advise my client not to respond," Shimoda said. "I believe this is sufficient for an initial interview."

Stevens ignored him, still focused on Omura. "I cared for Anchara. But not the way she wanted to be loved or deserved to be loved."

A long moment passed, raw and charged with the trifecta of grief, guilt, and regret he thought he'd carry forever now.

"Did you kill Anchara?" Omura's voice was a samurai sword slicing through silk.

"No. I tried to save her. I tried to save her!" Stevens felt his words coming out hard and tried to soften them. "In every way, I tried to save her. But I couldn't." And then, to his humiliation, his eyes welled with tears. He put his hands over his face. The tears burned like acid on his hands.

Chapter 8

Lei finally picked up her phone after she'd stripped out of the coverall down to her jog bra and Lycra shorts. She was dismayed to see multiple calls from Stevens, but no voicemail. Pono had left a message. "Something's happened. Come to the station immediately."

She looked up after trying to call Stevens back, but his phone was off. Torufu, also stripped down to sweat-soaked swim trunks, had his phone to his ear. He turned worried brown eyes on her.

"We have to get back to the station," she said.

He put the phone down and started the van. "You got that right."

"What is it? Stevens tried to call but didn't leave a message, and Pono just said to get back to base."

"Then we better get back to base."

That's when Lei knew it was really bad.

She and Torufu parked the ordnance retrieval van and jogged to the locker rooms. Lei's heart was thundering and she refused to let her frantic mind wonder what had happened—the possibilities were too endless, and terrible, and the list started with Stevens injured or dead.

She'd stowed the clothes she wore to work that
morning in her employee locker, but the sweat had been
so bad, she took five minutes to shower before dressing.
She took the stairs up from the locker room at a run and
met Pono at the top—Torufu must have called him.

"Come into my office." He sat her down on Gerry's
empty chair. "I'm going to tell you quickly because
they're interviewing him now, and I know you'll want to
hear."

"Who?"

"Stevens. Anchara was found murdered this afternoon.
He was at the scene, covered with blood. Says she was
stabbed before he got there and he was trying to save her.
And she was nine months pregnant."

Lei kept her eyes on her ex-partner's square,
handsome Hawaiian face, hyperfocused on his wide nose
and full, finely cut lips. He had new crow's feet she'd
never noticed before beside his dark brown eyes. There
were a couple of threads of gray in his thick black hair.
These tiny details anchored her while she tried to process
what he was saying. "Okay."

"They're looking at him for the murder," Pono said.

"Of course they are. She's his ex. His pregnant ex."
Lei was surprised at how calm her voice was. In fact, she
felt nothing right now—nothing but ice around her heart.

"Did you know Anchara was pregnant?"

"No."

"But Stevens says you saw her at the wedding. He says he never spotted her."

"I did. But only her face, and she was way in the back. She was wearing a big hat." Lei remembered that moment when their eyes had locked across the crowd, and Anchara had nodded, smiled, and given her blessing. "She was wearing something caftan-ish. I couldn't see anything, if that's what you're asking me. She was okay with us getting married."

"Well, apparently she wasn't okay. She called Stevens twice asking him to come to the Valley Isle Motel, and when he got there…" Pono's voice trailed off as McGregor, a large red-faced detective from California, appeared in the doorway.

"Prepping our witness, Kaihale?" he asked. "Texeira, you're getting interviewed next."

Lei stood. "I believe I have an alibi for the time in question. I can be viewed on KHIN 2 News, removing an explosive at the Maui Mall."

"We still have questions for you." McGregor took her arm. She yanked it away, giving him stink eye as she strode down the hall toward the interview rooms.

She got far enough ahead to peek into the glass windows until she spotted Stevens, dressed in prison orange, flanked by Shimoda and Bendes—and Captain Omura's sleek bob in the foreground.

Lei hit the push-down handle of the door and barged in.

Stevens had his hands over his face, but at the intrusion, he dropped them—and Lei saw an ocean of grief in eyes made even bluer than usual by tears. She took three running steps across the room, knocking the chair away from the table as she embraced him with all the strength in her body.

Stevens's long corded arms encircled her and drew her down onto his lap. He buried his face in her wet hair.

"Texeira!" Captain Omura rapped on the table. "You are disturbing an official interview!"

"I think we can take a tiny break," Shimoda said, and he got up and walked over to turn off the recording equipment.

Chapter 9

"Are you okay?" Lei whispered into Stevens's ear.

"No."

"Is it your baby?"

"Maybe."

"We'll get through this together." She kissed his closed, unresponsive mouth. She knew how many eyes were on them, and she didn't care. All she wanted was for Stevens to know that she had his back. He squeezed her tight in that way he did, and she felt his pain in the fine trembling of his big hard body.

"That's quite enough, Texeira," Omura said. "You can go with McGregor. He'll be interviewing you next door."

Lei straightened up. Stevens opened his eyes. They blazed with powerful, suppressed emotion. "I tried to save her. But I was too late."

"I believe you," Lei said, and saw him sag with relief.

She followed McGregor and Chun out and down the hall to the next interview room.

"I waive my right to counsel and union

representation," Lei said to McGregor, and sat down. "What do you want to ask me?"

What followed was the verbal equivalent of two pit bulls squaring off in the ring—making charges, tussling, retreating. Doing it again. Finally, Lei smacked her hand on the table. "We're covering the same ground. No, neither of us knew Anchara was pregnant, let alone if it's Stevens's baby. Neither of us saw her except for when I spotted her at our wedding. I had no contact with her; nor did I know where she lived or what she was doing. Do I have any idea who might want to kill her? No. But I do know there's someone out there who wants both of us dead." And she told McGregor about the shrouds.

McGregor glanced at his silent partner, Keith Chun, a wiry older man. "Did you guys start a case for these threats?"

Lei nodded. "Talk to Pono. He's been handling that since it happened."

"Can you check this out?" McGregor asked Chun, who nodded and left.

"What were the shrouds like, specifically?"

Lei shut her eyes, remembering the cardboard box containing them that the perp had sent to her dad and Aunty Rosario. "White unbleached linen, about a yard wide by twenty feet long. They're in the evidence room."

As McGregor made a note, Lei saw a flare of his eyes

that signaled he was excited about something. "What?" she asked. "Was there something at the scene that ties in?"

"You know I can't discuss that with you."

"Well, I don't have to discuss this with you either. I was just leaving, unless you have some charges to bring?" She stood and kept eye contact with the older man. She'd heard he was good, if new to the islands and their unique police work challenges.

A long beat went by. She saw McGregor waver, almost telling her whatever it was, but finally he flicked his fingers and looked down at his notepad. "We'll be in touch."

Lei wished the interview room door would bang behind her, but it was on a pneumatic hinge so there was no such satisfaction. She looked into the room with Stevens, and it was empty. Her stomach twisted.

She hurried to Captain Omura's office. Her boss was typing rapidly when she opened the door. "Don't make a habit of barging in here, or anywhere, Texeira. I'll write you up next time," Omura snapped, without taking her eyes off her monitor.

Lei shut the door. "Why did you take Pono and Gerry off the case?"

"You know why. Pono'd run and tell you everything. We have to rule you both out and run a clean investigation."

Lei knew that, but she couldn't help battling a feeling of betrayal. "Do you really think either of us had anything to do with Anchara's death? Because if so, here's my badge." She took the shiny, heavy metal medallion off her belt and smacked it down on the desk.

Omura finally looked away from her screen. "Really? You're making this personal? Both of you had motive to do that poor woman in. Fortunately, you are very publicly alibied—but Stevens could have done it, and we cannot have even a hint of favoritism or cover-up with this case. It's a gruesome, heinous murder with a baby involved—tabloid news heaven!" Omura threw her hands up. "So please. Keep your badge, do your job, and shore up your husband—but stay out of the investigation or you'll be suspended. I already put Stevens on admin leave for a couple days."

"On what basis? The news will get hold of that and run with it, implying he's guilty!" Lei exclaimed.

"On the basis of emergency family leave," Omura said, and her dark eyes were filled with compassion as Lei absorbed the body blow that Anchara's baby was also Stevens's.

Lei grabbed the back of one of the hard plastic chairs and collapsed into it. "So I guess the baby made it."

"Yes. He's in Kapiolani Hospital over on Oahu. They helicoptered him out to the neonatal unit there. He was deprived of oxygen, and they still don't know how badly it affected him—but the paternity test was positive. He's Stevens's son."

"Oh, God." Lei dropped her face into her hands. "This is so unreal. Poor Anchara." Lei felt her chest heave with grief she wanted to let out—she'd liked Anchara, once upon a time. Admired her courage, tenacity, and her will to survive. She'd only stopped liking her when Stevens had married the Thai woman. "We'll have to take the baby. And just when we were thinking of getting started with our own family."

"What?" Omura frowned. "I just assigned you to the bomb squad."

"I know. And I was wondering how to tell you and what to do about it. But it's a moot point now."

"So. Tell me you aren't already pregnant."

"Couple of weeks and I'll know."

Omura leaned toward her and tapped her pen on the desk. "I'm as feminist as the next woman. You know that. But I don't think bomb squad is the place for a pregnant woman—it's a very physical detail, as you know, and more stressful. I'd like you to consider light duty when and if you do start your family."

"That won't be happening with Stevens bringing home a baby right now." Lei's eyes prickled with tears. Having two babies that close together? Didn't make a whole lot of sense.

"Well, keep me posted in any case. Torufu tells me you did well at the Maui Mall ordnance retrieval incident today."

"That suit in the heat wasn't fun. I'll be honest, Captain. I've been struggling with this. Wondering if I'm the right person for the job."

Omura's black-olive eyes narrowed. "Sounds like I ought to be on the lookout for a replacement."

"I just—I don't know. You need someone with nerves of steel who can really focus. A lot of times, I struggle with that. Torufu's great that way. He says what I'm good at is locating the devices, interviewing the witnesses—the police work end of it. It's early days, but I wanted to tell you I'm not a hundred percent sure. And for this job, you should be a hundred percent."

Omura looked back at her monitor, and Lei felt the captain's disappointment in her averted gaze. "Duly noted. And if you're looking for your husband, I sent him home." She resumed typing, and Lei knew she was dismissed. She slipped out the door and shut it softly behind her. She had one more stop to make.

Lei jogged to Pono and Gerry's cubicle, stepped in, and closed the door. Both of them looked up from their computers.

"We aren't supposed to talk to you," Bunuelos said.

"Guys, I need to know what you found in the room

with Anchara that connects to the shroud threats," Lei said. "I know there's something, because when I told McGregor about the shrouds, he about shit a brick. Pono, I told him to ask you about our shroud case."

"Yeah. He came by." Pono inclined his head. "Anchara was lying on a length of white, unbleached linen, three feet by twenty feet long, folded up on top of the bed beneath her body. Sound familiar?"

"Oh my God. But this should clear Stevens!"

"Not necessarily. It could be argued he set it up to look that way. The knife used on her had no prints on it, so Stevens not picking it up doesn't help one way or the other." Pono's eyebrows were knit in concern. "More important—did you hear the paternity test came back?"

"Yeah. Omura told me."

"What do you think about it?"

"I think a newborn baby needs a home," Lei said. "I think we'll do the right thing and give it to him." She squelched the inner voice screaming that she didn't want to raise Anchara's baby, at a time she hadn't expected to, without any preparation whatsoever. Anchara's baby with Stevens. Not hers. And just when she'd been wrapping her head around having her own child with the man she loved.

The baby would forever remind them both of that first, ill-fated marriage. Poor Anchara. Murdered, about to give birth, all alone—and she hadn't so much as asked for a diaper from Stevens. It was all so wrong; it was hard to figure out where to begin to untangle her feelings. But Lei knew the right thing to do. "The baby needs a home, and we're his family. All that's happened—it's not the baby's fault," she said emphatically, and she knew the person she was trying to convince was herself.

Chapter 10

Stevens got in the shower the minute he got home. He washed his hair three times. He scrubbed his skin from head to toe with a washcloth until he was the red of a boiled lobster, and then he did it again.

He felt the shock unlocking slowly, and under the fall of water, he sat on the plastic bench they'd inherited with the oversized shower and wept for Anchara. Wept for the brave woman he'd married, with her indomitable will and fierce need for freedom. The one woman who'd escaped from the sex slavers who'd held her prisoner and lived off the land until she could find help. Anchara, the woman who'd testified fearlessly in court and helped shut down the ring of prostitution operating out of cruise ships. Anchara, the woman he'd married in a moment of impulsive need—a desire to help and a need to forget Lei.

She'd gotten pregnant with his child the day she left him, and she'd carried the baby alone, in a strange country, without anything but a part-time job as a waitress and the small alimony he paid her until she finished her culinary arts degree and got a solid job. Never said a word, never complained, and hadn't had an abortion. A mysterious woman, whom now he'd never know—except through the son she'd left behind.

If that weren't enough, he was a suspect in her murder, and he could tell he'd been carefully set up.

Stevens ground the heels of his hands into his eyes and stood up, turning off the water. The baby was his, and however he felt about suddenly discovering he was the father of a motherless newborn, he'd do right by the child. But it wasn't fair to Lei. All he could do was ask her to consider adopting and deal with whatever she said.

That's if they'd let him take the boy, with the shadow of suspicion over his head. He had to get the ball rolling as soon as he was able to get a little organized.

He got out of the shower, feeling a thousand years old, and dressed in his old LAPD sweatpants.

Keiki danced around, seeing this, and he patted the dog's large square head. Outside, in the sun-splattered backyard behind their cottage, he threw the ball for Keiki. She grunted with happiness as she caught it midair, waggling her cropped behind.

He looked around the unkempt patch of grass and overgrown hibiscus hedge. A plumeria tree dropped fragrant pinwheel blossoms on the weedy lawn. This place needed some work, work he and Lei always seemed too busy to put in. How the hell would they have time to raise a newborn?

It was one thing to think of Lei getting pregnant and having nine months to prepare, to make a plan. It was another entirely to bring home a baby as soon as next week. One of them would have to go on family leave, at least until they could find child care, and since it was his baby, it should be Stevens. He decided to get on with meeting his son and looked up the number for Kapiolani Children's Center on the neighboring island of Oahu.

"I'd like the neonatal unit please." Once transferred there, he had no idea what to ask.

"I'm the father of a child who's been admitted," he said. "A baby boy. Last name Mookjai."

"Just a moment, sir. Your name?"

"Michael Stevens."

A long pause. "We don't have you listed as a relative." The friendly voice had cooled.

"That may be so. My paternity was just confirmed on Maui. I'd like to come see him."

"You will have to speak to Child Welfare Services about that. He's a ward of the state."

"Is he okay? Is he doing all right?" Stevens almost couldn't believe how quickly he'd come to care about his child.

"I really can't say, sir, until your relationship with the child is confirmed and you're put on our access list."

"Do you have a social worker's name I can speak to?"

A long pause as she considered this. "Yes. Darlene Fujimoto." She rattled off a number.

Stevens called Darlene Fujimoto and left a voicemail identifying himself, offering verification he was the father, and Captain Omura's number to speak to regarding the situation.

He hoped Omura would support his effort, but there was nothing more to be done right now.

Except book a flight to Oahu, set up the nursery, and tie up all the loose ends at his station. Who would take over at his station? They were short-handed as it was.

That reminded him of the *Maui's Secrets* book he'd picked up on his way to Anchara's motel room. He needed something to do, something to keep his mind occupied other than with nightmare memories. Admin leave didn't mean he'd stopped working—just that he stopped getting paid and carrying his badge. Not that Omura would agree with that…

He got the book out of the car and sat on the back step, the sun drying his hair, as he leafed through it with a ballpoint pen and a stack of Post-its, circling the locations of the Maui *heiaus*. It was a start, and he had to keep working the case on the down-low, so that meant no cultural experts he had to coordinate with Omura.

The book was remarkably accurate, even providing

GPS coordinates for the locations in wilderness areas. He could see why the activists didn't like how accessible it made the *heiaus*.

Keiki whined and he threw the ball some more and finally returned inside the house. His cell phone was still being held as evidence, so he used the house phone to call Haiku Station.

After he'd told his second in command, Ferreira, that he'd be out a few days on leave, he asked for Brandon Mahoe.

"Yes, sir."

"Brandon, I'm glad you're there. What's the status of getting involved with the Heiau Hui?"

"I've decided to do it, sir. I met with Uncle Manuel already. Told him I was feeling a call to the cause and was putting aside my badge to answer it. He seemed to believe me."

"Well, be very careful. I don't have my personal cell, so I'm going to get my own burner phone and one for you, like we talked about, and we'll keep in touch that way. I'll tell Ferreira, who's doing scheduling, to schedule you so you can attend their meetings and patrols. Wait for me to get you the burner; I should be able to bring it by the station in an hour."

Getting back to his case renewed Stevens's energy. Hopefully, the rumors about him would wait a little while.

Galvanized, he drove the Bronco back into town. He bought two burner phones at Longs, and while he was at it, all the baby stuff he could find: bottles, formula, diapers in the tiniest size. One of the saleswomen, a Filipina with a kind face, saw him dithering over the various items.

"Baby shower?"

"You could say that. We have a new baby coming and I—don't know what we need."

She slanted him a disbelieving glance. "Where's the mama? Usually the mama like to shop."

"She's—in the hospital. We weren't ready yet," he fibbed.

The woman's apple cheeks creased in a smile. "Oh, I help you, poor t'ing. Here. You need these small-kine blankets. And these we call onesies. And you get one car seat?"

The cart was piled high when he pushed it to the checkout, and he actually felt a little queasy at the expense, so close after the wedding, which had wiped out their savings.

"Welcome to adulthood," he muttered. It reminded him of his father, dead the last fifteen years, clapping him on the shoulder and saying that to him the day he got his driver's license. But nothing said adulthood like parenthood, intended or not.

He loaded the Bronco, still feeling a little disembodied about making this commitment to a son he'd never seen. Driving back home, he wondered how long he would have to call the baby just "him."

What had Anchara wanted to name the child? He was sure she'd had that all figured out. She'd had an orderly way about her, everything in its place, tidy. She'd hum as she cleaned the house, and she'd seemed happiest working in the little ornamental garden they'd put in back. He wished he knew where she lived, that he could see what she'd bought for the baby and find out what she'd planned to name him.

He could look her up on the computer at the station— he was headed there now, to give Brandon the burner phone and tidy up his desk—but he was sure her living space was taped off as part of the investigation, and going there would be a very bad idea.

Maybe Pono could scout around in there for him, see what he could find out, what was going to happen to her belongings. Guilt twisted his guts at the thought—she had no relatives but those she'd fled in Thailand, and during their relationship, at least, only a few acquaintances. Maybe there were more people in her life now.

Why hadn't she told him about the baby? Why had she kept him, even? Probably she hadn't told Stevens because she didn't want him in her life anymore—even for the baby's sake.

These ruminations weren't helping his mood. He pulled into the modest parking lot outside the station and went inside.

"Can I speak to you, boss?" Ferreira met him, coming in.

"Of course. In my office."

He shut the door behind them and sat down, unlocking the drawers of his desk and looking for the little black address book he used to store confidential informant and other contact information. He'd never trusted keeping all that information in his phone or computer, and it had turned out to be a good thing.

Ferreira sat down in the chair across from the desk, potbelly straining his belt and his weathered face concerned. "I heard they're looking at you for the pregnant woman's murder in Kahului."

Stevens stopped rummaging—so much for his hope of no one at his station knowing for a little while. He made eye contact with the detective. "It's almost surreal, what's happened. I don't blame them for looking at me. She's my ex. She called me for help, and I got there as soon as I could, but she'd been stabbed. I couldn't save her life. Hopefully, the baby's going to be okay." Stevens looked down, turning to rotate the dial of the safe where he remembered stashing the book. "My phone's been taken for the investigation, so I bought a burner to keep in touch. Hopefully, this will blow over soon. It looks like

I'm going to be a dad rather suddenly, so it may be a little longer until I get things sorted out at home."

He glanced up. Ferreira's mouth had fallen open. "Damn, Lieutenant. What a shitstorm."

"You got that right." Stevens took the dog-eared black book out of the safe. "I don't know who Omura will send out to hold down the fort, but if it's you, here's where I keep things, and the password to my computer." He jotted the information down, passed it over to the other man. "Mostly I'm worried about the *heiau* case. Can you volunteer to take my place if Omura needs to replace me? Do you have the time?"

"I'll try."

Stevens and Ferreira had just been settling into a comfort level with each other, and he didn't really know how the other man was taking all this. "I'd appreciate a minimum of rumor spreading about this, if possible," Stevens said.

Ferreira frowned, looking insulted. "They'll clear you. I can't see you ever doing anyone wrong like that."

"It looks bad, though, I know. I think I'm being set up, but there's nothing I can do right now other than go through the process. I hope I'll have your support."

Ferreira stood, extended his hand. His grip was strong, encouraging. "You got it, boss."

"Can you send in Mahoe? He still needs some

seasoning—hope you'll keep an eye on him. I have him on a special confidential assignment, and he's going to need some flexible scheduling." He'd already decided not to tell anyone about Mahoe's role except Omura, in case of leaks.

"No problem. I'll give the kid whatever he needs. Good luck, boss." Ferreira saluted with two fingers as he left, his face serious. Stevens knew he could get no greater support from the grizzled older man.

He was clearing his desk off as Brandon Mahoe came in and shut the door. Stevens had taken the burner phone out of its packaging. "I've only told Omura about your assignment. No one knows here—and let's keep it that way. I programmed my own burner's number into your phone. Report to me daily, so I know you're okay—just a text is fine."

"Yes, sir." Mahoe's face shone with excitement. "They are having a rally at the *heiau* in Wailuku tonight. I'll call you afterward."

"Great. And, Brandon. If you hear some rumors about me, don't believe them. I'll be cleared eventually." The young man frowned, obviously confused, as Stevens went on. "I'm going to be out on admin leave for a short time. It changes nothing that we've set up here."

"Yes, sir."

"I'll look forward to your call."

"I'll keep you posted. Daily." And Mahoe left.

There wasn't anything more to do than make sure the desk was clear for the next guy, if there was a next guy, and go on home. He walked through the small open area in front, bolstered by the encouragement he received from his small team all the way out to the Bronco.

Evening had fallen and Lei was home when Stevens drove up to the house. One look at her face as she stood on the porch, lips tight and brow furrowed, and he knew it wasn't the right time to bury her in the avalanche of baby stuff he'd bought. He hoped she wouldn't spot the mountain of boxes and bags in the back of the Bronco as he got out and locked the gate.

Keiki greeted him with happy tail wags, but Lei greeted him with a poke in the chest. "Where were you? I was worried!"

"I had to go downtown, do some errands, stop by my station," he said. He pulled her stiff body in for a hug. "I had to talk to the guys. Make sure my cases were wrapped up a bit."

She relaxed, fisting her hands in the back of his shirt. "I wasn't sure where you'd gone."

"Thought I'd skipped town or jumped off a cliff?" He tried to make it light, but one look at her stricken face showed him she was still worried. He leaned down and kissed her. "Let's go inside. I need a beer. Or four. We have to talk."

"Do we ever." She hooked a finger in his belt as if she couldn't bear to be separated, and he looped an arm over her. "I made some chili."

He wanted to make a cooking joke, because chili was pretty much all she ever made—but the energy that had carried him this far seemed to have evaporated. The sight of the reddish sauce in the pan, the spatters on the white enamel of the stove, brought the nightmare from earlier bursting back in front of his eyes.

"I'm not hungry. I think I'll take a shower."

"That's a good idea."

He didn't resist as Lei took his hand, leading him into the bathroom—he understood her need to connect with him in the oldest way in the world. He wanted to as well, but felt muffled somehow, wrapped in cotton batting, unable to respond as she kissed him and touched him. He didn't resist as she undressed him, kissing her way down his torso, playing with the button of his jeans. Kneeling before him, she looked up at him, a position that had never failed to arouse him before. Today he felt nothing but a slight embarrassment for both of them.

"Are you okay?" Lei asked.

"I don't think so," he said. "I can't."

"I understand." Lei undressed briskly in that un-self-conscious way she had, tossing the clothes in the hamper and walking into the shower. He followed, more slowly, realizing it wasn't normal for him to want another shower after his earlier lengthy one, but still longing to feel clean. She sat him on the bench and this time she washed him, head to toe, with the washcloth and shampooed his hair herself.

He didn't feel any cleaner than he had before, after his long scrub-down earlier.

Sitting in the living room, he was grateful for Keiki's solid bulk as the dog seemed to sense something was wrong and pressed close to him as he sat on the couch. He drank a beer but refused the chili. Lei ate hers and finally set her bowl on the coffee table, picking up her beer.

"Where do we start? I want the whole story of what happened."

He took a sip, and the glass lip of the bottle rattled against his teeth. "I don't want to go there again today."

She gave him a level stare. "I need to know. Just the bare bones."

"Anchara called me and asked me to come help her." He filled in the events. "Omura got a call while I was still in the interview room, confirming the baby is mine, and he's on Oahu at the neonatal unit."

"About that. What are we going to do about that?"

"That? You mean the baby. My baby." He felt his neck

getting hot. He knew it was unreasonable, but he didn't like her tone.

"Anchara's baby, that you knew nothing about, and as far as I'm concerned, have no responsibility for." Lei's eyes widened and she clapped a hand over her mouth as if she wished she could take back the words, but they'd been said.

"I was wondering how you'd feel about this."

"Less than thrilled, to be honest." She got up, an abrupt movement, and carried the bowl into the kitchen. He heard loud and unnecessary splashing and crashing from the kitchen sink.

He knew he should follow her, say something, offer comfort. He couldn't find the energy. Every time he shut his eyes, he saw Anchara, her mouth moving, her hand reaching, that belly, astonishingly large, emerging from the pool of blood she lay in. Whatever they were going through was nothing compared to her suffering, her death.

Stevens set the empty beer bottle down. He got up and went to the little wooden bar where they kept other kinds of booze for when company came over. He took out a bottle of scotch.

His alcoholic mom's drink of choice. Maybe it held some secret cure he'd missed. He splashed four fingers into one of the glasses and downed it in two searing gulps.

Lei returned, wiping her hands on a dishtowel. She

watched him as he refilled the glass. "I'm sorry." Her voice was low, trembling. "I didn't mean it. It's not the baby's fault. You're his father. He needs a home, and he should come to us."

Stevens turned toward her. The alcohol had lit a fire in his belly, steadying the tremble of his hands. "I was hoping you felt that way, because I went shopping."

"What?"

"Yeah. Bought a few things. We can put it all in the spare room." He tossed back the second drink, and when he turned and headed for the door, he was a little unsteady—but the flashback was gone. He knew it was only a temporary reprieve.

"Oh my God," Lei whispered as he popped the back of the truck to reveal boxes and bags up to the ceiling.

"Yeah. Apparently, babies need a lot of shit." He handed her bags until she turned to walk back to the house, and then he filled his own arms.

It took four trips to empty the truck. Lei was silent, the tight silence that didn't bode well, but by the last trip he was feeling the booze buzz and ready to take her on.

"Say what you've got to say," he said, standing beside her in the spare bedroom doorway as they looked at the mountain of baby items.

"This was supposed to be our baby!" she cried. "Ours! Not hers!" She burst into tears. He didn't try to stop her when she ran into their bedroom and slammed the door. In a few minutes he heard the murmur of her voice between sobs—probably calling her friend Marcella. He went back to the living room, fetched a spare blanket, and lay on the couch with Keiki and the scotch bottle, the TV on mute keeping the terrible images away from his eyes.

Chapter 11

Lei woke up to the sound of screaming. Deep, guttural, the sounds of a man in mortal pain.

She grabbed her weapon out of the holster hanging from the headboard and ran to the door, stumbling in the dark as she got it open and then flicking on the living room light to see the threat.

Stevens was sitting straight up on the couch, screaming, his eyes wide open but seeing something else.

Keiki, agitated, pawed his leg and licked his face. Lei, still scanning for threats, saw Stevens wake as he hunched over abruptly and embraced the dog.

"Oh, God. Help me," she heard him say. And he wept into the dog's coat, his arms around the sturdy Rottweiler.

Lei set the weapon on the coffee table, unsure how he'd respond to her. "Can I do anything?"

The harsh overhead light cast dark shadows under his eyes, beneath his cheekbones as he sat up. She saw the shape of his skull for the first time, as clearly as if the skin were peeled back.

"No. I just need to get through this. Something to

drink would be great, though." His voice was a harsh rasp.

Lei went into the kitchen and poured a large glass of milk. Her own throat felt rough from all the crying last night, but she felt better. Lighter. Determined. She'd had her say, had her cry. Told everything to her friend Marcella, who understood her conflicted feelings. Now she'd set her course. She'd do her best to be a mom to this baby. Whether she chose him or not, he was coming to them.

She poured herself a glass too, and brought one to Stevens, along with a sleeping pill from her stash. "Drink this whole thing and come back to bed. I'm done being mad."

He took the glass, drank the milk, swallowed the pill. That was as alarming as the screams—he hated pills of any kind. He followed her into the bedroom and lay down. Keiki, keeping watch, hopped up and nestled at Stevens's feet on her ratty old quilt.

Lei left them there and went back into the living room. She looked up a number in her phone, dialed it. "Dr. Wilson? I'm so sorry. I know it's early. But this is an emergency. Can you come to Maui?"

Stevens woke up slowly. The sun was in his eyes. He expected the cottony pain of a hangover, but the milk and sleeping pill must have worked, because there was nothing but a slight ache behind his eyeballs, and he hadn't dreamed again.

Keiki licked his hand, trotting back and forth in front of the bedroom door, clearly needing to be let out. There was no sign of Lei.

He got up and walked through the sunlit, empty house. Unlocked Keiki's dog door in back and let her out. Lei had started coffee, and its aroma teased his nose with the memory of something he used to enjoy.

It didn't feel like he could enjoy anything ever again, with Anchara dead on a slab in the morgue, gutted like a fish to get the baby out. He shuddered at the horrible thought.

So much blood. So wrong. So unfair.

He poured the coffee, then went to the front and retrieved the *Maui News*. He took it to the back porch, bracing himself. Sure enough: HIGH-RANKING MAUI OFFICER A PERSON OF INTEREST IN GRUESOME SLAYING OF PREGNANT WOMAN screamed the headline.

At least they hadn't named him.

Yet.

He scanned the article and stuffed it in the nearby trash bin. Threw the ball for Keiki.

He was screwing together the wheeled legs of the crib the saleslady had encouraged him to buy when he heard the rumble of Lei's truck pulling up, the sound of voices.

He'd never combed his hair or put on a shirt, and he didn't care. Whoever had the nerve to arrive at their house unannounced had to take him as he was. That irritated thought was put to the test when he stood up, screwdriver in hand, to greet Dr. Caprice Wilson.

The petite blond psychologist had done something different with her hair, and she was wearing a pretty wrap dress. He'd heard she'd been through a hard time on Haleakala, but if anything, she looked better for it.

"Dr. Wilson. Welcome to our home. I assume you're here to psych me out after last night's screaming episode." He knew his voice wasn't welcoming.

Dr. Wilson kept her bright blue eyes on his, but he could tell it took an effort. "Michael, I hear you've been through a trauma. Would you mind putting on a shirt and putting down the screwdriver? You're giving me a bit of a hot flash."

Lei had gone into the kitchen, and he heard her snort of laughter, which echoed his own.

"Happy to get a break from 'some assembly required'." Stevens gestured to the lineup of tiny parts and detailed instructions surrounding the crib. "I'll be right back."

He went into the bedroom, pulled on a shirt, changed into boxers and jeans. Hot flash, right. He snorted again. He hadn't spent a lot of time with Dr. Wilson, but he'd seen how effective she'd been in working with Lei over the years, and he'd always liked her quick wit and down-to-earth manner.

He came out of the bedroom, combing his hair with his fingers. Dr. Wilson sat on the couch. Lei was gone already.

"She had to go in to work," the psychologist said. "She just went to the airport to pick me up and bring me back here."

"Oh." Stevens went back into the kitchen, poured himself a fresh cup of coffee, and joined her on the couch. "Better?" He gestured to his clothes.

She winked. "Much. I'm old, but I'm not dead. I can see why Lei had to marry you—to keep you away from other women."

He shook his head ruefully. "Too late, because Anchara happened." He took too big a gulp of hot coffee and burned his tongue.

"Anchara swooped in and snagged you when you were vulnerable. That's how I see it."

Stevens frowned. "Not how it was."

"How was it?"

"She was being deported. She had nothing, no one. I felt responsible, like I had to do something—and Lei, she'd just left for the FBI. Chose that job over us. I was trying to move on."

"We all know how well that worked out." Dr. Wilson

took another sip of her coffee. "I see you're making the transition to dad without a hitch."

He tightened his belly, then set down the coffee mug hard. "I've heard about your techniques, Dr. Wilson. Provoking. Well, I don't appreciate it."

"Angry, are you?" Dr. Wilson's blue eyes were guileless over her mug.

"Hell, yes, I'm angry. This!" He stood to his full height, lifted open arms in an encompassing gesture. He could feel heat in his face. "I didn't ask for this! This massive disruption in my life, becoming a murder suspect and a dad in one day! And as soon as I realize I'm angry about it, I remember Anchara and all she lost—her life. Everything taken from her. Horrific." He shut his eyes, pushed his fingers into them. He swayed on his feet.

"Why don't you sit down?" Dr. Wilson patted the couch.

"No. I'd rather do something useful." He went back to the crib, knelt on the floor. "A goes into B. B connects to C. I wish this situation were like that. And just when Lei and I were finally settling into life."

"How's she dealing with this?"

"I'm sure she told you on the way here."

"I want to hear what you think. You know her better than anyone."

He slanted a glance at her, screwing the wheel socket

into the crib's leg. "I'd say *you* do."

She flapped a hand. "Avoiding the question."

"Lei believes me, that I'm innocent of hurting Anchara. That I didn't know about the pregnancy. She wants to do the right thing, but her heart's not there yet. She wanted us to have our own baby."

"And why can't you?"

He rocked back on his heels. "Seriously. We can accept having one—but dealing with the hassle of two? You've got to be kidding."

Dr. Wilson shrugged. "People have twins all the time. Yeah, it's a lot of work at first, but having two close together ends up being less work later, and the siblings are close. Besides, once you take the parenthood plunge, one can be as much work as two. Trust me, I know. We only had one."

Stevens found the next part, screwed it together. Checked the instructions. Turned the slatted boxy shape over, set the struts to support it on the bottom and screwed them in while he digested this.

"So you think this shouldn't change the path we were on."

"You could think of this first baby as training wheels. The first one always is."

Stevens snorted a laugh again. "What did Lei say about that?"

"Client confidentiality. You should ask her yourself."

"Am I your client, too? Do I have confidentiality today?"

"Of course."

"So you're not fishing for answers for the prosecution."

Dr. Wilson stared at him. "What do you think? Unless you are planning to hurt yourself or another, this conversation is protected."

"All right, then." He shook his head. "No. I've stressed Lei out enough. Continuing with our plan seems crazy."

"Lei's a big girl. She can make up her own mind."

"Speaking of. Something that bothers me. Why did Anchara let herself get pregnant that last time with me? She was on birth control, and we hadn't slept together in months. She seduced me that morning. She was saying goodbye. She knew what she was doing."

"I don't know, and sadly, she's not here to ask."

"Anchara never told me she was pregnant, and we were in touch on e-mail, just little monthly updates. It seems like she might have got pregnant deliberately, and kept my son from me." He could feel his heart thudding, the heat of anger flushing his body a second time. "I think she was going to tell me she was pregnant—she'd emailed me that she had something important to say—but it was right before she was killed."

"It's unlikely she planned to get pregnant, but you could have worked this out with her if she'd been alive. Maybe she forgot her birth control. Maybe she decided to keep the baby for religious reasons. Any number of reasons, actually. Women who don't tell a man he's a father generally don't want the complication that relationship will bring into their lives, especially if things ended badly."

"They didn't end badly. But they definitely ended." Stevens inserted the crib's legs into sockets on the bracket he'd attached to the wooden bottom and stood it up. They both gazed at the small, pretty bed. Empty. Just waiting to hold an infant.

"Evocative. Makes me feel emotional just looking at it," Dr. Wilson said. "Been a long time since I've seen one of these up close and personal. What do you feel when you look at it?"

Stevens tightened the screws all around the legs one more time and finally sat back, looking at the crib. "What do I feel? Exhausted and scared. But some part of me really wants my son. The more I think about him, the more I want to see him. Hold him. Bring him home."

"Tell me about the murder."

He tossed the screwdriver down, still gazing at the crib. Trying to suppress the memories of Anchara's last moments. "I can't wait to be done telling this story."

"That's the thing about telling a story. The more you do, the easier it gets. The more it lets the poison out. Lei tells me you had a bad nightmare last night."

He went into the kitchen. Held up the coffeepot. She shook her head. He refilled his mug, remembered he hadn't eaten last night, and brought an apple back to the couch. He bit into it, tasting the juice, hearing the crunch of the fresh, firm fruit. "Life. It's so sweet, and over so quickly."

"You're thinking of Anchara's death."

"Her life was stolen from her. Her child, ripped out of her womb." He bit again, chewed. His hand, holding the apple, trembled. He told the story again, and this time, describing the bed, he frowned, remembering the odd length of sheet hanging out from under her body. "I think there was something there I didn't notice at the time."

"Will you let me hypnotize you? We can really walk through the scene. There might be clues there for the investigation, for your peace of mind. I can also leave you with some suggestions about letting go of your responsibility for what happened. You didn't kill her."

"I might as well have." He stood again. Keiki whined, watching him, brown eyes worried. "I want a drink. You want one?"

"No, thanks. It's ten in the morning."

"No shit? Well, that never stopped my mom, and
I'm beginning to understand the appeal." He went to the
sideboard, splashed scotch into his coffee mug. "I guess
we can try the hypnotizing. Will I remember what we talk
about?"

"Only if you want to."

"No, thanks. Can you make me forget the whole thing
ever happened? What I saw?"

"No, but you can be free from the flashbacks." Dr.
Wilson shook her head, got up from the couch. "I don't
do party-trick hypnosis. I do the kind that you are in
control of and that helps heal. I'll tape it, though, so you
can decide if you want to listen to it and see if there's
anything you forgot at the scene that might help the
investigation."

"But I don't have to give it to them if it implicates me,
do I?" He was pretty sure he hadn't done anything wrong,
but it never hurt to be cautious in the position he was in.

"Of course. You'll own the recording." She took out a
small recorder and held up a tiny cassette tape. "One copy
of this, okay? And it belongs to you. Now, why don't
you lie down on the couch, and I'll sit in the chair." She
took the armchair facing the TV and turned it toward the
couch.

Stevens swigged down the coffee and scotch,
grimacing at the taste, and lay down, shoving a pillow

under his head. His legs were so long that they hung off the end of the sofa. "I'll do anything to get rid of the flashbacks from the scene."

"And you no longer need to experience that trauma. That's right." Her voice had settled in to a lower register, soothing as his mom's hand on his brow when he'd been a sick child. "Notice your breath. Slow it down. You don't have to be anything to anyone right now. Just notice your breath. Breathing in relaxation, breathing out the tension. Relaxing. You're safe now. Nothing bad will happen here. You will remember as much, or as little, as you want to."

Stevens felt his body sink bonelessly into the couch, and his eyes closed.

Chapter 12

Lei got a call, the radio on her dash crackling to life, on the way back to the station after dropping Dr. Wilson off with Stevens. "Oh-four at Vineyard Street in Wailuku. G-15 and 16, respond."

Oh-four was a murder. Just what she needed—a heavy-duty new case, with all that was going on. "Ten-four, responding and heading to the scene," she said into the handset.

"Roger that. G-16 incoming," Torufu's voice confirmed.

Lei hoped like hell there were no new bomb threats today. Yesterday's relatively simple shell retrieval had taken all day, and meanwhile, the cases kept coming.

The modest, locally run inn on Vineyard Street didn't look like the kind of place for a murder. The landlady, an older Portuguese woman wearing a fuchsia muumuu and a pair of bright pink Crocs, was scolding the officers securing the scene when Lei walked up. "I have other guests, you know, and they have to get to their rooms! This is bad for business!"

"Murder is, generally, bad for business, especially for the victim," Lei said as she walked up to the landlady. "I'm Sergeant Texeira. We'll work as hard as we can to make sure the premises are safe for all your guests. Did you discover the body?"

"Yes!" She pointed to the upper floor of the two-story, false-fronted wooden building, one of several on the hundred-year-old street that had a feel of the old west. "Our apartment is up there. We heard a disturbance last night, yelling, thumping. My husband wen' shout downstairs that he was goin' call the cops if it didn't stop. The noises stopped, but when I went down, I found the guest all bus' up, lying on the floor."

Lei had her notebook out. She collected Claudine Figueroa's name, contact information, approximate time of the disturbance, name of the victim, a Norm Jorgenson, who'd paid in cash. She noted every detail she could get, while keeping an eye out for Torufu. Her partner finally arrived, at a jog.

The officer who'd responded to the call handed over the log for them to sign in. "Messy in there. You might want to wear booties."

Lei had brought her crime kit, and she bundled her hair into a ponytail to keep her own hairs from contaminating the scene. She slid blue paper booties on over her shoes and snapped on gloves, picking up her kit. "Dr. Gregory on his way?"

"He's been called," Torufu confirmed. Lei recapped the landlady's story as they walked down a creaky wooden hall with closed doors on either side. Dim lighting barely chased the shadows away. "Seems like a low-rent kind of place, but it's got historic atmosphere."

"It'll have more after this," Torufu said.

They arrived at the victim's doorway, crossed with crime-scene tape, another officer guarding it. He admitted them. Lei's nostrils crinkled at the powerful smell of blood, a sweetish metallic odor that she'd always thought had a texture to it. Today it was almost unbearably strong to her. She wished she'd brought Vicks to put under her nose.

The victim was facedown on the wooden floor, and even from where they were standing, they could see the back of his head was bashed in. Blood spatter had flown off the murder weapon to decorate the walls and ceiling in a criss-crossing pattern of blood droplets and chunks of brain.

This was worse than Lei had braced herself for, and her stomach did an uneasy somersault. Lei's shoe crunched on something as she moved forward. She stopped and bent to retrieve it. A shard of skull the size of a silver dollar reminded her of a chunk of coconut shell with the hairy husk still attached. She stopped where she stood, took out the camera, photographed the fragment, then picked it up carefully by a hair and set it next to the body.

Torufu put his hands on his hips. "Anger in this scene."

"Seems pretty brutal." She worked her way in closer to the body. The man's clothes were good-quality sportswear, and he wore lightweight European hiking shoes. She could tell he'd been physically fit, though the muscles had begun to assume the shapelessness characteristic of the dead.

"Someone didn't like the vic, that's for sure." Torufu looked through the man's possessions. "Check this out." He held up a metal toolkit, a yellow plastic case. "I think this is one of those hand-held jacks they use for mining and such. Expensive."

Lei straightened up from her study of the body. "This could be related to Stevens's *heiau* desecration case. He was telling me the petroglyphs were removed with some sort of hand-held jack."

They continued to process the scene. Lei breathed shallowly through her mouth as she carefully felt in the man's pockets, looking for ID. Empty. She didn't see any other obvious wounds on the body besides the bashed-in head. "Do you see the murder weapon?"

"Not so far." They both searched, looking under the bed, in the man's possessions.

Dr. Gregory, his assistant Tanaka, and their gurney,

appeared in the doorway. "Hey, Lei. Thought you were on bomb squad now."

"Multitasking, as usual." She grinned at the doc's aloha shirt, covered with lurid green sea turtles. "You brighten the place up."

"Glad I wore booties," Gregory said, turning his head to take in the spatter patterns. "You got photos of that?"

"Not yet. We were looking for the murder weapon."

"I can't imagine it went far. Whatever it was would be dripping with fluids and trace. In fact, did you see anything in the hall?"

"Good idea," Lei said. "Abe, you do the blood spatter photos and I'll check for trace outside."

Torufu nodded. She went outside the room, gratefully breathing fresher air, and thought of the scene Stevens had faced yesterday. No wonder he'd had nightmares. For a moment, an unbidden picture of Stevens stabbing Anchara bloomed in her imagination.

No. There was no way. Stevens wasn't capable of that, no matter the provocation. He'd never wavered in his support of Lei when she'd come under suspicion last year in the execution-style killing of her childhood molester Charlie Kwon. Now she had a chance to return the favor.

She hoped Dr. Wilson could work some of her psychology magic, help them get through this massive challenge. It was so overwhelming to think about that she was glad to have to totally focus on the job at hand.

Lei turned off the overhead light and shone the blue flashlight into the hall, swinging it back and forth. Proceeding down the hallway in a straight line were three sets of footprints picked out in blood from the victim.

She retrieved the camera and photographed the tracks, laying blotting paper on the most well-defined shoe prints to pick up one that might tell shoe size and type.

Nowhere, besides the footprints, did she see droplets or trace that might have fallen off an object used to beat the victim's head in.

After Lei recorded the footprints for later analysis, she walked back through the building and out, around into the weedy side yard outside the victim's window, which had been closed from inside. There, caught in the branches of a hibiscus bush, was a metal crowbar.

"Gotcha," she muttered. Crowbar—the weapon of thugs.

Lei photographed, then retrieved the tool. Such an ordinary thing, until suddenly it was lethal. Lei knew she'd never see a crowbar in quite the same way.

Blood marked one viciously-hooked end, and she tried not to picture the impact on the back of the fallen man's skull—and failed. The chunk of skull and scalp she'd stepped on had told the tale too well. She slid the iron into a large plastic bag the landlady fetched for her—none of the evidence bags she'd brought were large enough.

She went back into the victim's room, where Dr. Gregory and Tanaka, with Torufu's help, were prepping the body for removal.

"Found the murder weapon. Crowbar."

"Yikes," Gregory said. "That explains the skull fragments everywhere."

"Yes, and there were three sets of prints in the hall."

Torufu hefted the man's suitcase and the backpack with the tools. "Let's get these back to the station and see if they have any trace tying to the *heiau* desecrations."

Lei helped carry the victim's possessions. The landlady followed them. "Who's going to pay for cleaning the room?" she cried. "So disgusting!"

"The room is a crime scene, and sealed for the time being," Torufu said.

Gregory overheard the woman's comment and dug around in his kit for a card, handed it to her. "After they release the scene, you could try this special cleaning service. Unfortunately expensive, but you're the landlord."

They left her squawking in fury over the outrage that had been visited on her inn. After stowing the items and locking her truck, Lei tamped down irritation at Claudine Figueroa's insensitivity and returned to speak to the woman.

"So sorry this happened in your place," she said. "You seem like you know a lot of people—if you hear any rumors, anything at all about who might have done this, will you call me?"

"Yes! I still can't believe it; so shame this!"

Lei walked away from the voluble lady, leaving her describing her shock to a small crowd of neighbors. She took a deep breath, refreshing herself for a few seconds by resting her eyes on the sculptured, cloud-tasseled depth of Iao Valley behind Wailuku's funky collection of buildings. The cool green of the valley was a balm on eyes burned by what they'd seen.

In Lei's truck on the way back to the station, her cell rang. She saw Stevens had left a voicemail, but now wasn't the time to listen to it. Checking the caller ID, she picked up. "Dad! How are you?"

"Not so good. Your aunty, she's taking a turn for the worse. Her kidneys have failed. She's having emergency dialysis, but they're only giving her a week." Her father's voice was heavy and molasses-slow.

"Dad, no! I'm so sorry." Lei's mind scrambled as she tried to think of how she could get away and go back to California with Stevens under suspicion, custody of a new baby on the horizon, and a fresh murder on her hands. "Oh my God. I don't know how to get away. This is the worst possible time."

"Do you think there's a 'good time' for your aunty to die? Call me back when you can say something with even a little bit of love in it!" Her father banged down the phone.

"Dammit, I'm sorry." Lei bit her lip as she put the phone down, quick tears filling her eyes, but he was gone. Lei didn't feel like she could handle one more thing—but she had to keep trying. It felt like she was juggling live emotional grenades. She rubbed the rough white gold medallion at her throat.

Lei pulled into the station and told herself to focus on the job. When all else went crazy, there was always the job—even if it was its own kind of insanity.

Chapter 13

Stevens handed his boarding pass to the gate attendant. Dr. Wilson followed him onto the plane. It had been her idea that they travel to Oahu together, since she had more work to do on a case there.

In his pocket, not yet listened to, was the hypnosis tape. New information had come out from the session. Stevens had noticed an extra length of sheet beneath Anchara's body—a white linen shroud. Not only that, but worse—he'd recognized the knife she'd been stabbed with as his own. She'd taken the folding fishing knife when she moved out of their Wailuku house, and he hadn't seen it since.

He'd been set up by a pro.

Dr. Wilson turned to Stevens as they sat together for the brief flight. "You sure you didn't want to bring Lei for this?"

"I know she can't get away. I heard she pulled a fresh murder this morning. Those first twenty-four hours are critical, and I left her a message."

"I hope she's not upset with you."

"No more than usual, I'm sure." He tried to smile. "We've been doing okay through all this. I know she's got my back and I've got hers, and that's what we need most right now."

"Okay. Just imagining myself in her shoes. I'd have wanted to come support you seeing the baby for the first time." Dr. Wilson turned away, gazed out the oval window at the iconic view of Diamond Head. The jagged outline of Waikiki's hotel district, stark and white against the lush mountains and bright ocean, was just coming into view. Billowing piles of cottony clouds slid by the window as they began their descent.

Stevens knew Dr. Wilson was right in what she was saying, but he also knew Lei wouldn't be available during those first twenty-four hours on a new case. He just couldn't wait to see the baby—needed to see him. He reclined his seat and closed his eyes, replaying in his mind the conversation he'd had with the social worker in charge of the child.

"I spoke to your captain, and she faxed me the results of your paternity test," Darlene Fujimoto said. "However, I need to interview you and assess your readiness to care for the baby, the situation you'll be bringing him home to. Not to mention ruling out the question of your involvement with his mother's death."

"I understand," Stevens said, keeping his voice soft, though he'd felt defensive. "I just want to meet with you and begin the process. Everyone has to be confident ours is the right home for my son and that it's a healthy environment for him. I get that. As to my 'involvement,' it's an investigation. It will take as long as it takes. I hope that doesn't keep me from at least showing my support and care for him."

A long pause. "I look forward to meeting you. Let's rendezvous at the hospital in the lobby," Fujimoto had said.

Stevens said goodbye to Dr. Wilson at the airport and got into a taxi for the hospital, wrinkling his nose at the cab smell of old cigarettes—the pine tree dangling from the rearview wasn't cutting it. He tried Lei's cell again, and this time she picked up.

"Just going into the evidence room." Lei sounded a little breathless. "I saw you left me a message?"

"Yeah. I'm on Oahu. Trying to see the baby, maybe bring him home."

A pause.

"Oh. Okay." Her voice was downcast.

"I'm sorry I'm here without you. I heard you pulled a fresh one, and I know you won't be able to get home, so after Dr. Wilson and I talked, I thought I'd get over to Oahu and see if I can get the wheels moving."

"So inconvenient, all this happening at once." He could tell Lei was struggling to stay light.

He switched gears. "Can you ask Pono, or McGregor—somebody—if we can get access to Anchara's living space? I really want to find out what she wanted to name the baby. It's so weird calling him Baby Boy Mookjai, which is what's on his birth certificate now."

"I'll try." Her voice sounded hesitant. "But I don't know if they'll let me in there, or tell me anything. You know that."

"Of course I do." The taxi took a turn a little fast, bumping him against the window, and Stevens glimpsed the ocean from the elevated freeway, a gleam of peaceful blue. "I just want to find out more about him. The social worker is meeting me at the hospital for an initial interview, but said she needs to 'rule out my involvement' with his mother's death, and God knows how long that will take. He'll go into foster care, probably." Stevens ran a hand through his hair. "I just want to see him. Maybe hold him."

"We have to get you cleared as soon as possible, then. Speaking of your involvement, Pono told me they found one of those shrouds under Anchara's body. I thought that was going to clear you, but he says no."

"I know. I remembered it after Dr. Wilson hypnotized me. I was too distracted at the time. I also recognized the murder weapon."

A long beat. Stevens raised his eyes to check on the

taxi driver. The man had his eyes on the road, but he decided not to say more. "Can't discuss it now. But Dr. Wilson was really helpful. Thanks for bringing her in."

"I didn't know what else to do. How to help you."

"I love you. Don't believe I said it yet today."

"I love you, too. We'll get through this. I don't quite know how, though." Lei told him about her aunt dying. "I have to find a way to get back there. They only gave her a week."

"Holy God." Stevens ran his hand through his hair again. "And I mean that as a prayer. I'm so sorry. I'll call you as soon as I know what's happening with the baby."

"Sounds good. Come home soon."

She hung up, and when he pressed Off on the phone, in spite of all the challenges, his chest was lighter, his breathing easier, and he noticed the color and buzz of Honolulu's downtown swirling around him for the first time. He shut his eyes and prayed for strength for both of them.

Stevens waited in the lobby after a quick trip to the bathroom to make sure he'd combed his disordered hair and brushed down the blue shirt Lei had bought him. He looked respectable, if a little stressed out. Acceptable under the circumstances.

Darlene Fujimoto approached him, a round middle-aged woman with a name badge clipped to her large Lycra-wrapped bosom. She eyed him over thick glasses and shook his hand. "Nice that you could come, Lieutenant Stevens."

"I'm eager to see my son."

"Yes. Well. Let's talk first." She led him to a couch and sat him down. "I checked with my supervisors, and what we'll do here today is begin the process of screening you for guardianship. We will also have to interview your wife and check your home and make sure it's safe and prepared for a newborn. Then there's the situation with his mother's death."

Stevens kept his face blank. "I am happy to go through whatever screening we need to do. My wife as well. If you check us out, you will see we're both dedicated civil servants."

"Be that as it may. We are not comfortable releasing the baby into your custody until you have been ruled out in his mother's murder. I'm sure you understand." She pushed her glasses farther up her nose and fiddled with her clipboard, clearly uncomfortable.

Stevens squelched his dismay. Who knew how long this thing could drag on? But he saw it from their point of view, too—for all they knew, he'd killed Anchara to get the baby for himself.

"I understand. I hope, in the meantime, we can at least

visit the baby. Supervised, of course," he said, hoping to diffuse her tension. He needed this woman on his side.

"Of course!" She smiled, clearly relieved he wasn't going to fight her on the terms of custody. "He is stable and doing well since he got into the neonatal unit, and actually, he's due to leave the hospital tomorrow if his vitals stay good. We've set up a very nice placement for him, and you can arrange visits with the foster family when you and your wife are able to come."

His son was definitely going into foster care.

Stevens fought to keep his voice even. "Thank you. Please do the very best you can for him."

"Oh, I did." Fujimoto handed him the clipboard. "Some background information, here, while I tell you about the placement." She proceeded to natter on about the foster family, how many babies they'd cared for with the state, how wonderful they were. Stevens kept his attention focused on filling in the little boxes on the form. He was done with it all by the time she'd begun to wind down, and he handed it back to her.

"Any chance we can go look at him in the nursery?"

"Of course." Fujimoto stood up and led the way to the elevators. "Tell me a little about your home situation. I understand you were recently married?"

"Yes." He didn't know how to address the thorny issue of Anchara's pregnancy so close to his own wedding, so he left it at that.

They got on the elevator. "And according to your captain, you weren't aware the baby's mother was pregnant?"

Stevens felt a flash of heat on the back of his neck at her insinuating tone. He reached out and punched the Stop button. Fujimoto's eyes got big behind her glasses, and he held his hands up in a "surrender" gesture. The last thing he wanted to do was scare her.

"Let me just tell you the situation as best I can, now that we have a little privacy. Anchara was my wife. We probably shouldn't have married—we had issues from before day one—but I was trying to make it work. It wasn't enough for her. As soon as she knew she was getting her green card, she left me. She slept with me on her way out the door, literally, and must have gotten pregnant. I never saw her in person again, and even though we were in contact through e-mail, she never said a word about the baby. I paid her support every month and wished her well—there was regret between us, but nothing more. She even came to my wedding to Lei, but I didn't see her there." He drew a breath, pushed a hand through his hair. "Then, out of the blue, she called me, asking for help. Claimed to be 'injured' and unable to meet me at a restaurant I asked for. She insisted on meeting at that motel."

"That was when you found her, already dying?"

Fujimoto frowned.

"Yes. She was bleeding out from stab wounds. I did first aid and CPR. The paramedics took her away, and the baby was delivered by emergency cesarean. That's why he was deprived of oxygen." He forcefully suppressed the memory of Anchara's pale face and thready voice, begging him to take the baby sooner.

While she was alive.

Stevens found himself trembling at the memory of the scene and steadied himself by putting a hand on the wall. "So, I understand why I'm being looked at as a suspect, but I swear to you, on a stack of Bibles, I had nothing to do with her death."

"So what makes you think you should be the person to raise her son?"

"Because, however things started, he's my son, too."

"Well, he could have brain damage. Disabilities. Because of the oxygen deprivation. Are you prepared to deal with that?"

"He's my son. It doesn't matter what needs he has. I'll stand by him."

"And your new wife? How does she feel about raising your ex's child? One who might even be disabled?"

"She's just as committed as I am." He bit the inside of his cheek, hoping that was true.

Fujimoto turned to the control panel and pressed the floor number. They started moving again. "I appreciate hearing your version of events."

They rode up to the neonatal floor in silence.

As he stood in front of the glass viewing window into the nursery, Stevens's heart raced. He could see Fujimoto inside, talking to the nurse in front of one of the square, glass incubators. Around the open room, he could see babies in various levels of care, from tiny preemies in isolation units with spaces where hands could be inserted into gloves inside, to ones like the one his son was in, a rounded Plexiglas orb. He couldn't see much, but his eyes fastened, as if magnetized, on the tuft of dark hair not hidden by Fujimoto's bulk.

As if he'd conjured a response, Fujimoto turned and gestured to him to enter.

Chapter 14

Stevens's hands broke out in sweat as he pressed down on the door handle. His heart pounded. Was he scared? Excited? He didn't know. He wished suddenly and desperately that he hadn't undertaken this alone and that Lei was by his side.

He navigated the unfamiliar setting and came to stand in front of the unit, gazing in at the tiny swaddled form.

The baby's eyes were closed, and even though he looked as anonymous as any newborn, there was a pleasing symmetry to his round head, rosebud mouth, and delicate, shell-like ears. His hair was jet-black, thick and long, and reminded him of Anchara, which brought a stab of sorrow. He'd heard the baby was almost full term, but Anchara had been a small woman, so perhaps that explained how ridiculously little the child looked, no bigger than a football.

Blood was roaring in his ears so loudly it was hard to understand the nurse. "You can sit and hold him," he heard her say. "Put on this gown and gloves. He's doing great, but we keep a sterile environment in here."

"Okay." Stevens got the gown on over his clothes, put on gloves and a mask. Fujimoto put one on, too. He sat down on the rocking chair next to the unit, feeling stupid, inept, terrified—as if poised at the top of a roller coaster ride that would change his life forever.

The nurse opened the pod. Stevens felt a draft of the warmth that surrounded the baby, and the next moment she handed him the child, wrapped in a pale blue blanket.

His son's head fit perfectly into Stevens's palms, and the baby's body lay easily on his forearms. There was a light, springy quality to the tiny body in his arms, as if any moment the child could arch into the air and fly. He could feel the baby warming him. Stevens stroked the tracery of an eyebrow, and as his finger brushed the baby's cheek, the pink mouth opened, making kissing movements.

"Rooting reflex," the nurse said. "Touches to the face activate the baby looking for the breast."

"Afraid he's going to be disappointed in me." Stevens's voice sounded squeaky.

"Not necessarily. Would you like to feed him? It's almost time. He eats every two hours."

The baby's eyes opened. He arched his body, stretching, a surprisingly strong movement, and yawned. His gaze steadied, fastening on Stevens's face. His eyes were cloudy gray, a shade somewhere between blue and brown. He yawned again and turned his head to mouth the side of Stevens's glove-covered hand.

Stevens felt something powerful seize hold of his heart, and he knew he'd just fallen into a love as strong as the one he had for his wife.

The nurse had been preparing a bottle, and she handed it to Stevens. She showed him how to tuck the child against his chest in the crook of his arm and to keep the bottle at an angle to minimize bubbles: "or else he'll get gas and be all fussy."

Stevens felt like he could gaze at the child's face all day. The baby seemed equally smitten, staring up at Stevens as he worked the rubber nipple, jaws pumping energetically.

"What are you going to name him?" Fujimoto asked softly.

He glanced up at her, surprised. "I get to name him?"

She shrugged, avoiding eye contact. "The child needs a name."

"I have Lei looking into what Anchara was going to name him. She deserves that we do our best to honor her wishes." Stevens looked back down into the baby's hypnotic face. "What color are his eyes going to be?"

The nurse answered. "Probably brown, given his hair color—but with your blue eyes, they could be green. You won't know for a few months."

Stevens stayed through feeding, burping, and changing under the nurse's tutelage until Fujimoto began getting restless. Finally, reluctantly, he handed his son back to the nurse. "How soon will we know if he's sustained any brain damage?"

"There's no easy way to tell. All his reflexes and vitals are normal at this point. It could take as long as school to show up, perhaps as a learning disability. You just have to stay positive," the nurse said.

"I will definitely do that." Stevens tore his gaze away from the baby as the nurse put him back into his pod. Stevens stripped off the scrubs and threw everything in a bin, and made himself walk away. His heart lurched at the thin wail he heard from the unit.

Fujimoto patted his arm, and he realized he'd forgotten she was even there.

"You'll do fine," she said, and he heard support in her voice. He blinked hard, and as they stepped into the hallway, he turned to Fujimoto and shook her hand.

"Thank you so much."

"I'm sorry how things started for this little guy, but I think they're going to end up fine." Fujimoto's eyes were misty, too. "I'll be in touch to give you the foster family's contact information."

"Is it okay if I just stay here awhile?" He thought he could still hear the baby crying.

"Of course. Perhaps you can see him again tomorrow."

"Definitely. Please, if you can make the time. I'll get a hotel for tonight. I have some police business I can do here, but I want to see him every minute I can."

"In that case, I'll sign a waiver that you can visit him as long as the nurse stays with you. I'll leave it at the front desk."

"Thank you." Impulsively, he bent and kissed her cheek.

Darlene Fujimoto flapped a hand and blushed. "See you tomorrow, Lieutenant."

He was already looking back through the window into the nursery.

Chapter 15

Lei uploaded the dead man's prints into AFIS and Interpol. Though they'd found no ID at the scene, the sleek hair and pricey clothing of the victim spoke of Europe to her. She and Torufu logged the evidence items in one by one, but even as she worked on building the case file, one part of her mind was on Stevens.

Going to Oahu to see his baby.

They had to clear him in Anchara's murder quickly, or the child would go into foster care. Probably no way around it, the way things were going.

She remembered her own stints in foster care way too well; the one where she'd slept in a bed with another little girl who wetted. Nightly humiliation, sheet-changing, and doing laundry with the foster mom yelling at them and the other little girl blaming Lei. The home where she got on a truck with the other kids every afternoon and worked on a taro farm, knee-deep in mud from when school ended to dark, for "character-building." The one where "Uncle Joe" and "Aunt Sarah" had them pray for hours, on their knees, and fast once a week. Most of all, never belonging, minimally cared for by people who couldn't emotionally afford to love her.

Even as she typed the scene report, the last resistance to the idea of adopting the baby evaporated. However unprepared, she and Stevens were the baby's family, and she wouldn't let him stay stuck in foster while there was breath in her body to stop it.

"Abe." She turned to her partner. Torufu looked up from the hand-held jack on the worktable—he was dusting it down for prints. "I need to go talk to someone. Can you finish up here?"

"Sure." He had one of those toothpicks he liked to chew between his front teeth. "Everything okay, Mrs. Stevens?"

"Not really." She described the situation with the baby. "We need to get Stevens cleared on his ex's murder as soon as possible."

Torufu's expressive brown eyes were compassionate. "You know it looks bad."

"I know. But that shroud tells us it's the perp who threatened us. We just need to prove it. I want to see what's going on with the case."

"Go." He flapped a hand. "I'll say you're out on a smoke break, if anybody asks."

"Right." She snorted a laugh. "I'll be back soon."

Lei found her ex-partner and oldest friend on the force, Pono, in his office with Gerry Bunuelos. "Got a minute?"

Pono followed her into the empty break room. She poured a mug of coffee. "I need to know what's going on with Anchara's murder."

"You know I got taken off the case." Pono had a line between his brows, and he rubbed his lips under the bristly mustache. "For this very reason."

"I get it, but we need to get Stevens cleared ASAP. Our baby's going into foster care for as long as it takes for him to be removed as a suspect." She described what was happening. "Also, we need to find out what Anchara wanted to name him. How prepared she was for him."

He took down a mug and filled it beside her. "Ready to call the kid 'our baby' huh? Okay. Well, I've been keeping my ears out, and I think the shroud thing does have them tracking down who bought it—but I'm afraid they'll find a receipt planted somewhere at your house. You should do your own search before McGregor comes by with a warrant."

"Crap," Lei said. "I agree." The house was empty but for the guardianship of their faithful Keiki—but if the receipt or other evidence was planted, it would have been done earlier. She should check Stevens's car—and follow up with the GreenDeath Place, where the shrouds were purchased. She'd better move fast. On the way out to her truck, she called Stevens.

He picked up right away. "What's up?"

"Where are you?"

"In the hall outside the nursery, watching the baby." Lei heard a wondering note in Stevens's voice. "He's beautiful, Lei."

"I bet." Lei felt a jealous twinge, followed by guilt—how could she be jealous of a baby? Perhaps it was because she knew that, with Anchara's beauty and Stevens's good looks, the kid had a head start in the gene department. But he'd lost his mother because of the shroud killer's vendetta, and for that Lei felt responsible. "Listen, I have a lot to tell you. I want to search your truck and our house for planted evidence related to the shrouds or something from Anchara's murder. Pono thinks McGregor is going to serve us with a warrant and they'll find something. I'm also going to go by the GreenDeath Place myself, ask them about the shroud. Where did you park the Bronco at the airport?"

"The Bronco's in stall J-14." She heard the frown in Stevens's voice. "That's good you want to check out her place, but I worry about you duplicating their investigation. It could muddy the waters. Give the wrong impression, if they find out."

"Do you want to go to jail? Or bring home the baby?" Lei found she couldn't say Anchara's name.

"You know the answer to that. Now, more than ever."

She heard him sigh as she turned on her Toyota truck. "But we have to be careful. I also need to check in with Mahoe, see what he's been able to pick up about the Heiau Hui from the inside."

"That's the other big thing that's happened." Lei filled in the details on the bludgeon murder. "Torufu and I think this could be connected to your *heiau* desecration case. This guy had a jackhammer with him. Torufu's testing the residue, but I wouldn't be at all surprised if it matched rock dust from your *heiau* site."

"I better get ahold of Marcus," Stevens said. She could tell he was walking now. "I was planning to see him anyway, but now I should tell him about your case. I wonder if the Heiau Hui had anything to do with the bludgeon murder."

"Right, we were thinking that, too. There were three perps, and the murder weapon was a crowbar. Not exactly sophisticated, but definitely effective. When are you coming home?"

"I was going to stay overnight, visit the baby some more. I'm still not cleared for duty."

"I'll miss you," Lei said, and hung up. She stuffed down her mixed feelings about the baby and opened the Toughbook computer on her dash. She typed in Anchara Mookjai's name. The Department of Motor Vehicles address didn't mean that was where the woman currently lived. Still, it was a place to start. She was sure the team investigating the murder would be done searching Anchara's residence by now—but it was still worth going by to see what she could find out about what the woman had wanted to name her son, and who might have murdered her.

At the airport, Lei parked near Stevens's Bronco and felt around for the magnetic key box in the wheel well. It was crusted with red Maui dirt, but she slid it open for the spare key and unlocked the vehicle.

She didn't bother with gloves, because her prints would be expected in the car, but she found her hands prickling with nervous sweat as she searched it.

In the front seat, shoved down in the crack where she located it by feel, she found a receipt for one pure white linen shroud from the GreenDeath Place. Hidden enough for Stevens to miss it but in a plausible location to have been lost.

She slid it into an evidence bag, her heart hammering, and relocked the vehicle. Getting into her truck, turning it on, waiting a minute for the air-conditioning to blow her frizzing curls off her face, she considered what to do with the incriminating scrap of white paper.

The receipt was evidence in a murder case, but if she turned it in, it would only confirm Stevens as a suspect. She doubted there were any prints on it, but if she sprayed it with ninhydrin to check and then decided to submit it, they'd be able to tell it had been tampered with. She needed to turn it in, but how?

That paper was as deadly as a grenade, and it had been intended to blow them up.

Lei drove to the GreenDeath Place location. The little storefront in Haiku was shuttered and closed, and a handwritten sign on the door said BY APPOINTMENT ONLY, listing a cell number.

She couldn't use her phone to call for an appointment—if her phone were subpoenaed, they'd know she was investigating. She pulled the silver Tacoma in next to a pay phone and called the number.

A male voice answered. "GreenDeath Place."

"I'm here near your establishment and would like to speak to you about your products."

"Sure. I live next door, so I'll come right over and unlock for you."

The owner had the lean, oiled-looking muscles of a yoga practitioner and was decked out in wooden beads, clad only in a sarong. He was bald, but even his head was tan and toned-looking.

The GreenDeath Place interior was dimly lit, with spotlights on plain wooden coffins. A strong herbal smell, not unpleasant, infused the room. Lei identified herself and told the man that she needed to know about a purchase.

He shook his head. "I talked to the cops yesterday."

Lei nodded. "I'm just following up." She showed him the receipt. "See the date? I need a description for who purchased this."

The proprietor frowned. "Cash. I remember this because we usually get orders online or over the phone. Yeah, this was a medium guy, dark hair. Asian. Wore a ball cap. Didn't get a good look at his face."

Lei felt a thrill. That description could match Terence Chang, heir apparent of the Big Island crime family—and a known enemy.

"Did the other cops ask you already about working with a sketch artist on a drawing of this man?" Even as she said it, she worried. Terence Chang wouldn't be caught so easily. Surely he hadn't bought the shrouds in person. Still, as long as this physical description didn't match Stevens, she wanted to pursue and document it.

"Yeah, they said they were sending someone, but he hasn't come yet. He bought two more," the proprietor said, tapping the plastic-bagged receipt with a finger. Lei felt herself stiffen in shock.

"Did he pay separately for them? With cash?"

"Yes."

"Did you tell the other detectives this? About the description and the other shrouds?"

"I didn't have this receipt with the exact date, but I did tell them about the transaction—it was odd enough for me to pay attention. Hey, aren't you working together?"

"Of course. We've all just been running around so much I haven't had time to coordinate all the information our team has gathered." Lei snatched back the receipt with a smile she hoped was reassuring. "We'll be in touch about the sketch artist." Now that she knew McGregor and his partner knew what she knew, there was no point in turning in the receipt right away.

She could only hope this witness didn't tell them about her visit.

Lei took a breath of fresh air outside and went to the nearby market to pick up a Spam musubi and an apple for lunch. She'd learned the benefit of having something, anything, in her stomach.

She also picked up an island map. She didn't want to enter any addresses into her truck's GPS. Back in the car, munching her lunch, she plotted the route to Anchara's address, somewhere in the heart of Kahului in a neighborhood that she knew—a sprawl of elderly cement block homes punctuated by rusting cars and parked boats.

On her way, she put the Bluetooth in her ear and checked in with Torufu. "I'm still processing the vic's belongings, but his fingerprints came back: Norm Jorgenson, Norwegian. Wanted for art theft by Interpol."

"This is definitely connected with the *heiau* desecrations, then. I'll let Stevens and Kamuela know."

"Be back by three p.m.," Torufu said. "We're meeting with Omura to update her on the case."

"Roger that."

Lei texted Stevens the man's name and connections while at a stop sign, and he sent her a thumbs-up and told her that he was meeting with Kamuela downtown about the *heiau* case. Lei paused, considering telling him about the receipt and her visit to the GreenDeath Place—and decided not to, for the moment. The less he knew about her activities, the better.

Twenty minutes later, she pulled into a chipped cement driveway, peering ahead through the windshield. It appeared, by the crossed crime-scene tape over the door, that Anchara had lived in a small *ohana*, or mother-in-law cottage, tucked under the spreading limbs of a mango tree in the backyard of the main house.

As she got out of her truck, a dog burst into barking inside. Someone shushed it, and Lei knew there was no way she could just sneak into the cottage. If McGregor and Chun found out she'd been there, she'd just have to tell them she was looking for information about the baby—and that was the truth.

A paunchy older man opened the screen door of the main house. "Thought you cops were done back there."

"Not done until we release the scene," Lei said, holding up her badge. "Is it locked? I need to do one more check inside."

"I'll unlock it for you." He disappeared and then reappeared in the garage, pushing his feet into rubber slippers. "This way."

Lei snapped on gloves and bundled her hair into a ponytail as they crossed the patchy, dry grass of the backyard.

"What are they going to do with all of her things?" The man's back was to Lei, his worn Primo Beer shirt stretching as he unlocked the door. "So shame, this whole thing. What happened to the baby?"

Lei kept her face impassive, suppressing an inner quaver as the man turned to her, pushing the door open. "I'm sorry. I can't discuss the case. Perhaps she had a next-of-kin? Do you know of anyone?"

The landlord shook his head. "Few friends. No family. She was one sweet girl, though, and so excited about the baby."

"We'll let you know if we find a place for her belongings to go."

"Make sure you folks do—rent will be due at the end of the month, and if we don't hear anything, we're going to send it all to Goodwill."

Lei felt her chest tighten, grief prickling the backs of her eyes. She didn't want to be here, doing this, poking through the remains of Stevens's ex-wife's life. She didn't want to be reminded of all Anchara had been through, all she'd lost. It was sickening, and so wrong.

She kept her expression neutral, lifting the tape and stepping inside. "I'll be a few minutes. I'll lock up when I leave," she said, dismissing the landlord.

He nodded. She shut the door and turned around to face Anchara's home.

Chapter 16

Stevens got out of the cab at the Honolulu Police Department's modern downtown building. Marcus Kamuela had agreed to meet him, and came down the wide stone steps to give him a shoulder-clap man hug. "So you're here. Why? Surely not to see me. We could just Skype it, like before."

"Yeah, personal business. Lei and I are going to be parents."

"Damn, man, knocked her up already?" Kamuela gave his trademark white grin as he led the way back into the building.

"No, not that simple. My ex got pregnant as we were separating." Stevens tried to think of how to put the whole terrible situation into as few words as possible.

"Say no more. I heard about your case." Kamuela's eyes were serious now. "Didn't realize you were the father. A bad business—and a good setup by someone who has it in for you."

"You have no idea." Stevens breathed a sigh of relief that he didn't have to tell the story again and that

Kamuela appeared to believe his innocence. "When they clear me as a suspect, we're bringing home a baby boy. I went to the hospital to see him and grease the wheels with Child Welfare."

"Then I hope they clear you soon." Kamuela led him into a conference room. The walls were decorated in crime-scene photos of the various sites looted for petroglyphs, sacred carvings, and statues. Another wall was filled with mug shots. "These are the suspects we're running down."

"I've got something really good for you," Stevens said, digging his phone out of his pocket. He consulted Lei's text. "Norwegian art thief wanted by Interpol was killed at the inn he was staying in last night." He sent the name and Interpol link Lei had texted him to Kamuela's phone.

The big Hawaiian frowned down at the name and mug shot appearing on the phone in his hand. "Norwegian, huh? That European connection seems like the artifacts might be going out of the country."

"I hope not. Maybe they're just using pro art thieves to collect them. Anyway, this guy was bludgeoned to death with a crowbar. Makes me think of some of the hotheads in the Heiau Hui. Lei tells me there were three perps at the crime scene. I have an inside man; he told me there was going to be a rally of the Hui on Maui. Do you know anything about it?"

"Yeah. We have the Hui leader's phone tapped."

"How'd you get an order for that?" Stevens glanced at Kamuela in surprise.

"God bless the Patriot Act. We suspect these are domestic terrorists," Kamuela said. "And now we get to surveil them night and day and on all technologies. So far there hasn't been anything but chatter about spreading the word to recruit more people to participate in guarding the sites and such."

"Let me get ahold of my confidential informant," Stevens said, digging the burner phone out of his pocket.

"Sure. Take a look around at all this; see if it sparks anything for you. I'm going to update my captain on this Euro guy's death and Interpol connection."

Kamuela left. Stevens called Brandon Mahoe.

"Hello?"

"Brandon? This is Lieutenant Stevens."

"Yes, sir! I was just going to call you."

"What have you found out?"

"There's a lot of anger. I know this is supposed to be about guarding our sacred sites and artifacts, but it seems like there are a lot of other agendas happening."

"Like what?"

"Like focusing on that book, *Maui's Secrets*. They wanted to organize boycotts and demonstrations outside the retailers carrying it, and a campaign in the media pressuring the publisher to pull it down, at least until the author revises it and takes the sites out of the book."

Stevens thought of his copy of the book and how he'd bought it to find out where the main *heiaus* were located. "Like I said before, it's closing the barn door after the horse is gone."

"Right. But there's a lot of anger here about a lot of things. High taxes on land Hawaiians have owned for hundreds of years. So many families unable to own a home, while rich off-islanders buy everything up. The streams getting diverted for big agriculture. Corruption in our local government. Somehow the rally turned into all that, and people were jacked up afterward."

"You should know there's been a murder that's very likely related." Stevens told Mahoe about the Norwegian thief's bludgeoning. "Stay very careful. They can't know you're reporting to me."

"I understand. I heard about your ex's murder, boss. I'm sorry." Mahoe's voice was strong and steady, and once again Stevens was heartened by the support around him.

"Thanks. I need all the help I can get. I'm here on Oahu, seeing my son and helping coordinate with HPD's end of the investigation." Marcus Kamuela returned, his commanding officer with him. "In fact, I have to go. Stay safe and check in with me tomorrow."

Stevens shut the flip phone and slid it into his pocket.

"Michael Stevens, this is Captain Bards." Captain Bards was a dapper, muscular man with a neck that strained the tight collar of his uniform.

"I hear you're at the front of the case on Maui," Bards said.

"You could say that, but we have a whole team on it," Stevens said, unwilling to disclose his leave status. "What do you make of this beating death of the Norwegian art thief?"

"Do you have confirmation that the vic was looting the *heiaus*?" Bards said.

"I don't, no. The lab is working on samples from the mini jackhammer retrieved from the man's possessions. I happened to be over here on personal business and thought I'd pass on the latest from our side of the investigation."

Kamuela gestured to the wall. "As you can see, we have plenty of evidence gathered—but no one we're looking for yet. Too bad they killed the guy—he could have put us onto who his crew is."

"We'd never have found him if he wasn't dead. This has been a slick operation—as you know even better than I do. I just got off the phone with my inside man, who's in the Maui branch of the Heiau Hui," Stevens said. "He reports conflicting agendas and a lack of unity within the group. It seems to be generating a lot of unfocused anger."

"Yeah, we've had two random beatings of tourists who visited the *heiaus*. We really need to solve this case before a ripple effect inflames the community further," Marcus said.

"Are you following money trails? Because whoever is behind the looting is paying top dollar for expert thieves."

"We're looking at that," Bards said. "Or we would, if we had a lead on where to look. Maybe now that you have that Norwegian on a slab, you could trace his accounts and see who's paid him recently."

"Seems like we're starting to need the FBI now that we're getting into Interpol territory," Stevens said.

"I've been discussing this with Special Agent Scott," Kamuela said. "They've got a case file open, just waiting for the word that we need them."

"Well, tracking international payments and bank accounts is definitely an area we'd need them for. Our office can't handle that kind of tech," Stevens said. "Seems like it might be time to bring them in."

They reviewed the case thus far, and Kamuela agreed to contact Captain Omura to coordinate involving the FBI.

Walking toward the front of the building, Kamuela clapped Stevens on the shoulder. "Married and a dad in the same month. How's it feel?"

Stevens slanted him a glance. "You really want to

know? Great. And terrible. Don't do what I did. If you're in love with her, marry her if you can; wait until she's ready if she isn't. Be there. Don't give up."

Marcus Kamuela's eyes widened at the sober, heartfelt words, and he ducked his head. "Sorry, man. I shouldn't have joked about it."

"Just remember what I said," Stevens said. "If you think Marcella's the one, don't let her get away. Now I'm back to the hospital to see if I can feed my son his evening bottle."

Chapter 17

Anchara's cottage had a small front room and kitchen combo with a bedroom and bathroom in back. The walls were white, the space tidy, and she'd decorated with bright fabrics. Lei could hear the squabbling of mynah birds in the mango tree outside, and the rooms smelled a little musty from being shut up.

The evidence search team had not been careful. The pillows from the couch were tossed on the floor, cabinet doors hung open, and the bedding had been stripped off the bed, leaving a stark white mattress. Lei coughed to clear her throat, constricted by emotion at the sight of the violation of the simple, pretty space.

Lei decided to start in the bedroom and immediately sucked in a breath at the sight of the small, beautifully carved rocking bassinet near the bed. Under the window was a changing table, fully stocked with everything a new baby coming home from the hospital would need.

Anchara had prepared so carefully and lovingly. It was really a shame Stevens had gone to Longs and bought all that cheap stuff. Lei sat for a moment on the bed, letting the tears she hadn't allowed herself to cry for Anchara well up. Using these items would be a way to remember her and to share with the baby, when the time came, how much his mother had loved him.

Lei shook her head briskly, pulling out a tissue from beside the bed and blowing her nose, blotting her eyes. She stuffed the tissue in her pocket. She had to get in and get out. Every minute that went by was a minute her trespassing could be discovered.

Where would she find the name of a baby not yet born? And were there any clues to her killer the search team had missed?

There might some sort of baby book, and given Anchara's other careful preparations, she probably had one.

Lei scouted around the bed. Nothing. She flipped through the stacks of tiny shirts, cloth diapers, folded flannel blankets. Wow, Stevens was right—babies needed a lot of stuff.

Nothing here. She went back into the living room and over to a low bookshelf under the small TV in the corner. A blue cloth-covered book drew her eye, and she took it out. The cover held a decorative medallion shape on which Anchara had written something in Thai.

She flipped open the book. It was a baby book, all right, with monthly notes in that beautiful script she couldn't read.

Lei wondered why they hadn't taken this in for evidence. Maybe they'd flipped through it and decided it wasn't relevant—after all, Lei couldn't see any mention of Stevens's name, nothing but the monthly journal and, at the end, a photo of Anchara, smiling, her hands cradled around her huge belly. Lei covered her mouth with her hand—Anchara was beautiful, her body full and ripe, her smile radiant.

All gone. Stolen. Snuffed out.

Thank God the baby, at least, was alive. Lei wondered how Stevens would have survived a blow like losing both of them. It was hard enough as it was…she tried not to think about the crime scene she'd heard about, but the mental images came anyway.

Lei shut the book. She was pretty sure the writing on the cover was the baby's chosen name, and the color of the binding indicated Anchara'd known the sex of the child. She slid the book into a paper evidence bag for the landlord's benefit and, after one more pass where she found nothing of interest to the case but a lot to grieve over, Lei closed and locked the door of the little apartment, making a decision as she did so.

She stopped back at the landlord's door. Knocked. The dog's barking summoned the man, and she took out her card. "I think I have an idea of a family that's adopting a new baby unexpectedly and may be able to use this stuff. Can you call me before you do anything with it? They'll even be able to pay you something."

"Good," the landlord said. He rubbed his eyes, and she saw they were red-rimmed. "I just hate what happened to her. If some family would use the stuff for a baby in need…"

"We'll make sure that happens." All Lei was keeping quiet about stuck like a chicken bone in her throat. "Call me when you go to clear her place out, and I'll make sure the baby things are used and appreciated."

Out in her truck, she leaned her head on the steering wheel for a long moment and then sat up and turned on the engine to return to work. She had to find someone who read Thai.

There was only one person she knew who did. Sitting in her truck, with the engine idling for the AC, Lei took a photo of the medallion on the front of the baby book with her phone and texted it to Special Agent Sophie Ang at the FBI.

Can you translate this for me?

As Lei hit Send, she realized she hadn't talked with her other FBI friend about the mess they were in. She'd called Marcella in tears the other night after she'd left Stevens to sleep in the living room, but she and Sophie weren't as close and she'd had the energy to tell the tale only once that night. She remembered Marcella's bracing words: "You two have been through worse, and I've got your back, no matter what. I'll even learn how to babysit and give you guys a date night out when all this gets sorted out."

She'd been able to fall asleep after talking to Marcella and was sure Marcella would tell Sophie Ang about the situation. She pulled out and headed for the police station.

As she pulled in to the station parking lot, her phone rang.

"Lei!" Sophie Ang's slightly accented voice was hurried. "My God! Marcella told me what happened to Stevens's ex-wife!"

"Yeah." Lei shut her eyes. "It's terrible. In every way. Stevens is on Oahu now, actually, visiting the baby at the neonatal unit. I'd appreciate if you guys called him, kept him company. This has been really rough, and being at the top of the suspect list doesn't help."

"I can only imagine. So does this photo you sent have to do with that case?"

"Yes, but not directly. We're trying to discover the name she had chosen for her son." Lei still couldn't say Anchara's name out loud. "This is on the front of a baby book she kept, but it's all in Thai. You're the only person I know who reads or speaks that language."

"Yes. I can translate the whole book for you, if you like."

Lei's stomach knotted at the thought. She didn't want

to read about Anchara's hopes and dreams for her son month by month. It would be too sad. But it might be a priceless gift for a motherless boy someday. "That would be great. Next time we get together, I'll give it to you."

A long pause.

"Well, do you want to know what the writing says?" Sophie asked, her voice a little tight with tension.

"Yes. Lay it on me. I can call Stevens, and he can put it on the birth certificate at the hospital."

"Kiet. Kiet Mookjai." Sophie took a breath, blew it out. "Kiet is spelled K-I-E-T, and it means 'Honor.'"

Lei's eyes filled with tears, and she bit her lip. *Honor.* Naming the child Anchara's choice was a way to 'honor' her memory. "Thanks, Sophie. I owe you."

"No, you don't. I'm your friend. Let me help. What else can I do?"

"Call Stevens this evening and you and Marcella distract him. Find a way to make him laugh." Lei struggled with how much to tell her friend and finally said, "I'm worried about him."

"Don't worry. We'll take care of him. Now, go call him about Kiet, and you can decide if you want to keep the name."

"Oh, we will," Lei said, and blinked again as she hung up. Kiet. It sounded good when she whispered it.

She called Stevens. "Where are you?" he asked. "I tried the house phone."

"I'm sitting in my truck, outside in the station parking lot," Lei said, looking around at the parked personal vehicles and rows of squad cars outside the fortress-like building. She spotted McGregor and Chun coming out the sliding doors. She saw them heading her way, and McGregor pointed at her truck.

"Listen, I can't talk. I found something with the baby's name on it, and I got it translated. His name is Kiet, spelled K-I-E-T. And it means 'honor.'" A pause as Stevens absorbed this. McGregor was getting closer. His choleric face was frowning, and she could see a white paper in his hand. "I think we're about to be served with search warrants. I have to go, but I was thinking you might put your dad's name in as a middle name. A way to remember him." McGregor reached her, knocked on the window. "Whatever you decide, I support. But I love the name Kiet already."

Lei hung up the phone. She took a deep breath, rolling down her window. "What can I do for you, Detective?"

Chapter 18

Stevens put his phone back in his pocket. He was standing in the hallway of the hospital nursery, still in the scrubs and gloves he'd been wearing. The baby was being discharged the following day to the foster home.

He hadn't had a chance to say anything to Lei, to answer her at all, but he didn't need to.

"Kiet," Stevens said aloud. "Honor." And he knew it was perfect, as perfect as adding his father's name as his middle name. Edward Stevens had been a firefighter and had died on the job when Stevens was sixteen. He'd been a hero. He'd saved three people before the fire in an old motel with faulty wiring claimed him and the rest who were trapped inside.

Stevens had stepped into his father's oversized shoes and done his best to be the "man of the house," but his mother's drinking, until then a little problematic, had tipped into raging alcoholism with the loss of her husband. Stevens escaped to the military and his brother, Jared, two years younger, had followed their father into firefighting.

Kiet Stevens. It had a ring about it.

He called the caseworker next. "Ms. Fujimoto? My wife found out what our baby's mother wanted to name him. I'd like to get the paperwork started for his birth certificate, and to adopt him. His name is going to be Kiet Edward Mookjai Stevens."

McGregor handed Lei a folded white paper through the truck's window. "Warrants to search your house and cars."

"Mine, too?" Lei frowned. "I alibied out on TV during the time of the murder."

"Doesn't mean you weren't in on it together," McGregor said, but his eyes shifted away.

Lei snorted. "Do what you gotta do." She got out of her truck, gathering her backpack that served as a purse, where the blue cloth-covered book was stowed. The receipt she'd found planted in Stevens's truck felt like it was burning a hole in her back pocket.

She handed her keys to McGregor. Neither of them would meet her eye, and as she headed into the station, she felt a shiver of terror: Maybe whoever had killed Anchara had planted something in her truck, too. She'd been so preoccupied, she hadn't searched her own vehicle; nor had she had time to return to check the house.

Her palms were sweating. She needed to get rid of that receipt, but not to McGregor and Chun.

Lei knocked on Captain Omura's office door. Her boss looked up. "What is it?"

Lei shut the office door and approached the desk. She set the receipt in its plastic evidence bag on the captain's desk and slid it over to her.

"I found this in Stevens's truck at the airport. Hidden in the driver's seat."

Omura looked up, frowning, studied the receipt. "Why didn't you give this to McGregor and Chun? I know they were headed out to serve you with warrants."

"I don't trust them," Lei said. "I trust you." And she turned on her heel and left the office with her boss holding the receipt.

In the women's room, Lei washed her hands and face, decided to leave her unruly hair in the ponytail, as it had completely frizzed once it had been restrained. She put on a touch of mascara and a dot of lipstick. Maybe looking better as she and Torufu went into the meeting with Captain Omura would help calm her nerves.

Still, Lei knew she wouldn't rest easy until she found out if McGregor and Chun's searches had come back empty. She'd turned in the receipt. She'd had to. Destroying evidence in a murder investigation went against every case she'd ever worked on. Damning as the receipt was, she had to hope the process would clear Stevens in spite of how thoroughly he'd been set up.

There was nothing to do but stay busy until then, and with a fresh body, that wasn't going to be hard.

On her way back to the cubicle, Torufu headed her off. "We need to meet the captain, update her about the Norwegian."

"Right. Did you get anything off that jackhammer?" Lei asked.

"I did. Rock dust consistent with samples from the *heiau*."

They turned in to the captain's office. Torufu handed her a folder. He'd prepared copies of all the data they'd collected on the Norwegian's death for her, as well as for Omura. She gave him a grateful look. "Thanks, man."

Omura was sipping on a Diet Coke through a straw in a rare moment of relaxation as they came in. There was no sign of the receipt; nor did she indicate in any way that Lei had been in the room only minutes previously. She set the soda aside, turning to her keyboard. "Report."

They took the chairs in front of her desk, and Torufu handed the captain the folder he'd prepared. "Norm Jorgenson. At least according to his fingerprints in Interpol. Wanted for international art theft. We found no ID at the scene."

Omura leafed through printouts from the crime scene. "Crowbar. Messy. Where did you find the murder weapon?"

Lei described the process of elimination that had led to the iron's discovery under the window of the inn. "There were three perps in the room." They all looked at the shoe print photos Lei had taken.

"Were you able to surmise which pair of shoes actually connects to the murderer?" Omura asked, eyeing Lei over square reading glasses that made the Steel Butterfly look even more fashionable.

"We haven't had time to do a scene reconstruction," Torufu said. He went on to tell her about the samples and the hand-held jack. "The victim probably had something to do with the *heiau* desecration Stevens is working on."

"So. Any hint of any connection to the Heiau Hui?"

Lei shook her head. "Nothing direct. Stevens has his inside man keeping an ear out, and he's on Oahu. I told him this vic was likely connected to the *heiau* case, and he said he was meeting Marcus Kamuela and would bring them up to speed."

"He's supposed to be on admin leave, but yes. In fact, just before this meeting, I got a call from Kamuela's captain on Oahu, asking us to bring the FBI and Interpol in on tracing this man Jorgenson's financials and identity. He's the first solid connection we've got to whoever's looting the sites, and none of us here have the kind of online tracking the Feds and Interpol do."

"Do you want to make the calls, or should we?" Lei

asked.

"I need to sign off on an official request, but since you're our FBI liaison, you call over there first. Let's move on this. One last bit. What are you liking for motivation for this murder?"

Torufu and Lei looked at each other. They hadn't had time to do the usual brainstorming about motives. Torufu led off, turning back to the captain. "I see a possibility he was killed by his own crew. Wasn't going along with their agenda or was going to sell them out or something. No honor among thieves."

Lei cleared her throat. "We both think there was a lot of anger in the way Jorgenson was bludgeoned. Blood spatter flew all over the ceiling from multiple blows to the back of the head, when he probably died after the first blow. So it's also possible this was someone from the Heiau Hui who tracked the thieves and let their emotions gain the upper hand. There were three people there, which speaks to some sort of grouping."

They sat for a long moment; then Omura turned back to her computer. "I'll compose the request for FBI help and fax it over to Oahu, and, Lei, you let me know the name of the agent we'll be working the case with."

"Yes, sir." They both got up and left for their cubicle.

Lei took the blue cloth book out of her backpack. She wanted to photograph the pages and send them to Sophie

Ang, but first she needed a quiet place to make a call to Marcella, updating her on everything.

"Back in a few," Lei told Torufu.

The Tongan just nodded, sitting down in his office chair. The chair squeaked in protest as Torufu opened the case report. "Just hope we don't get any bomb calls today."

She liked that about Abe Torufu. He didn't bug her for anything she didn't want to tell him. Lei ducked into Conference Room B, currently empty, and opened the case folder as she used the triangular phone in the middle of the table to place a call to Special Agent Marcella Scott.

"Lei!" Her friend sounded rushed. "Just got back in the car after another bank robbery downtown."

"The fun never stops," Lei said. "Do you have a minute? Omura's putting in an official request for FBI assistance regarding this victim whose case I pulled this morning." Lei rattled off the details.

"I'm swamped right now. Better go up the chain with this one, let Waxman assign it." Lei could hear Marcella turning on the AC of the black Acura "Bucar" her team used. "What's going on with Anchara's murder? That's the case I'm really interested in."

"Me too, obviously. Stevens is over on Oahu bonding with the baby."

"I knew that. Sophie, Marcus, and I are taking him out tonight."

"Good. Well, I've been doing a little poking around myself. I know we're being set up." She told her friend about her visit to the GreenDeath Place and finding the receipt. "An hour ago, I was served with search warrants. I'm hoping McGregor and Chun come up empty, but I'm not at all sure. The GreenDeath guy told me two more shrouds were purchased. The only person left in my life who hates me this much is Terence Chang. What do you think about reopening the investigation into him?"

"Already done," Marcella said. "The file on him was barely closed, anyway." Last year Lei had been at the forefront of a case in which the scion of the Chang crime family had been involved. His hatred for the Texeiras had been activated by Lei's deadly encounter with his grandmother. "We haven't found anything solid on him, but word on the street is that he's assumed the reins of the Chang operation. On paper, and online, he's clean as a whistle, with a nice little import/export business in Hilo and nothing more. I've got local PD keeping an eye on him, too, and he seems to be in Hilo most of the time."

"I am hoping a sketch artist can get a description out of the GreenDeath Place owner—not that it will show much, but all it has to do is rule out Stevens. The man described an Asian guy with a medium build."

"Someone was also with Anchara in the motel,"

Marcella said. "With any luck at all, someone there saw that man."

"I forgot about that! Though McGregor and Chun aren't exactly telling us anything. Seem to be running things totally by the book. I just want to see Stevens cleared." Lei rubbed the white gold pendant around her neck. "We can't bring the baby home, out of foster care, until he's ruled out."

"Are you in a hurry for that? Really?" Marcella sounded skeptical. "I mean, I think you're a saint to take him on at all. Anchara's baby."

"Well, the more I think about it, the more I'm okay with it. It's not his fault, poor little guy, and we can't leave him in foster. But still, with this investigation, all our cases, and my aunty dying, it's not exactly a good time." Lei told her friend that Aunty Rosario was going downhill fast. "I just hope I can get away at all. I haven't even asked the captain yet—I know she's going to say no. Between the bomb squad and a fresh murder, this isn't the time for compassionate leave."

"Yeah, about the bomb squad. I don't like that assignment for you, Lei." Marcella seemed to be gathering her thoughts. "I don't think it's a good fit for your personality. All the bomb techs I know are tinkerers who like figuring out how things work. They're loners, and they're emotionally under-reactive. The only part of what I just described that fits you is the loner thing."

"Yeah, and I'm an ex-loner," Lei said. "I've been worrying about this, too. I don't have cool nerves, and I don't like the pressure." She told Marcella about the simple ordnance retrieval they'd done and the massive public pressure and TV reporting. "I hated it."

"Talk to your captain sooner rather than later. And what if you get pregnant?"

"Oh, God, Marcella. I'd succeeded in forgetting that." Lei groaned. "I'm not getting pregnant now, with a baby already on the way."

"Why not?" Marcella echoed Dr. Wilson's words. "When you've already taken the plunge, what's one more? You could stop at two and have a complete family. Voilà!"

"You make it sound so easy," Lei said. "I gotta go. I've taken too long for this call as it is. Abe has been patient with me disappearing all day."

"I'll let you know anything I hear on Chang's activities," Marcella said.

"Thanks. And give my husband a kiss for me tonight."

"I will. But I promise, no tongue with Marcus right there."

Lei laughed as she hung up. Marcella always made her feel better. Thinking how important that friendship was to her reminded Lei that two shrouds were left. She didn't like wondering what plans the killer had for them.

Chapter 19

Stevens was on the way to the airport the next morning in yet another taxi when his burner phone rang. "Lieutenant Stevens."

"Lieutenant, sir! This is Mahoe. I have a tip for you on the *heiau* case."

"Go ahead." Stevens kept his eyes on the sparkling horizon line of the ocean as the taxi rose in elevation on the expressway into the airport. His head ached from drinking with Marcus and Lei's FBI buddies, and his heart felt sore, too. He'd said goodbye to Kiet that morning at the home where his son was being cared for, and he'd been able to assure himself that the foster family were caring and kind.

"I overheard something. Some of the higher-up organizers were talking about where the artifacts might be going, and they mentioned an art dealer on Maui. Magda Kennedy."

The woman's name instantly conjured her in Stevens's mind: lava-black hair, blue eyes, beautiful face—and an attitude. He and Lei had dealt with her on another case a couple of years ago—the same case that had brought Anchara into their lives. Could there be a connection?

"Anything more? What her role is?"

"I didn't get anything more. I was just trying to get in and hear what they were talking about, and they shut up."

"Were they going to do anything about this?"

"I believe what's going on is that the Hui is conducting their own investigation. They are trying to figure it out on their own and shut it down. I know that's dangerous to all involved, sir."

"You got that right." The taxi swung in to the drop-off zone for Hawaiian Airlines and he got out, handing the driver cash and waiting for a receipt. "I need to pass this on to Captain Omura right away. Anything else? How's Okapa doing?"

"Uncle?" The young man's voice contained a smile. "He's having the time of his life. All fired up, comes to every meeting wearing his *kihei* robe and war paint."

"Well, you should be aware there's been another development, and it means you need to be more careful than ever." Stevens reminded Mahoe about the bludgeon murder of the Norwegian. "Keep your ears and eyes open for anything about this."

"Will do, boss. Talk tomorrow." They hung up, and Stevens called Omura next on her direct cell phone line.

"Keep it short. I'm going into a meeting," Omura said.

Stevens passed on the tip from Mahoe. "I'm done over here on Oahu. My son is going into foster care until I'm cleared in Anchara's murder," Stevens said. "I'd like to return to work. My station needs me, and there are some developments in the case." He passed on Mahoe's tip. "I'd like to bring Kennedy in for an interview."

A pause. He could picture Omura frowning even as he went through the Hawaiian Airlines automated check-in kiosk. He had only a small backpack, so the process was short.

"Well, let me take a moment to bring you up to speed on what's been happening," she said. "The *Maui's Secrets* people have agreed to pull down and revise the book. They've issued a statement that should be on the news tonight that they want to show 'respect and collaboration with the Hawaiian culture.' So that's good. I also went ahead and contacted Marcus Kamuela's mother, Moani Kamuela, as our cultural expert. She came in and helped our team map out the sites of the *heiaus*. We've organized and begun supplementary patrols. All that is underway, but I really do need you back on the job. So, yes. Come back to work today."

"Thanks, Captain. Any breaks in Anchara's case?"

"You know I can't discuss that with you. But I will say, the team on that case is following some interesting leads that don't involve you or Lei."

"That's a relief." Stevens rose on the escalator toward

the boarding gates, his spirits lifting at the thought of being back in his home office. "The sooner I'm cleared, the sooner I can bring Kiet home."

"Kiet? That's an unusual name. How is the baby doing?" Omura's voice was hesitant. He knew without being told that she wasn't thrilled about how the sudden addition of a newborn was going to complicate the lives of two of her best officers.

"It's Thai. Means honor. And he's doing well. Healthy, so far."

A long pause. "Seems appropriate to 'honor' his mother's memory with that name," Omura said. "Well, give me a call when you're able to come in. I have another meeting with the Hui leader scheduled, trying to get him to accept our help patrolling the sites."

Stevens cleared his throat. "Yes, sir." He slid the phone into his pocket. He got to return to the job, and things were moving in another direction on Anchara's murder case. He couldn't hope for more.

He pictured placing the tiny newborn in the crib he'd assembled at home. He couldn't wait to bring Kiet home—there was nothing like the feeling of the child's soft weight in his arms. He hoped Lei felt the same, but told himself it wasn't realistic. She hadn't had the experience he'd had: a lightning bolt of love that made any sacrifice seem worthwhile.

On the plane, looking out the round oval window for the short twenty-minute flight to Maui, Stevens wondered who could possibly hate him so much that they'd killed his ex-wife and set him up for murder. He rubbed the tiny purple heart on his arm thoughtfully. There weren't many names. Just one, an enemy he'd gained with his marriage to Lei.

Terence Chang.

Lei walked out of the morgue, leaving an early-morning meeting with Abe Torufu and Dr. Gregory over the art thief's body. There were no big surprises about cause of death and no new breakthroughs.

Lei sucked a few deep breaths of fresh air, walking briskly across the hospital's parking lot. Her phone rang. She checked the little window and held up a finger to Torufu. "I have to take this. I'll catch up with you at the station."

Torufu nodded and Lei picked up the call, greeting a woman she hadn't spoken to in at least a year.

"Mrs. Ka`awai."

"Hello, Lei." The Kaua`i wise woman's resonant voice never failed to calm Lei's heart rate. She immediately pictured the woman's regal bearing, her graceful muumuu, her waist-length hair in a coronet of braids. "I thought I should give you a call. There are some disturbances going on here on Kaua`i."

"Am I the right person to call? Shouldn't you be contacting your local police?" Lei couldn't help wondering what kind of "disturbances" Esther Ka`awai meant.

"I have." Lei heard the dismissal in the older woman's voice. "But I felt Spirit telling me to call you."

"Oh. Okay." Esther had been important in the uncovering of a serial killer on the remote Garden Island where she lived and worked as a kumu hula. Her "words of knowledge" had provided some insight to the baffling and extensive case Lei and Stevens had worked on there. Lei unlocked her truck. Even as early as it was, the vehicle was hot. She lowered the windows and turned on the engine to cool it down with AC while they talked. "So how can I help you?"

"No, it is I helping you," Esther said. "There is a new one coming into your life, and you are both in danger."

Lei stiffened. Even though she'd experienced Esther's psychic moments before, she still didn't know how to take them. Esther must be referring to baby Kiet. "Where is this danger coming from? And what are these 'disturbances' you are concerned about?"

"They are two different things. First of all, I am concerned about some of the attitudes within the Heiau Hui group that has formed here on Kauai. Are you familiar with the Heiau Hui?"

"Yes, we are. They're a vigilante group protecting the Hawaiian sacred sites from these desecrations that have been going on."

"Yes, and we have a branch on Kaua`i. I have been involved because of my interest in protecting culture. But recently I have come to suspect that some of the Hui members are not as honest as they should be about what the group is doing."

"Tell me more."

"I cannot. Only that some are violent, and some other agendas are behind the organization."

"We are aware of that, but thank you for telling me Kaua`i is having the same issues," Lei said. "What other disturbances are going on?"

"Just that I am getting the impression that there is someone behind all these thefts. Someone who thinks they are doing a good thing."

"Do you have anything harder than that? And why call me?"

"You are a daughter of my heart," Esther said simply. "You were given to me to pray for. I sense danger to you in this, and to the new little one coming to you."

"Thank you, Esther." Lei knew the gift she was being given, to be chosen in this way. "I'll tell Stevens. We *are* getting a baby unexpectedly, and he's in foster care. We'll alert the people working with his case. His mother was murdered, so you are right to be concerned."

A long pause. Lei could picture Esther's wide, smooth brown forehead, her finely modeled lips, and her shining brown eyes as she contemplated this.

"That is not the baby I'm concerned about," the wise woman said, and hung up the phone.

Lei frowned. She set the phone in its holder and navigated out of the parking lot. She'd never yet had a phone call with Esther in which something confusing wasn't said. Did she think Lei was pregnant?

She'd never known what the woman meant until after the fact—but so far, all her "knowledge" had checked out, even if only in hindsight. Lei pulled in to the station and met Torufu in Omura's office, where they updated her on the progress in the art thief's murder.

"The FBI is now tracking the man's identity and financials." Omura tapped her fingernails on the case file. "Now that we've brought them in, and the man is wanted by Interpol, our responsibility is the 'boots on the ground' aspects, such as this autopsy report."

"Right," Torufu said. "Nothing too interesting. His tox screen was clean, and obviously, blunt force trauma to the head was cause of death."

Omura pushed a paper over to them with contact names and numbers. "This is the FBI team working on the man's background and Interpol agents looking for his residence in Norway. Please coordinate any new information with them."

"Sounds good." Lei took the paper. "I was planning to go back to try to establish which set of footprints dealt the killing blow. I'll reinterview the landlady and then release the premises for cleaning."

"You do that while I get ahold of the Feds and Interpol and fax them the autopsy report," Torufu said. "And please, God, no bomb threats today."

They stood to leave, but Omura gestured to Lei. "Stay back a moment."

Lei sat back down as Torufu headed out. Omura told her about Stevens's phone call that morning and the lead on the Hui related to Magda Kennedy. "I'm putting him back on the job."

"That's good," Lei said. She took a breath, blew it out. "On another subject, I need to ask permission for some compassionate family leave. My aunt is dying." She told Omura about her father's phone call.

Omura frowned, a crease between her immaculate brows. "This isn't a good time."

"I'm aware of that, sir."

Omura sat back, twiddling a pen. "You are aware that once you're officially on bomb squad, you need to be available on call twenty-four seven."

"That's why I've really been thinking it over. Talking

with some people I'm close to, including Dr. Wilson, the psychologist. I'm very sorry to tell you, but I don't think I'm the right person for that detail."

Omura sat forward. The line had deepened between her brows. "I won't lie and tell you I'm happy to hear it. I liked how you stepped up to the challenge and dealt with your demotion to sergeant, and though I heard mixed reports on your training, I was hopeful. I guess I'm glad you're not wasting more of our time and resources getting trained for a job you don't really want."

"I'm sorry, sir," Lei said again. She sat upright in the chair, her hands on her thighs to keep from rubbing the pendant at her neck. "I really like working with Torufu. We make a good team. But especially now, with my aunty dying and this newborn coming into our lives—I don't think I'm the right person for the job."

"Can't say I didn't see it coming. You gave me some hints, and so did the instructors with Homeland who ran that training—they thought you didn't have the confidence or mechanical aptitude," Omura said. Lei felt her pride smarting but tried not to let it show as the captain continued. "All right. How about this? Finish your interviewing today and wrap up what you're doing, and I'll release you for a week of leave tomorrow to go be with your aunt. I'll see if Torufu can carry on with your cases alone or if I need to reassign someone."

"Thank you so much, sir." Lei stood. "I really

appreciate your understanding. I won't forget this."

"See that you don't." Omura flicked her nails. "Now get out of here before I change my mind."

Lei pulled her truck into the municipal parking lot outside the Vineyard Street Inn in Wailuku. Her body felt sticky with stress-induced sweat from her conversations with Omura and Torufu. She'd told her partner she'd resigned from the explosive detail and was making flight arrangements to California. She'd just hung up the phone from calling her father to tell him, and that conversation hadn't been easy either. He'd confirmed Aunty Rosario really was going downhill. Hospice was in, and she wasn't leaving her bed except for dialysis.

Getting out of her vehicle, Lei looked up at the deep green cleft of Iao Valley directly behind the taller municipal buildings of Wailuku, the oldest town on Maui. A cool mysteriousness about the valley, usually wreathed in clouds, wild and yet so close to civilization, never failed to calm her nerves. She'd loved the year or so she and Stevens had lived in Iao Valley...

She slammed the door of her truck and walked briskly across the worn two-lane road to the inn. She found the door marked MANAGER and checked the name in her notebook before she knocked on the jamb. "Mrs. Figueroa?"

The petite landlady looked up from behind a battered metal desk. "Yes? Who's asking?" Today she was wearing a muumuu decorated with papayas and a pair of lime-green Crocs. Lei wondered if she had a different pair to match each muumuu.

"Remember me? Detective Lei Texeira with the Maui Police Department."

"Of course. Come to release my guest room for cleaning? The place stay stink inside. I like clean 'em already!"

"Yes. But I'd like to look around one more time and ask you a few more questions." Lei sat down on one of the wicker chairs next to the woman's desk. "Remember I asked you to keep your ears open on who might have done this?"

"Yes, and I been asking. I no like say, though." The woman appeared to have loose dentures, which she played with, lined lips working like she was sucking a lozenge.

"Why don't you want to say? This crime was a terrible thing. It brought danger to your inn and cost you a lot of business."

"I no like say because I no like more bad things come to my inn."

Lei frowned. "Is someone threatening you?"

"No."

"Is this something to do with organized crime?"

"No." Mrs. Figueroa slapped her hands down on a

pile of paperwork. "I no like say. The guy was one stupid Euro. No one cares he wen' *make* die dead."

Lei hadn't heard that pidgin English phrase in a while, and she was taken aback by the woman's attitude. "I'm sure his family would disagree. No one deserves what happened to him."

Mrs. Figueroa sucked her dentures, clearly considering. "I only heard rumors about who done him. But you didn't hear it from me, right?"

Lei mentally crossed her fingers. If she needed to call this woman as a witness, she would. "Anything you can tell me would be great, and of course, this is a confidential conversation."

"I heard it was da boys from the Hui went done 'em."

"What Hui?"

"You know, the Heiau Hui. They found out this guy one of the thieves that took the petroglyphs from Haiku, and they came here and killed him."

Lei made a note on her spiral notebook. "Who told you this?"

"Rumors. I no can say."

"I need a name, Mrs. Figueroa. Someone I can follow up with. A lead."

Mrs. Figueroa worked her dentures for a long minute. "I no like them get piss off with me."

"I understand that, and I won't say how I got the lead."

More coaxing, and Lei finally got the name of one of the local organizers of the Hui, a man related to Mrs. Figueroa's second cousin. He'd told her it was a Hui hit and to shut up about it. "So I no like get more trouble for my inn."

"Well, we still have to figure out which of the three sets of footprints are the ones of the person who actually killed the man. The others were accessories. Please don't worry."

"Be sure you keep me out of it." Mrs. Figueroa's anxiety seemed genuine. "I only want to do the right t'ing. The Hui, they're doing a good thing for our island, protecting the artifacts."

"Of course. We couldn't possibly guard the sites as well as I'm sure the Hui is doing," Lei said. She jotted the cousin's name, George Figueroa, in her notebook and, after more assurances that Mrs. Figueroa wouldn't be quoted in a way that would get back to her, Lei walked down the hall to the door marked with crisscrossed crime-scene tape.

She'd brought her camera, because even though Torufu had shot the scene, she wanted to be able to assess the footprints near where the body had been found and see if she could find the pair that had dealt the death blow. They really should have done that at the time, but

Lei remembered getting distracted by finding the murder weapon.

Mrs. Figueroa, still grumbling, unlocked the victim's door. The foul smell of rotting blood hit Lei hard. She stepped back out of the doorway into the hall.

"Phew!" Mrs. Figueroa held her nose. "So stink!"

Lei dug in her backpack purse for the little vial of Vicks she carried for just these occasions. "Please stay outside, Mrs. Figueroa."

"You don't have to tell me." The landlady pulled the door shut behind her, leaving Lei, breathing shallowly and nauseated by the smell, snapping on gloves.

The blood spatters had dried black all over the room, and the smell, sweet and cloying with a metallic aftertaste, was cut by the Vicks but far from gone. Lei gulped repeatedly, feeling the urge to vomit and annoyed with herself because of it. She turned on her blue light and shone it on the floor. Blood trace immediately lit up, and she set the light down at an angle so that it shone across the negative space where the killers had stood and on the blank area where the body had lain. Smeared spots where the perpetrators had walked through the blood led toward the door.

Lei was able to identify one set of prints, approximately a men's size nine, that had faced the victim and were outlined in negative space and spatter. Trace on either side outlined other shoe prints. She photographed the positions.

"They held him down and the guy wearing size nine beat his head in," Lei muttered, chilled by the brutality of the slaying. She suddenly needed more air. She turned and slid up the screenless window where the murder weapon had been ditched.

She stuck her head out and breathed fresh air until her stomach settled and dizziness subsided. "Good thing Abe wasn't here; he'd laugh me right out of the room," she said aloud.

Finished checking the shoe prints, she stripped the tape off the door and left it unlocked, stopping by Mrs. Figueroa's. "You can have the room cleaned now," she said. "Be sure to use the firm Dr. Gregory referred you to. You don't want to handle blood yourself."

"No one will want to rent that room," Mrs. Figueroa grumbled. "I going have to paint the whole thing."

"Not a bad idea," Lei agreed. "But I think this will blow over quickly, and as long as you keep renting to tourists, they'll never know."

She hurried out to the truck, eager to pass on the lead she'd picked up to Torufu along with the identification of the murderer's shoe print. At least she wasn't leaving him with nothing to follow up on as she took off for the mainland.

He'd taken the news she wasn't sticking with bomb squad stoically. "I guess that means we'll be reassigned partners," Torufu said. "Too bad. You're good in the field, Mrs. Stevens."

Lei had apologized again. She felt like it was all she did these days.

With any luck at all, Stevens would be home soon, and maybe they could meet in the shower. She couldn't wait to get the stink of rotten blood off her body.

Stevens drove up to the house in the cool blue of evening after a long day of catching up at the station and working the Heiau case. The interview with Magda Kennedy was set up for the following day, and he'd caught up with all his station business. A light was on inside. Lei's truck was already parked in the driveway, and he felt his battered spirits lift.

She was home. The last few days had felt like an eternity. He was doing much better after meeting with Dr. Wilson, so much so that he was looking forward to sleeping in his own bed—with his wife.

Keiki greeted him happily, with a woof and a tail wag, but as soon as Stevens stepped inside the house, chaos hit him.

Everything had been moved or was awry and out of place. The cushions were off the couch, bedding on the floor, cupboards hung open, drawers gaped ajar. He recognized the aftermath of a search. McGregor and Chun had been in his house, and they hadn't even had the courtesy to clean up after themselves.

Rage surged up inside. Stevens stormed forward to slam the doors of the cupboards and shove the drawers back in. He knew he was overreacting, but he couldn't stop himself.

"Lei!" he bellowed. "Where are you?"

She opened the bathroom door, wrapped in a towel, hair dripping and eyes wide. The freckles stood out on her nose like dots of paint. "What are you yelling for?"

"This! This, dammit! Those assholes, tearing up our house. No respect!" He held up the mattress of the baby's crib. The backing had been ripped off to check inside the box spring. "What, I was going to hide something in my baby's bed? Seriously?"

"I know. They did a really rude, crude job. It sucks, and they were in a hurry. They did it quickly because I told them to. I came hurrying home, hoping you'd be here, and instead they were waiting to be let in because of our alarm and Keiki. So I was right outside while they tore through here in fifteen minutes. I told them to hurry."

Stevens's fists were clenched, his jaw tight. His chest heaved with anger. "So you told them to trash our house like this."

"No, of course not. I told them to hurry up and not to bother cleaning because I wanted them out before you came home."

Stevens strode over to the sideboard and splashed himself a glassful of scotch. He tossed it back in quick gulps, the bomb of warmth that went off in his empty stomach almost dizzying.

"It's a shitty thing to come home to." Lei slid up under his arm, her wet hair touching his shoulder, a towel around her slender body. "I just wanted them gone."

He set the empty glass down with a thump. A wave of desire rose in him—a fierce need to bury himself in her, to be obliterated there, if even for a moment. He craved her in times of pain. She was his haven, the only person who knew every broken place in him and matched it with one of her own. Lei was the only one who could take all he had and give it back to him, pressed down, shaken together, overflowing.

"I want you," he said, through gritted teeth. "Now."

Her tilted eyes flared wide, and she let go of the towel. "You got me."

He could barely wait, both of them tearing at his clothes to get them off. He was consumed by frantic want, and with no finesse whatsoever, he took her among the discarded couch cushions on the living room floor, the coffee table shoved aside.

She met him with an explosion of equal fire, bite, and power. In the tangling clash of their damaged hearts and wild emotions, he found a measure of peace.

For a brief moment they were that one body—the one safe and welcoming place in the world.

Chapter 20

Lei lifted herself onto one elbow as she and Stevens lay facing each other on the floor. Stevens's arms were still locked around her, their legs entwined. Her skin complained from several rug-burned spots, but the knot of tension she'd carried in her chest, queasiness left over from the blood-spattered crime scene, and the anxiety she'd felt at getting home from work to find McGregor and Chun in the driveway—all of it was gone.

He'd buried his face in the juncture between her neck and shoulder, her damp curls covering his face. He'd instantly fallen asleep, but his arms were still clamped tight around her.

Lei pulled back slightly so she could see his face. There was tension in his squared jaw and shadows under those blue, blue eyes, hidden from her by a fan of lashes. She smoothed the crease between his brows with her thumb, stroked her hand down the plane of his cheek, and massaged the muscles between his neck and shoulder. Gradually, the grip he had on her body loosened and his muscles went heavy and slack.

She eased away, picked up the towel and wrapped

it around herself. Went into the bathroom, washed. Squelched some Curl Tamer into her hair, slipped into her robe, and moving as quietly as she could, she let Keiki in. She went around the house and tidied up the mess left by the search.

A search that, thankfully, had yielded nothing.

It was Chun who'd given her a subtle thumbs-up as he followed his partner out, with a murmured, "Sorry for the hassle."

She'd banged the door shut behind them, and after her afternoon in the crime scene, she'd wanted nothing more than to get clean in the shower.

Lei hadn't counted on Stevens's explosive response to the mess or she'd have picked it up first. She put some hot water on and made spaghetti, heating up some canned sauce as he slept on in the living room. Finally, when the food was almost ready and she'd poured them each a glass of Chablis, she woke him up, kneeling down in front of him and kissing his closed mouth.

"Michael. Dinner's ready."

He blinked awake, and she saw the remnants of a bad dream in the whites around his eyes, the tension that surged back into his tall frame, the way he leaped to his feet, reaching for his weapon, which had been discarded and now lay under the coffee table.

"Michael, it's me. Dinner's ready." Her smile felt

strained. She saw when he recognized her. He cleared his throat, grabbed his pants.

"I need to get into the shower. I'm sorry about all this." He made a gesture that covered the mess of couch cushions, discarded clothing, and rough sex.

She held up a hand and he tugged her to her feet. "No need to apologize. We both needed that. Come eat when you're done."

He nodded and went into the bathroom. She heard the water running and frowned as she went into the kitchen, drained the pasta and set it out, then set the table.

He didn't seem okay. And now she was leaving tomorrow to go watch her aunt die. Sometimes it was all just too much. She wanted to cry, and took a sip of wine instead. She grimaced at the taste.

He joined her at the table in his terry-cloth bathrobe, rubbing a hand through damp dark brown hair. "What, no chili?" He gave the ghost of a smile.

"Variety is the spice of life. Thought I'd show you my full range of cooking skills now that we're married."

He dug into the pile of pasta. "Delicious."

"Flattery will get you everywhere."

When they were both sated, Stevens sat back and lifted his glass to toast her. "Thanks for getting the guys out of the house quickly. I'm not sure I would have been in control if I'd gotten home and they'd been in here. With my mind, I know they're just doing their jobs, being cops. I'd have to do the same thing in their shoes. But another part of me is just—raw." His voice caught. "It's better, but I still see Anchara. Those last few minutes she was alive. What was done to her, so wrong and terrible. And then, trying to save her and being treated like a criminal—I can know what's going on with my mind and tell myself it's okay, but I can't seem to make my emotions behave."

"Dr. Wilson thinks you've got some post-traumatic stress symptoms. Her murder has activated old traumas that never got dealt with—your dad's death, your mom's alcoholism, your stint in the army, all the blood from all the crime scenes you've walked through in your career… and then this. Dr. Wilson told me what to expect." Lei took another sip of her wine, just a small one because it tasted funny, metallic and strong. She set the glass down and pushed it away. "She said you might have trouble sleeping. Mood swings. Angry outbursts, emotional overreactions. Flashbacks. You should see her a few more times. It'll help you get better, faster."

Stevens pushed his plate away and buried his face in his hands. "I feel like shit for doing this to you. To us. Even the baby. Forcing him on you."

"It's okay. You've put up with so much crap from me over the years. For richer, for poorer, in sickness and in health, remember?" She tipped his chin up with her hand and kissed his hard mouth until he responded to her, coming alive gradually as if she were breathing life into a statue. Finally, his arms came around her and he drew her onto his lap and held her there for a long time, and there were no more words.

Chapter 21

Lei got off the plane in San Francisco, retrieved her bag, and waited at the curb until Wayne Texeira drove up in the huge extended-cab F-150 he drove. Her dad leaped down from a doorframe so high there was a step to get in and embraced her with all the strength in his strong arms. "Lei-girl. Sweets. How are you?"

She hugged back. "I'm okay, Dad. More importantly, how's Aunty?"

"Not good, honey. I'm so glad you could come. They're saying only a few more days."

Lei found she couldn't answer. She let her dad heft her bag into the truck bed, and she grabbed the door handle and stepped up into the solid-feeling cab. "I know why you drive this beast. You want to feel like you're going to win any kind of encounter on a California freeway."

"You got that right." Wayne grinned, his teeth flashing handsome. His curling hair, shot with silver, looked long. Lei knew Aunty cut it for him. It was a sign of Rosario's illness that now he had a rock-star-wild hairdo. "When I want to turn, everyone gets out of my way."

"Must be murder on the mileage."

"Speaking of murder, I saw a news story that Stevens's pregnant ex was killed and that he's a person of interest. When were you going to tell me this little bit of news?" Her father's voice rose with distress as he pulled the truck away from the curb and merged into traffic.

Lei sighed. "I'm sorry, Dad, that you had to hear it that way. I wanted to tell you in person. I should have remembered you always watch the Hawaii news."

"Did he do it?"

"Of course not. It's the shroud thing again. He was set up." She filled him in on the case so far. "You can't talk to anyone about it, but I don't want you thinking your son-in-law is a murderer, especially when we're going to be parents."

"What?" Wayne took his eyes off the road, swerved. "I thought you said nothing happened!"

"She was pregnant, remember? With Michael's baby. The goodbye screw on her way out the door had consequences, apparently." Lei wondered when she'd be able to speak Anchara's name, and she couldn't quite keep the bitterness out of her voice. She also wondered when she'd really accept baby Kiet's existence, when telling the story wouldn't rub salt in the wound left by Stevens's first marriage, when her grief for Anchara wouldn't be mixed with guilt and jealousy, too.

"You sure you want to be a mama to this baby?" Wayne frowned.

"I'm sure. He's in foster. We're his family. We have to do the right thing by him. Stevens is totally committed." She told her father about coming home to her husband's truckload of purchases. "He can't wait to bring Kiet home, but we can't until he's cleared in her murder."

"I don't know what to say. I wanted to be a grandfather, but not like this."

"I know." Lei turned her head to watch the lights of Marin County stream by, the rounded, dark velvety hills garlanded in colored lights of civilization.

They drove on in silence. Lei heard muttering from her father. "What are you saying, Dad?"

"I was praying. Asking God to give me peace."

"You can pray in front of me."

"Oh, God." Wayne's voice vibrated with emotion, his large rugged hands squeezing the steering wheel. "Help my daughter accept and love this child who's lost his mother. Help the detectives find answers to who did this evil thing, and surround all of us with protection that no arrows of darkness can penetrate. Give Lei and Michael wisdom and strength to be loving parents, and give me a right heart to help them. Amen."

Silence filled the cab. Lei looked back out at the lights, surprised at the calm that followed his words.

"Thanks, Dad."

"You can pray anytime. God is always there for you."

"I forget. I try to do everything on my own."

"We all do." He reached over and patted her hair. "I'm so glad you came."

They pulled up at the little 1940s stucco bungalow on D Street, with its scrap of lawn and clipped junipers in front, the porch light casting a welcoming pool of amber. Wayne parked on the cement driveway and hefted Lei's suitcase out. She followed him up the walkway, waited as he unlocked the door, and followed him into the small front room.

A smell assaulted her nose—a chemical reek covering something darker—the smell of serious illness. Lei rubbed the pendant at her throat, taking some calming breaths.

"You're in your old room, as usual," Wayne said. "Go in and see her. Momi was waiting for us to get home."

Lei made her legs carry her down the short hall to her aunt's bedroom. The drapes were closed, and Rosario Texeira was a small mound in the middle of the bed. Gentle light from a lamp fell over her aunt's best friend and business partner, seated beside her.

"Aunty Momi. I came as soon as I could." Lei hurried to the statuesque older woman, and Momi stood up and embraced her.

Momi brushed tears off her cheeks. "Just when I think I'm done crying, I find a few more tears leaking out. She will be so glad to see you."

"It was hard to get away. Crime never sleeps." Lei tried to smile but failed. "How's she doing?"

"Weak. Hospice has her on a morphine drip, so she's as comfortable as she can be."

"What's that smell?" Lei whispered. It was making her queasy.

"It's the cocktail of medicines they've got her on. Kidney medicine, pain medicine, and her catheter." Momi gestured to the clear, dangling intravenous bag on the steel pole beside the bed. "Her kidneys are failing, as Wayne probably told you. They're doing dialysis every couple of days. She doesn't want to go into the hospital anymore, so now it's all about keeping her comfortable."

"This is so hard." Lei felt her legs fold up, and she sat abruptly on the bed. The movement startled her aunt awake, and Rosario's deep brown eyes opened.

"Lei! You came!" Her voice sounded thin and rusty.

"Aunty. I love you." Lei embraced her aunt carefully around the cords and wires. She was dimly aware of Momi's departure as she lay down beside her aunt, plumping one of the pillows so she could lie facing her aunt with her head on it.

"I love you too, Lei-girl." Rosario had continued to

lose weight since Lei had been there a month ago. The bones of her skull were prominent, and her thick braids had gone almost entirely white. She still had her hair because she'd opted not to do chemo. "I'm so glad you got here in time. It won't be long now."

"Don't say that, Aunty." Lei could hardly speak through the tears pouring down her face. She dabbed her eyes on the sheet. "I have good news. You're going to be a grandmother, sooner than we thought. You have to hang on to see him." She told her aunt about baby Kiet—that his mother had died and they were adopting him.

"You're going to be such a good mama." Her aunt's skeletal hand, soft and pink on one side, bony and brown on the other, stroked her hair. "I am so happy for you. She will be such a beauty."

"No, Aunty, he's a boy," Lei said, but her aunt had fallen abruptly asleep, eyelids crepey over her sunken eyes.

Lei kicked off her shoes and reached over and turned off the light, snuggling down under the covers beside her aunt. She fell asleep as if tumbling down a rabbit hole.

Stevens and Captain Omura sat in Interview Room B with Magda Kennedy and her lawyer. He felt like they were pressing Play on a recording of the interviews he'd watched a few years ago, when the gallery owner was interviewed in connection with art smuggling and money laundering. Her hair was a shimmering blackbird's wing under the harsh fluorescent lights, icy blue eyes haughty as she gazed at them.

Her lawyer paced behind her. "I wonder how we can help the Maui Police Department today," he said. "As quickly as possible. My client is a busy woman."

"Thanks for coming in." Omura opened a file. "We're working on a case that's been in the news a lot lately—the *heiau* desecrations. Someone is, apparently, looting Hawaiian sacred sites for petroglyphs and other artifacts."

"I've heard about that," Kennedy said. "Terrible thing."

"What do you know about the case?"

"I know there have been lootings and lost artifacts on Oahu, and now Maui. I don't know why I'm here."

"You're an art dealer. Have you heard anything in the art world? Rumors about where the artifacts are going?" Omura asked.

"The art world is a small one, but it's a competitive one. I don't generally spend a lot of time with other gallery owners, talking about dealing in stolen objects." Magda Kennedy kicked a pedicured foot, irritability in the way she tossed her hair back. "Besides, the value of these items seems to be in their antiquity and scarcity more than any artistic merit."

"If you have any specific questions regarding this investigation, please just ask them," the lawyer said.

"We're on a schedule."

"Well, your name has come up in connection with the distribution of the artifacts," Stevens said. "We think they may be going overseas. What can you tell us about that?"

"Ridiculous and insulting." Magda made as if to stand.

"I wonder if you've heard about the recent murder of a visitor to our islands. His name is Norm Jorgenson, and he was a professional art thief." Omura opened the file and pushed over a picture of Jorgenson's bashed-in head. "There is evidence linking him to the *heiau* desecration here on Maui. We'd like permission to search your gallery and check your computers to see if you, or anyone in your employ, has a connection with this man."

Magda Kennedy gave a delicate snort and stood. "You're wasting my time. Show me a warrant."

Her lawyer followed her as she went to the door, but it wouldn't open. Stevens unlocked it, and she picked up speed as she walked down the hall, gold sandals winking and creamy Grecian-styled dress billowing.

Omura came to stand beside him as they watched her go. "She was right about one thing. That was a waste of time."

"I need to check in with Brandon Mahoe. Get more on where and who he heard that from, because we aren't getting a warrant on someone with her clout with so little probable cause," Stevens said. As if on cue, his phone rang. He recognized the number as Mahoe's. "Speak of the devil." They walked out of the interview room and down the hall as Stevens picked up the call. "Hey, Brandon. What you got for me?"

"This isn't Brandon; it's his mother. Who is this?" The woman's voice throbbed with emotion.

Stevens stopped in his tracks. "What?"

Omura looked at him and frowned but continued on to her office.

"This phone was in his pocket and this is the only number he called, so I'm calling you before I turn you into the police!" the woman yelled. "So I'm asking one last time, who are you!"

"I'm Lieutenant Stevens, Brandon's commanding officer," Stevens said, his throat closing. He coughed. "What's happened?"

The woman burst into tears. "Oh, Lieutenant Stevens! We're at the hospital and Brandon, he's in a coma from being beaten!"

"I'm on my way."

Stevens shut the phone and broke into a run for the front doors. In his truck on the way to Maui Memorial, he got in touch with Dispatch to find out who'd been sent to take a statement. He was able to intercept the responding officers and called Ferreira from his own station for backup. He'd also called Omura on her personal cell to apprise her of the development by the time he screeched into the portico of the hospital.

Showing his badge, he was quickly escorted to the intensive care unit, where Brandon's mother, several cousins and siblings had already gathered in the waiting room.

"Lieutenant Stevens." He held up his badge as he strode forward, heading for the distraught-looking woman in a Hawaiian-print shirt and capri pants, her black hair wound into a tower held up by chopsticks. "Are you Mrs. Mahoe?"

"Yes." She straightened her shirt, standing tall to look him in the eye.

"I'm so sorry for what's happened. What can you tell me?"

"You first. What was Brandon doing that yours is the only number on his phone?"

Stevens looked into the window of the ICU. His stomach dropped at the sight of his young recruit. The man's head was wound in bandages, his sturdy frame motionless on the bed, his robust color gone gray. A nurse moved around inside the room, monitoring the equipment.

"I'm here to take your official statement and begin investigating what happened," Stevens said, looking back into Mrs. Mahoe's tear-stained face. "Is there anywhere we can speak privately? My partner will be joining us."

A young man, burly and brown in a wifebeater T-shirt emblazoned with a pit bull, elbowed through the relatives toward him. "I saw the whole thing."

"Okay. Let me take your statement first." Stevens looked around for hospital personnel, approached the nurse's station, and held up his badge. "How is Brandon Mahoe doing?" he asked.

"He's being treated for head trauma," the nurse said. "He's currently in a coma. We are hopeful."

"Hopeful for what?" Stevens rapped out, aware of the audience behind him.

"Hopeful that he'll recover. His skull is fractured. The coma is medically induced, to let the swelling in his brain go down."

Stevens drew a quick breath in shock, feeling guilt twist his guts—but now was a time to focus on the job at hand. He could second-guess his decision to send Brandon in undercover later. "Is there anywhere I can interview these witnesses more privately?"

"The chapel." The nurse pointed.

Ferreira arrived, recoiled at the sight of Mahoe in the ICU, but didn't comment. "Boss, where do you want us?"

"We're going to the chapel to take statements." Stevens gestured to the young man in the T-shirt. "Follow us, please."

The room was a dim square filled with rows of plastic chairs. At the front squatted an altar that reminded Stevens of his grandmother's old walnut TV cabinet from the 1950s. A wall-mounted box with a plastic dove that pulsed glowing light overhung it.

Stevens rearranged several of the chairs into a triangle with Ferreira in one, himself in another, and the witness in a third.

"What's your name?" He took out his notebook with the stub of pencil.

"Mana Guinamo." The young man smoothed his shirt self-consciously, and Stevens spotted dirt and scuff marks on his pants and clothing.

"Mana, I'm Lieutenant Stevens and this is Detective Ferreira. Did any other officers respond to a call at the scene of the attack?"

A long pause. Guinamo looked down at his hands. Stevens noticed the knuckles were swollen and split. "No, sir."

"So we are the first police officers to talk to you?"

"Yes."

"Tell us what happened."

"We were at a Hui gathering. Just a small one, where we were learning to be team leaders for our patrol groups. Do you know about the Heiau Hui?"

Ferreira spoke up. "Yes, we're aware. I hear good things about what you're doing."

"I don't understand it." Guinamo shook his close-cropped head of wiry black hair. "We were listening to our leader, Charles Awapuhi, when suddenly he pretends to be sniffing the air. 'I smell a rat,' he says. 'I smell a piggy rat.' Everyone starts looking around all confused, and then he points a finger at Brandon." Guinamo looked at his hands again. "Mahoe, he's my friend; we go back to small kid time. He stands proud. Doesn't say a word. Awapuhi comes over, pokes him in the chest. 'Who you been ratting to, boy?' and Mahoe, he says nothing. Then Awapuhi punches him right in the stomach. Suddenly, everyone starts punching him, and one guy he even had a bat! I jumped in and started fighting, trying to get them off him, but once he was down, on the ground, Awapuhi called them off. "Nuff already," he says. "We just want to send a message." And they all walked off. I called nine-one-one for an ambulance and they came. I called his mom. I know her. She went through his pockets and found the phone with your number on it."

"Why didn't some officers respond to your nine-one-one call?" Stevens asked.

"I don't know."

"Did anyone besides you know Brandon was a police officer?"

"Yes. Plenty people knew. He wasn't trying to hide it."

"Are there any other police officers in the Heiau Hui?"

"Yes." Now Guinamo looked down. "But I'd rather not name them."

"Tell me more about the Hui, how Awapuhi runs things."

"Until now, he's been hard but fair. We all knew he was the boss, but this was the first time I saw him target anyone. Why Brandon?"

Stevens didn't answer, enduring his guilt. He took down Guinamo's contact information. "Can you send in Mrs. Mahoe, please? And thank you for sticking up for Brandon. Who knows? You might have saved his life."

"I just hope he's okay," Guinamo said. "Least I could do for my friend."

"Get those knuckles looked at," Stevens said, as the young man stood up. "I think you might have cracked something."

Mrs. Mahoe came in next. Stevens peered past her. "Is there a Mr. Mahoe?"

"No," she answered shortly, taking a seat. "What was my son doing for you that put him in this kind of danger?"

"I'm so sorry for what happened, Mrs. Mahoe. Your son is a brave man. He's a hero."

"You don't have to tell me that." She folded her arms over her considerable chest and narrowed her eyes at him.

"You haven't answered my question."

"I'm sorry. I mean no disrespect, but I can't discuss an open investigation. May I have the phone, please?" A long moment passed; then Mrs. Mahoe reached into the pocket of the capris and smacked it into his hand. "Thank you. What can you tell me about the Heiau Hui and their activities?"

"Don't know much. I work at the Lahaina Luau. I'm a fire dancer." Stevens blinked, trying to keep the surprise off his face, but she must have seen it, because she gave a tiny smile. "I'm very good at juggling flaming coconuts and pretty much anything else. Anyway, too busy to get involved when Brandon told me he was starting to work with them—but it seemed like a good thing, organizing to protect our *heiaus*. Now I'm starting to think they're only a gang of thugs."

"What do you know about Charles Awapuhi, the leader here on Maui?"

"I went to school with him."

Stevens looked down, took a note as Mrs. Mahoe went on.

"He was always a little radical. Liked risks. Liked to push things. He got his first head tattoo in high school. Even then, he was declaring he didn't want to have to live like other people. He did that tattoo knowing it was going to make it hard for him to get a job."

"Why do you think he targeted your son?"

"Because he found out Brandon was reporting to you on the Hui activities." Her eyes were hard. Stevens had to resist the desire to look away from her gaze. "I hope whatever Brandon told you was worth it."

"It could never be worth what happened to your son," Stevens said, and extended his hand to Mrs. Mahoe. "I'm so sorry."

The woman's eyes filled with tears as she took his hand in both of hers. "Brandon loves being a police officer. He thinks so much of you."

Now it was Stevens who had to blink. "This is enough for now. We have enough to move on."

Ferreira stood up and embraced Mrs. Mahoe. "He's going to be okay," the grizzled detective said. "Keep praying."

As they walked down the hall, Stevens glanced at Ferreira. "We still have to remind ourselves the Hui isn't the real problem." They brushed through the automatic doors of the hospital. "They're a problem, all right, but they arose as a result of the desecrations. If we can stop the looting and retrieve the artifacts, there will be no reason for the Hui to exist."

"Unless they decide they want to take on another cause," Ferreira said.

"Well, let's hope this whole thing subsides when we

get the looters and whoever's paying them. I'll coordinate the arrest warrant for Charles Awapuhi with Captain Omura. You get back to the station and keep an eye on things," Stevens said.

"Right, boss."

They peeled off to their separate vehicles.

Chapter 22

Lei woke up the next morning to the unfamiliar twittering of blackbirds in the California oaks outside. She was curled up next to her aunt, and for a moment she savored the feeling of safety, belonging, and love that Rosario's nearness brought her. She'd gone to live with her aunt when she was nine years old, after her mother's death, and had slept in her aunt's bed for the first two years. She'd been unable to tolerate the anxiety of being alone.

The memory of her aunt's condition crashed in on Lei, and she felt herself curling up tight against the pain of the oncoming loss. There was no doubt death was coming—it was all around Lei in the smell that filled the room.

Lei turned her face into the pillow to muffle the sound of her sobs. In spite of that, she felt her aunt's hand, light and soft, stroking her hair.

"You're here," Rosario said. "You're here."

Lei reached out and put her arms around her aunt's shrunken form. She pulled her close. "As long as I can be."

Even as she held her aunt close, the reek of the IV

and the smell of her aunt's body rose up to make Lei's stomach roil. She shut her eyes and weathered the waves, horrified that she could be having such a physical reaction to her aunt's illness.

Finally, it was too much, and she let go of Aunty Rosario, getting out of bed. She hurried to the bathroom, shut the door, turned on the water full blast, and made it to the toilet just in time to vomit.

Weak and trembling, she rested her head on the cool porcelain and wondered what she could have eaten that was getting to her.

But maybe she was pregnant. The thought made her heave some more, just from pure terror. It was one thing to think it might be a good idea to let nature take its course. It was another entirely to deal with the real effects.

A knock on the door. "Lei? You okay in there?" Her dad's worried voice.

"Yeah. Just ate something funny on the plane, I guess. I'll be out in a few."

She heard his footsteps pad away.

She stood up carefully, feeling another wave of dizziness and nausea, and turned on the shower. Under the fall of water, she took inventory of her body, running her hands down her arms to feel the familiar ridged lines from past self-injury, across her collarbone to feel the knot of scar left by a perpetrator's bite, and around her breasts, which felt tender and sore.

She'd worried she was pregnant before and been wrong, but that night a while back with Stevens might have done it—and if it hadn't, it certainly hadn't been for lack of trying. She smiled at the memory of how good that whole night had been. In spite of everything else, their love and passion were only growing.

She'd better get another one of those tests and see what was going on, and if something was, she'd have even more good news for her aunt, maybe enough to keep Rosario alive a little longer.

Lei scrubbed briskly, energized by the thought even as she quavered at the idea of not only dealing with bringing home Kiet but adding their own child to the mix when the baby was less than a year old. But maybe it was like Dr. Wilson had said, that two wasn't much more work than one. In any case, no point in obsessing until she knew one way or the other.

Lei got dressed and met her dad in the kitchen. He handed her a mug of coffee. "Feeling better?"

"Yeah." She didn't feel able to say more. "What's the plan for today?"

"I thought you and Rosario could sort all those pictures she took of you as a kid and put them in albums. I brought the photos down from the attic and bought the albums already."

"Oh, Dad, that's a great idea. She's always been working so hard. She used to say she'd do this when she had time," Lei said. Her eyes welled. "I'm so sick of crying already!"

"Just get used to it. It's how we roll around here," Wayne said, his face unashamedly wet. "I don't feel right if I haven't cried at least three times a day."

She hugged his lean body, feeling his hard, tattooed arms come around to squeeze her. "Okay. I'll just let whatever happens, happen."

"That's my girl." He tweaked her wet curls. "Though you never have been good at that."

"I think I'm getting better."

"Well, here are the photos and albums." He'd set everything out on the little square dining room table. "I have to get to the restaurant soon. I've been picking up Rosario's work."

"Can I take a quick run to the store before you leave?" Lei had dressed in her running clothes. "I have to pick something up."

"Sure. Just hurry. They want me in by nine a.m. I'll try to get her eating some breakfast while you're gone."

Lei jogged the several blocks to the pharmacy, feeling her angst lift with the movement of running. "God, grant me the serenity to accept the things I cannot change, the courage to change the things I can, and wisdom to know the difference." She'd learned that one from her father and knew it was one of the cornerstones of the twelve-step programs. That prayer had a lot of uses, including accepting that a loved one was dying—or that she might be pregnant.

It is what it is. Another good saying, one she owed to Dr. Wilson.

Lei bought a pregnancy test along with a bright bouquet of sunflowers and jogged back to the house. She put the flowers in water and scraped up her nerve to do the pregnancy test. The sooner she knew, the sooner she could share the news with Aunty, if there was any news to share.

She went into the bathroom and did her business on the stick. She shut the two sides of the plastic slide for the minutes required and got up to wash her hands. Finally, she looked at herself in the mirror, took a deep breath, and opened the slide.

"Blue," she said aloud, and for a long moment couldn't remember what that meant. She scrabbled around for the instructions, hands trembling as she read aloud, *"A blue result indicates pregnancy. Congratulations!"*

She looked up into her own scared eyes and said aloud, "I'm going to be a mama. Of two." And clapped her hand over her mouth and gave a little scream. She didn't know if the feeling surging through her was terror or excitement.

She went back out to the kitchen, picked up the vase of sunflowers, and took them in to her aunt.

"Aunty, I brought you something."

"Oh, honey, I love them. So cheerful!" Rosario looked brighter today. Wayne got up from the chair beside the bed and the bowl of soft cereal he'd been coaxing Aunty to eat.

"Off to work," he said, dropping a kiss on Lei's head. "I'll bring you home something for lunch."

"Hold on a minute, Dad. I've got some news to share with both of you." She made sure she had both of their full attention. Her mouth trembled as she said, "I'm pregnant."

"What?" her father exclaimed. "I thought you said it didn't work!"

Aunty Rosario clapped her hands. "I knew it!"

"Aunty, oh my God." Lei felt her cheeks burning, and tears filled her eyes. "I can't believe it. I don't even know how I feel about it really. I was just getting used to the idea of having Kiet, and now we're going to have another one."

"This is just the news I needed to hear," Aunty said. "Come give me a hug." Lei leaned down for that and then was caught up in her dad's arms.

"I can't wait to be a grandpa," he said gruffly. "Take it easy, now, you hear? No more bombs."

"Dad. None of your business," Lei said, but she smiled and patted his shoulder.

"Call that husband of yours," Wayne said.

"I want to tell him in person," Lei said. "He's got a lot going on right now, and I don't want to distract him."

"Well, I'll be back in a few hours and will bring you girls some lunch. Have fun with the photos, and you really made my day." Wayne kissed her on the top of her head and left.

Lei spent a pleasant couple of hours sorting the box of photos with her aunt, pasting them into the photo albums her father had bought with a glue stick. "Remember Girl Scouts?"

"How could I forget? Lei, the girl who already knew how to fix a meal from stuff she found in the woods and who chased off a bear with a stick before any of the grown-ups knew it had wandered into camp!"

"I liked getting a medal," Lei said, smoothing the photo of her receiving her "Courage" merit badge. "I think that's why I'm good at police work. You get to do stuff, and then you get promoted when you do good. The rules are clear, even though I don't always follow them. I don't think I would like civilian life. Too fuzzy."

"Well, for someone who likes clear rules, you sure knew how to break them. Remember prom?" Her aunt held up a photo of Lei in a white dress uniform standing beside a scared-looking boy in a tux.

Lei had been surprised to be asked to prom at all. He'd been a shy boy who'd had a crush on her for years. She decided to go so as not to miss out on a high school ritual, and she'd worn her Reserve Officers' Training Corps uniform, a high school training elective that focused on preparing college-bound students as officers for the army. "I was proud of being in ROTC. I didn't see anything weird about it until I got there and saw everyone else was in dresses."

"That boy had such a crush on you, but I don't think he said a word all night."

"He didn't. I didn't, either. It was a disaster. Really added to the rumors I was gay."

"I didn't know that was going on."

Lei shrugged. "I punched out the girls who started the rumors. They stopped. Anyway, I'm glad I went to the police academy instead of the army," Lei said, gluing in the final photo, one of her in uniform, graduating from the police academy. "I wonder what happened to the first nine years of my life. Now that we're having our own family, I guess I wish I had a little more record of growing up."

"I don't know, Sweets." Her aunt yawned, her hands fluttering on the spread. "You didn't come to me with anything but a suitcase. I have a few baby photos of you I took and some that Wayne sent me before he went to prison." She gestured to the dresser. "Top drawer. Now, if you don't mind, I'm going to take a little nap." And that suddenly, she was asleep.

Lei had to lean in close to see if Aunty's bony chest was rising and falling. Very small movement, but it was. She got up and opened the top dresser drawer, taking out a small cardboard box.

She tiptoed out of the room and sorted through the pictures, feeling the bittersweet squeeze of grief as she looked at her mother's fresh, young, beautiful face beside her own: straight black hair beside curly brown. Lei's eyes were tilted like her mother's, but were larger and the golden-brown color her father and aunt shared. Her family tree was truly multicultural.

That blend would be even more mixed in a child she and Stevens would have. Would the child have straight hair or curly? Round eyes or almond-shaped? Brown, green, or blue? They'd just have to wait to find out, just as they would to see what baby Kiet ended up looking like.

Lei stacked the photos together and put them in the box just as her father returned. "Brought you your favorite," he said. "Beef stew and poi rolls."

"Thanks, Dad." Suddenly her upset stomach rumbled with hunger. "That sounds perfect. Aunty just fell asleep."

"The nurse is coming by in a few hours to do her daily care," Wayne said. "How was the photo album project?"

"Great. It really seemed to take her back in time. She told me stories about when I came to live with her that I barely remembered. But I was wondering—do you know where any more photos might be, from my first nine years? With you and Mom?"

Wayne looked down as he served the stew from a round cardboard carton. "I'm sorry, Sweets. I remember Maylene had a baby book for you, but after I went to prison, I don't know what happened to anything."

"I don't know either. At some point—after they took you away—we lost so much. Started living in cheap rentals with lots of other people. Mom was using drugs every day she could get them. I don't remember anything in those rooms but my toys and clothes in one suitcase."

"You know, we've hardly talked about that time before," he said. "It hurts to hear how my screw-ups affected you."

"Water under the bridge," Lei said, as he handed her a bowl of stew. "I would like to have more pictures, though."

"I wish I had them for you." Wayne sat down beside her, folded his calloused hands. "Bless this food to our bodies, Lord. And bless my daughter and her family." He smiled at her and dug in with his spoon. Lei followed suit, suddenly ravenous.

When they'd eaten, Lei prepared a bowl on a tray for

her aunt and peeked back in on her. Rosario opened her eyes. "Oh, there you are."

"You took a little nap." Lei came in with the tray. "Please eat a few bites."

"I'm still full from breakfast."

"Come on, Aunty. I saw how little you ate this morning." Lei pushed a second pillow behind her aunt, helping her sit upright. "How are you feeling?"

"A little better." And Rosario did look better, a little more color in her cheeks. Lei set the tray over her legs and she lifted the spoon, spilling some but eating.

"I'm going back to the restaurant. You girls have fun," Wayne said from the doorway.

"Thanks for the stew, Dad," Lei said. He nodded and left.

Rosario ate a few more bites, then pushed it away. "I want to tell you something," she said. "It's time for me to get it off my chest."

"What?" Lei cleared the tray, setting it on top of the bureau and getting in bed beside her aunt. "You had so many good stories this morning. I had a wonderful childhood after I came to you."

"I did the best I could." Rosario took Lei's hand, smoothed the back of it with her own silky-soft palm. "But I told you before. I made mistakes."

"Yes. Keeping my father's letters from me. But that's all in the past."

"That wasn't the only one. I'm talking about that phone number in your grandmother Yumi's things that got you in all that trouble."

Lei straightened up, turned so she could see her aunt's face. "What do you know about that?" Last year, a phone number for Bozeman, the assassin who'd killed her childhood molester, Charlie Kwon, had turned up in Lei's deceased grandmother's collectible box.

"Your father told me about the trouble you were in with the FBI's internal affairs because of it."

"Yeah, it was a scary time." Lei almost shuddered, remembering the investigation into her past and how close she'd come to being charged with Kwon's murder.

"Well...I have a confession to make. I guess it counts as a deathbed confession." Rosario laughed, a damp chuckle. "Your grandmother Yumi contacted me. She had found the hit man's number, and I was the one to call it. I sent her money, and she paid Bozeman over there on Oahu when the job was done."

Lei recoiled, jumping up off the bed. "Aunty! You're telling me you...you and my grandmother hired Bozeman?"

"We didn't agree on much, your grandmother and I... but on Charlie Kwon, we agreed. The man was sick. He raped little girls. Some dogs just need to be put down before they bite again." She plucked at the hand-sewn Hawaiian quilt that covered her lap, looking down.

"Holy shit." Lei sat down hard on the chair beside the bed.

"Told you I wasn't perfect. You can charge me if you need to."

"Aunty, oh my God. How can you put me in a position like this?" Lei felt her vision narrowing in a return of her PTSD symptoms, and she pinched her own leg, hard, to ground herself. She picked up her aunt's hand, squeezed it in both her own. "Kwon was a terrible man. It's just not how things should be done." Lei's mind flashed to her own confrontation with Kwon, the man on his knees before her, the Glock wobbling in her gloved hands

"I know. But I can't bring myself to regret he's dead. No price was too high to pay to make sure no little girl ever went through what you did." Rosario stroked Lei's hair. "I'm tired again. So exhausted today. Let me know if you're turning me in to the cops."

"Oh, Aunty." Lei sat up. "I need some time to take this in. To think of what to do."

Rosario's eyes filled with sorrow as she gazed at Lei. "Don't take too long." And her eyes shut again.

Chapter 23

Stevens finished updating Omura about the attack on Mahoe. "I need a judge's signature on this arrest warrant due to Awapuhi's high profile," the captain said. "I'm faxing it to him now, but I don't know when he'll get it back to me."

"I'll go back to the hospital," Stevens said. "Keep an eye on Brandon. We know where Awapuhi is. We should have all our ducks in a row with a guy like him."

"I want a couple of units to go out with you when you arrest Awapuhi. No telling what kind of response he's going to have."

"Makes me wonder why he went after Brandon like that. Surely he must have known there would be blowback from us."

"I don't know. According to your witness, he stopped the beating before it was terminal, but it was still very severe, and he knew Brandon was a police officer. To me, this signals a change from minimal cooperation with MPD to outright warfare. I have no intention of sweeping Mahoe's beating under the rug."

"Thanks." Stevens held her eyes. "I appreciate it. I feel responsible."

"We both took a chance sending him in there. It's on me, too." She smoothed her sleek bob back behind her ears. "Now, get back to the hospital, and take a fruit basket to the mother from MPD, why don't you? Gather your arrest team and be ready for my call."

"Yes, sir." Stevens hurried off down the hall, already working his phone to alert Ferreira, Torufu, Pono, and Gerry Bunuelos, along with a couple of backup patrol units, for when the warrant was ready.

On the way to the hospital, he phoned Lei. "I love you," he said when she answered. "There. That's out of the way."

"I'm glad you called. Something's come up." Lei's voice sounded thin and stressed. "Let me get some privacy."

"While you're getting that, I need to tell you we've had a break in the case—or not really, there's nothing direct—but you remember Brandon Mahoe, the recruit I sent undercover? He was severely beaten. He's in a coma."

"No, Michael! That's terrible!"

"Yeah. We have a witness that says Awapuhi fingered him as a snitch and then everyone attacked him. What I'm wondering is, why that response? So many other ways they could have handled it, kept him out of anything important, fed him false information. In fact, the one thing he did give us, a tip on Magda Kennedy, dead-ended right way."

"Maybe Brandon'll have more to say when he wakes up."

"Yeah. So I'm going back to the hospital, waiting on the arrest warrants for Awapuhi. So what did you need to tell me?"

He heard her sigh. Even as he drove he could picture her putting the phone against her shoulder, squeezing the web between her thumb and forefinger, one of her stress management techniques. "It's about Aunty. And there's something else."

"How's she doing?"

"Not good, but she perked up a bit after I got here. She told me something today. Something big. I'm having trouble deciding what to do."

He just waited, the speakerphone in its holder emitting a tinny buzzing, as he stopped at a light.

"She told me that she and my grandmother, Yumi Matsumoto, hired the hit on Kwon."

"No shit!" Stevens exclaimed, his foot coming down too hard on the accelerator so that the truck leaped forward as the light changed. "That's messed up. Thought those two hated each other!" Lei's Japanese mother had broken with her family to marry *paniolo* Wayne Texeira when she was only eighteen. Rosario, Wayne's sister, had resented Maylene's parents' judgmental attitude, especially after Lei was without a guardian at age nine and the Matsumotos made no effort to reach out or support their grandchild.

"After Kwon got out of prison, according to Aunty, my grandmother contacted her with the hit man's number. Yumi couldn't be bothered to contact me, but she finds my aunt and proposes they kill the man who raped me as a child?" Stevens could mentally see Lei's head shake. "It *is* messed up. But they did it together. Yumi found the hit man, Rosario paid for the hit, and Yumi delivered the money when it was done. Now Yumi's dead and Aunty's dying."

A long pause. Stevens pulled in to the hospital. "Other than agreeing with you that it's messed up, what's your question?"

"If I should turn Aunty in for hiring Bozeman."

Stevens snorted. "What's the point?"

"It's the right thing to do."

"Call Marcus. It was his case. Throw yourself on his mercy and see what he says."

"I'm tired of throwing myself on his mercy."

Stevens knew she'd had to do that the year before in trying to get herself cleared of suspicion in Kwon's murder. "Well, as you say, it's his case, and it's closed now. His team decided not to try to track Bozeman's clients. So I'd just call Marcus, see if he thinks any further action should be taken against Rosario. I'm guessing none will be merited."

Lei sighed. "I love you. Let's talk longer when you have more time."

"You said there was something else."

"No. I'll tell you when I'm home. Stay safe."

"I'll do my best." He hung up and parked the truck in the sprawling lot. Inside the hospital, he bought a basket of fruit and flowers and charged it to the MPD reimbursement card he used for departmental expenses. Brandon Mahoe had been moved, and Stevens found him in a private room a few floors up.

Mrs. Mahoe greeted Stevens, setting down a lapful of crocheting. "You came back."

He held up the flower-studded fruit basket. "With Maui Police Department's best wishes. I don't know how long I can stay, but I wanted to keep you company while I could."

"Thank you." She appeared calmer, taking the basket and setting it on the wide windowsill. "They seem to think he's going to be okay, but it's hard to tell with head injuries."

"I know." Stevens took a chair beside the bed.

Brandon appeared as inert as before, the strong young body slack on the bed, his color yellowish. Monitors beside the bed beeped steadily. "Why don't you take a break? Go make some phone calls, get a snack."

She considered this a long moment and finally stood. "I'll go down to the cafeteria."

"Good. I'll sit with him."

She left. Stevens glanced over at the young man on the bed. It felt like he'd been running full speed ever since he came back to Maui from Oahu, and this was the first moment he was sitting quietly, just being with someone. That made him remember Kiet.

He took out his phone and thumbed to a photograph of the baby. The boy's changeable eyes were open, his little face serious, that thatch of black hair comically upright like the crest on a bird. He'd taken the photo for Lei, and in all the chaos of the night before she left for California, he'd never shown it to her.

He texted the photo to her: *Kiet Edward Mookjai Stevens. It's on his birth certificate.*

Almost immediately she texted back, *Thanks. I wondered what he looked like. Cute! What color are his eyes? Is that gray?*

To be determined, Stevens texted back. *But probably brown, hazel, or green.*

He's going to be gorgeous.

Of course.

It felt good to have this moment, even sharing the trace of proud humor with her that he felt. He slid the phone back into his pocket, looked up, and was surprised to see Mahoe's eyes were open.

"You're awake."

"Hi, boss." Mahoe's voice was scratchy, but his eyes looked clear as he gazed around the room.

"How are you feeling?"

"Fuzzy. Head's sore."

"You were in a coma, and I thought you were going to be out for quite a while." Stevens poured some water into a plastic cup from the carafe by the bed and held it for the young man to drink. Mahoe finished the cupful thirstily.

"Gotta admit, you aren't who I expected at my bedside," Mahoe said. "Where's Mom?"

"She went down to the cafeteria for a minute. She's been by your side every other minute." Stevens handed the young man another cup of water.

"You'll be glad to know we've got a warrant in process for Awapuhi. Gonna pick him up as soon as the order comes through."

"Awapuhi?" Mahoe looked confused, frowning. He shut his eyes.

"Yeah. Charles Awapuhi, the Heiau Hui leader. Your

friend Mana Guinamo told us he saw the whole thing."

Mahoe's eyes popped open and he tried to get up, falling back in agitation. "You mean he was the one who beat me!"

"What?" Stevens felt his brows snap together. "He told us the whole story, how he fought the Hui leaders off to save you."

"He's the one who did it!" Brandon's face congested and his mouth worked. Alarmed, Stevens pushed him back against the pillows, restraining Mahoe gently.

"Take it easy," Stevens said. "Go slow. Take all the time you need." He took his phone out and thumbed it to the audio feature. "I'm going to record this."

Brandon's throat worked, and for a moment Stevens was afraid the young man was collapsing again, but instead tears welled in his eyes. "Mana's been my friend my whole life. He really got into the Hui thing and was all excited I got involved. But then I overheard him talking with another guy—Red Toaman. Red and him, they been making trouble since we were in junior high. Anyway, I overheard them talking about 'doing the Norwegian.'"

"You mean the murder vic found in that Wailuku inn? You think he had something to do with that?"

"Yeah, I do. Mana saw me, but I pretended I hadn't heard anything. Later he confronted me when we were alone. Told me he thought I was a snitch for the MPD and told me to get out of the Hui. I told him no way. I cared about the cause. He attacked me." Mahoe looked down at his hands. Stevens saw they were as bruised as Mana's had been. "I was doing okay handling him until someone came up and hit me on the head. Then it was lights-out."

"Did you ever see who it was who hit you?"

"No."

"Did you see Awapuhi anywhere around? Because Mana pointed the finger at Awapuhi."

"No, but they call Awapuhi 'Kane' for the Man. And when he and Red were talking about the Norwegian, I heard them say that 'the Man wanted it done.'"

"So why would he lie and point the finger at Awapuhi?"

"To get you to arrest him, maybe. I don't know."

Stevens stood. "We'd be arresting him for the wrong reason, and it would make it harder to get charges to stick later. I have to make some calls. Your mom is going to be back shortly."

"All right."

Stevens pushed the nurse's button so they could come see that Brandon was awake. Stevens was already calling Omura with the latest developments as he walked down the hall.

"I was just going to contact you to tell you the warrant

is signed," she said. "We have to change the charges. Go ahead and mobilize your team to bring him in, and that young man Guinamo, too."

Stevens broke into a run as he got ahold of Dispatch to activate his team. His cell was ringing again in his pocket as he pulled the Kevlar vest out of the backseat of the Bronco and shrugged into it.

"Stevens," he barked, the phone against his ear as he tightened the Velcro straps on the vest.

"Michael? This is Esther Ka`awai. On Kaua`i." The *kupuna*'s deep, authoritative voice stopped all movement.

"Mrs. Ka`awai," he said cautiously, checking his weapon, racking the slide, reholstering it. "This isn't a good time. Can I call you back?"

"No. It's about the Heiau Hui. I was in touch with Lei a while back, and this morning when I called, she told me to contact you immediately with this information."

Stevens got into the Bronco, shut the door, turned on the ignition, and blasted the AC. Pre-raid adrenaline combined with the hot vest was already ratcheting up his temperature. "What is it?"

"I don't know exactly what's going on, but I've found out who's taking the artifacts and why."

Stevens went very still. "I'm listening."

"The artifacts are being collected by a man who believes that's the best way to preserve them. He's hired those art thieves from Europe so it won't get back to him. He's a politician. Councilman Muapu."

"Mrs. Ka`awai. This is a very serious charge to be making. What's your evidence?"

"Councilman Muapu contacted me, asked me to be part of his Board of Five who will be custodians of the artifacts."

Stevens knit his brows. "Is there any evidence we can use? We can't just bring in a man of his stature on your say-so, all due respect."

"I know where the artifacts collected on Maui are being stored. They're at Charles Awapuhi's place. They're buried in his yard, behind the kukui nut trees."

"How do you know that?"

"They called out to me and told me where they are. They want to be returned to their proper place at the *heiau* in Haiku."

Stevens felt a chill from the AC ripple across his arms, raising the hairs. "So there's nothing hard we can use to search Awapuhi's house and grounds?"

"I thought you were on your way to arrest him."

"I never told you that."

"You didn't have to. I'll be prepared to testify against Councilman Muapu when the time comes." She hung up.

Stevens shook his head, blew out a breath. This was

getting deep. First thing was first—execute the raid on Awapuhi's house. Once the man was in custody for being involved in the Norwegian's murder, he could search the house. Never mind telling anyone about Esther's psychic tip with the location of the artifacts—he'd just go have a look and hope she was right. Stevens lifted the cop light out from under the dash, turned it on, and peeled out from the parking lot to meet his team.

Chapter 24

Lei left her aunt sleeping after their conversation—it had seemed to relax her, truly giving her some peace of mind, while Lei felt wound up with so much tension she knew the only cure was a run. She left the bungalow and jogged around the semi-urban neighborhood, enjoying the sight of squirrels, crows, and live oak trees, letting her thoughts wander free-form over the case, her future motherhood, and her aunt's confession. She left a message on Marcella's voicemail telling her to call, and finally she cooled down, returning to the house and stretching in the little patch of front yard.

She'd made a decision. She dialed a contact on her phone.

Marcus Kamuela's voice was surprised. "Lei! To what do I owe the pleasure? Is this about your art thief murder?"

"No. It's something else entirely—though I think Stevens has some developments over on Maui to catch you up on. I have a situation. A hypothetical situation."

"Okay." His voice had gone cautious.

"Remember how Bozeman's phone number had turned up in my grandmother's things?"

"How could I forget?"

Lei paced, rubbing the pendant at her throat. She looked up at the sky, down at the cracks in the cement, over at the little house. The junipers beside the stoop were getting long; she should remind her dad about cutting them. "Suppose I found out how that phone number got there, and it implicated someone very close to me—who's dying. Would that person be under investigation for obtaining Bozeman's services?"

"I need more information." His voice was brisk.

"This person is definitely dying." Lei pressed the medallion at her throat, the roughness of embedded diamonds digging into her skin as she forced the words out. "Got a few days, maybe a week, to live. And as a sort of conscience-clearing deathbed confession, this person told me that, together with my grandmother who is now deceased, she obtained Bozeman's services to kill Kwon."

A long pause and then Kamuela gave a rough bark of a laugh. "Never a dull moment with you, Texeira. I don't see this moving forward at all with the district attorney. Why waste the state's money prosecuting someone who won't be alive for the trial? Not to mention the case itself—a dying person hired a hit man, now dead, to shoot a child molester. No one would touch the case with a ten-foot pole—no one benefits from it."

"What are you saying? That you don't want to charge the dying person?"

"That's what I'm saying. Bozeman's murder is closed. Kwon's murder is closed. I got to put them in my solved stats, and I can guarantee the DA will not want to reopen either one just on a deathbed confession. Who would it serve?"

"It would be the right thing to do," Lei said, closing her eyes.

"Well, I can run it up the flagpole, if you insist."

"I'd like to leave this up to your professional judgment."

"Then my professional judgment is, let sleeping dogs lie. Both cases are closed and tied up with a nice little bow. Prosecuting a deathbed confession is a waste of time and money."

Let sleeping dogs lie. That phrase had come up a lot in Lei's life, and she'd never been much good at it. Relief made her smile. "Thanks, Marcus. That's how I would have handled it if this came across my desk, but I can't be responsible for suppressing information like this. It just wouldn't have been right to decide on it myself."

"I'm sorry you're going through this, but on a personal note—I think your family is badass."

"I guess they are," Lei said, trying to imagine the conversation between Rosario and Yumi, the lengths the two women had gone to avenge Lei. "It's a little scary."

"You stack right up with the rest of your family," Kamuela said. "Looking forward to getting together with you guys soon—Marcella and I are overdue for that Maui R and R."

"Our door is open." Lei wrapped up the call and tucked the phone into the pocket of her running shorts with relief. She'd done the right thing and could sleep better knowing that—and also knowing that she wasn't going to have to turn her beloved Aunty Rosario in.

Lei went into the silent house and cleared the beef stew bowls off the table and washed up. As she was finishing, the front doorbell rang. Wiping her hands on a dish towel, she went to the door and peeked through the peephole.

A woman dressed in green scrubs with a floral apron over them stood on the porch, holding a white briefcase.

Lei glanced at the clock above the sink—two p.m. This must be the nurse who was scheduled to do her aunt's home care. Lei opened the door. "Hello."

"Hi. I'm Sylvia." The woman held up an ID badge that hung around her neck. Sylvia Crypton, Home Health Marin County was emblazoned on the plastic badge. "I'm here to work with Rosario Texeira."

"Sure, of course. I think she might still be sleeping. I wore her out this morning." Lei led the nurse down the hall to Rosario's room. "Are you from hospice?"

"Yes. We contract services with them."

Lei eased open her aunt's door gently. Rosario was sleeping, still as a wax doll on the bed.

Lei frowned. "She was looking better earlier in the day," she whispered to the nurse. "She ate a little breakfast and half a bowl of beef stew. Had some good color in her face."

The nurse focused all her attention on Rosario, picking up the fragile wrist and feeling for a pulse. "Looks like she must have been a little pooped out. I'm going to have to wake her up. I plan to give her a sponge bath today."

"Oh. All right. Do you need me to do anything?"

"Sure. Why don't you fill me up a bowl with warm water, and bring a washcloth, some soap, and a second bowl of clear warm water. I'll check all her vitals now. Come back in fifteen minutes."

"Sounds good." Lei went back into the kitchen. She finished tidying up. She felt so relieved by what Marcus had said about Aunty. As disturbing as it was to realize her aunt had been capable of paying for a hit on another human being, on some level she wasn't surprised. She'd always thought her dad might be behind Kwon's slaying. Rosario was his sister, and not nearly as religious—a branch from the same rugged tree.

Her grandmother Yumi, according to her grandfather, whom she'd reconnected with while living on Oahu, was a bitter and angry woman. A woman whose expression of support for family wouldn't be something obvious, like sending a greeting card. No, her grandmother had procured a hit man. Lei wondered why Yumi had approached Rosario with the idea and hadn't just done it herself. Perhaps she couldn't have explained the money expenditure to Soga. Her grandfather had a samurai side, but it was honorable. She couldn't see him going along with such a devious plan.

Lei filled the biggest bowl in the kitchen with warm water, dropping a snow-white washcloth into it. Then she draped a clean towel over her shoulder and dropped a white square of soap into the water.

She'd bring the rinse water next, when her hands weren't full. Lei checked the clock. Only ten minutes had passed, but maybe they needed the water now, or she could help with something. Lei walked down the hall and pushed the bedroom door open sideways with her hip, her hands occupied with the bowl.

A white sheet was pulled up and over Rosario's head. The sight struck Lei with all the force of blow. Her mouth fell open, and she spun to where the nurse had been sitting beside the bed, spilling water on the floor in her abrupt movement.

The nurse was gone. The window was open, the

screen had disappeared, and the curtains, which had been shut to shield Rosario's sensitive eyes, billowed inward in a mocking suggestion of flight.

"Aunty!" Lei cried, and set the slopping bowl on the dresser. She lunged forward to grab the sheet, stopping herself by sheer act of will. If the nurse had killed her aunt, as it appeared she might have, this was now a crime scene. Lei had better not mess with it. She grabbed a tissue from the nearby box and used it to lift the sheet off her aunt, feeling grief strangle her breath and turn her stomach inside out.

Her aunt looked utterly peaceful, and just as when Lei entered the room with the nurse. She had a gentle curve to her mouth, as if she were dreaming. Her thick white braids lay undisturbed on her shoulders—and on her aunt's belly rested a bomb.

Lei recognized the device instantly, even as she registered that a timer was counting down, a round plastic kitchen timer whose loud ticking seemed to echo in her ears. "Aunty!" Lei cried loudly, hoping her aunt was just somehow asleep, but her aunt didn't move.

She focused on the dial—it was counting down five minutes.

"Oh, shit," Lei muttered, leaning in to assess the threat. A brick-sized chunk of gray C-4 was visible between wires wrapping it so deep it dented the claylike explosive. Probably had a blasting cap embedded in it, and there might even be a trip wire or pressure switch that would prevent her from just throwing it out into the backyard.

First things first—maybe she could reset the timer and get longer to deal with the explosive. She scanned around the device and couldn't see anything—but her recent brush with motion-sensor activation made her wary of touching the bomb. She used a tissue to try to turn the dial, but it wouldn't budge backward, clicking relentlessly on.

This had been set to go off when she returned to the room in fifteen minutes, and if she'd been late, this much C-4 was still enough to blow the house apart, splattering her aunt to kingdom come and killing Lei. Even in another room.

Lei whirled and ran back into the kitchen, scrabbling through the utility drawer for the pair of heavy poultry scissors she'd spotted there. Running back, she leaned down carefully, dismayed to see her hands trembling. Shaky hands—this was why she wasn't the right pick for bomb squad, Lei thought. She dug the heavy utility scissors into the clay, the wires wrapping the bundle— wire that would become deadly shrapnel upon detonation. She cut all the way around the ticking timer, one eye on its countdown as she tried not to apply too much pressure in case of a pressure switch underneath.

The scissors caught on something: the blasting cap,

a small, tube-like explosive device that, when triggered, ignited the C-4. Lei clipped the wire leading to it and, using her hand and the scissors, pried it gently out of the clay. This one was a three-inch metal rod, which could still go off and take off one of her hands with it.

She hurled it out the window. Separated from the timer, it should be neutralized, but she didn't want it anywhere near her, her aunt's body, or the menacing block of wire-wrapped C-4. She was shaking and soaked with sweat as she turned back to the remains of the bomb. She still couldn't be sure there wasn't a pressure switch linked to a second blasting cap on the bottom of the block—but even as she considered what to do, the timer went off with a cheerful *ding!*

Lei jumped and shut her eyes involuntarily.

Nothing happened. It appeared there was no secondary trigger, but she still didn't want to move the device.

Lei put two fingers on her aunt's throat, feeling for a pulse, shock and grief making every movement jerky. She couldn't feel anything. She leaned down and put her ear on her aunt's chest, listening for a heartbeat, for a breath.

Nothing.

Lei straightened up and pulled her phone out, dialing 911. "I need to report a bomb and a homicide."

Only when the first responders were on their way did Lei throw back her head and let out a terrible cry of anguish. Holding the sheet away from her aunt with the tissue, tears rolling down her cheeks, Lei noticed the rough quality of the sheet. It had a loose weave, a nubbly texture to it, and the threads were creamy natural linen.

Lei was holding a shroud.

Chapter 25

Awapuhi's house was a modest ranch at the end of a quiet road, sheltered by towering kukui nut trees, their palmate, light green leaves casting dappled shade over the house and yard. The front door was reinforced by a steel-grilled security exterior door, and a ten-foot chain-link fence surrounded the house. The one large picture window was curtained.

Stevens parked behind two squad cars. Gerry, Pono, and Torufu leaped out of Torufu's black Escalade as the officers parked the squad cars to block the driveway, where several trucks were parked. "Let's hope he comes quietly," Stevens said to the other team members. "But be ready for anything."

Steven led the approach, using the cars for cover, darting from one defensive point to the next. As he climbed the steps quickly and stood to the side of the door, he could hear voices inside—and someone began playing ukulele. The distinctive smell of barbeque wafted to his nostrils.

Stevens straightened up from his defensive position. This should be a peaceful takedown; no one was expecting them. He rang the doorbell, realizing as he did so, how much he loved what he did. Being what he was. These charged moments, when anything could happen. The other officers ranged along the stairs, a few still positioned by the cars. Stevens heard the sound of footsteps, and someone checked the peephole.

The wooden inner door opened suddenly, reminding him of opening the motel door to see Anchara. The terrible flashback tightened his chest. Charles Awapuhi, his frown fierce and his tattooed head like some otherworldly demon, confronted him from the other side of the grilled door, holding a sawed-off double-barreled shotgun. The gun was theatrically huge in the dim light of the house's interior, the black bores like twin empty eyes.

"Gun!" Stevens yelled, and dove to the side as the shotgun tore a hole the size of a grapefruit in the steel-grille door. He hadn't had time to identify them as MPD, he thought, as he smashed into the metal porch surround and flipped over it into the yard on the other side, landing awkwardly. His ankle gave with a crunch that sent a spike of fire up his leg—but that would be nothing compared to the holes the shotgun would leave. Stevens swung himself sideways to flatten against the house.

The air erupted in gunfire as officers returned fire. Awapuhi's cannon replied, and Stevens crouched, making himself as small as possible.

"Maui Police Department! Hold your fire!" he yelled.

"Pull back!" Who knew how many people were inside the house? They needed to retreat and get a plan. His detectives and the officers managed to withdraw back to the vehicles, but Stevens was still pinned against the house with no cover.

The gunfire stopped.

"Charles Awapuhi!" Stevens bellowed. "This is the MPD! Put down your weapon and come out peacefully! You are endangering everyone in your house!"

"What the hell are you cops doing here?" Awapuhi's voice sounded jittery with adrenaline.

"You are under arrest for the murder of Norm Jorgenson," Stevens called. "Come out with your hands on your head and you will not be harmed."

"Norm who?" Awapuhi sounded angry and confused. "I never murdered nobody!"

Stevens persevered. Talking the man into surrendering was by far the best scenario. "Come out and we'll sort this out. Maybe there's been a mistake."

A long pause. "Who told you I killed someone?"

"You'll be able to ask all the questions you want down at the station. Now, drop that weapon outside the door and come out with your hands on your head, and we'll figure this out."

Another long pause, and then Stevens was surprised to see a gleam off the shotgun's barrel as the man set it on the welcome mat. Awapuhi followed it out onto the porch, his hands interlaced on that gleaming, tattooed head.

Torufu made it to the man first, pulling his hands behind his back and cuffing him as the doorway filled with Awapuhi's guests, yelling and demanding answers.

Stevens pushed away from the wall of the house. His ankle buckled. "Sonofabitch," he muttered, limping quickly across the lawn, highly aware of his exposed back and head, and not taking a deep breath until he'd made it behind the squad cars.

"Take Awapuhi down to the station and put him in an interview room," he told the two officers driving the vehicle in which the Hui leader had been stowed. "The rest of you, clear the people out of this house. I want to search it. We have warrants on the way." He got on the radio and updated Omura of developments. "I'm going to search for evidence related to the Norwegian's murder and anything to do with the artifacts," he told her. "I had a tip-off phone call on my way here." He told her what Esther Ka`awai had shared—everything but her description of where the artifacts were hidden.

"Go for it, and get back here ASAP. I want to interview Awapuhi with you present. And send a team to pick up Mana Guinamo and his friend Red. Maybe we can flush out 'the Man' between the three of them."

"On it. I'll let you know when the search is completed." Stevens hung up the radio in his truck and winced as he set his foot on the ground.

Torufu, Pono, and Gerry came toward him. "We've got the house clear."

"Call a few more units and go pick up Mana Guinamo and his friend Red Toaman. We need them down at the station for questioning in the Norwegian's murder. I'm going to search the house. Pono, you're with me."

"You got it," Gerry said. He and Torufu peeled off.

Stevens's phone buzzed again and he looked down—it was Lei. He didn't have time to talk to her right now. He snapped on a pair of gloves, picked up a crime kit and a box of evidence bags, and headed for the house with Pono and a couple of officers in tow.

Chapter 26

Lei hung up on Stevens's voicemail in frustration. Things must be really hot on the Hui case if he wasn't taking her call.

The response team officers who'd responded to her 911 call had been skeptical of her claim that the nurse had killed her aunt, though the bomb on Rosario's body, disposed of by their explosive disposal team, lent credibility. She'd known it would take some convincing because her aunt was so clearly very ill, even on the hospice services list. Lei had shown her badge and endured their verification calls home to speak to Omura, but she resented the implication one of the young officers had made, that this had been a good thing, sparing her aunt further suffering.

Bullshit. Her aunt might have had only a few more days, but they were days she was entitled to. The bastard doing this to Lei and Stevens had stolen those days from her.

Lei dashed tears off her cheeks, waiting in the kitchen as they searched the scene and the ME worked on her aunt's body. She'd called her dad and he'd told Momi;

they were on their way home.

And still, tears kept welling up.

Lei went outside and paced back and forth on the lawn, doing her breathing exercises. Being unable to help with the investigation, track down the 'nurse,' or anything else, was driving her nuts. And whenever she stopped physically moving, grief was waiting, a black well she felt dragging at her.

Her father and Aunty Momi pulled up, and in moments Lei was surrounded by their arms, their tears releasing her own. "It was the nurse," Lei sobbed. "She did something to her."

"What?" Her father lifted his streaming face. "I thought she just passed away!" In the hectic moments of informing Wayne on the phone, she hadn't had time to tell how Rosario had died, or about the bomb.

"Let's go in the kitchen. They're still in the bedroom, checking the scene, but we should go inside."

The two officers came out of the bedroom. One of them was carrying a large evidence bag labeled SHROUD. "We might as well hear you tell it again," they said, and Lei told Momi and her dad how she'd opened the door to a nurse who identified herself, wore ID, and came at the right time.

"I had no reason to suspect anything," Lei concluded.

The medical examiner entered. He was a short, round

Hispanic man, and he carried an old-fashioned doctor's bag that reminded Lei of Dr. Fukushima on Oahu.

"I know you're saying this is a murder," he said, frowning. "But so far I see no signs of foul play. No petechial hemorrhaging, no needle marks, no signs of swelling, bruising, or other trauma. Are you sure your aunt was alive when you took the nurse into the room?"

Lei paused, her hands on her hips. She remembered the total stillness, the waxy tinge of her aunt's skin when she took the woman back into the room. "I don't know. I left her sleeping, went for a run, and brought back the nurse. I did notice that her color was poor, and I commented to the woman on it."

"Well, I won't know until I do the autopsy, but I suspect your aunt may have died of natural causes—either that, or this nurse was so good she injected her with something I can't find visually. Tox results should tell us more. I'll let you know as soon as possible."

"Well, because of the shroud, I think I was the real target and the bomb was the intended weapon," Lei said. "Aunty is collateral damage." She'd gone over all this with the officers, but they wanted to hear again how she'd known how to deactivate the bomb.

Lei, her father, Aunty Momi, and the ME moved aside as his assistant wheeled the body past them, the belted-down black body bag looking tiny on the gurney. Lei held on to a wave of nausea until they'd all followed the body out of the house. She made it to the bathroom just in time.

Resting her head on the lid of the toilet, she remembered she was pregnant. But that just made the tears come again, because it was another thing she wouldn't be able to share with her aunt.

Stevens and Pono walked into the modest house. Pono flipped on the light switch. Behind a tape barrier the patrol officers had erected, Stevens could hear the muttering of a gathering crowd, watching with folded arms and frowns that echoed that of their leader.

"We should work fast," Pono said. "And clean up after ourselves. We don't want to piss off his supporters more."

"Agree. Shut the interior door and lock the grilled one. We don't need someone barging in on us." Stevens flicked on his hand-held light. He told Pono about Esther Ka`awai's call. "So we want to look for anything related to the Norwegian's murder, or the artifacts themselves. I'll take the kitchen, back porch, and backyard." Stevens went off, moving fast as he searched, but replacing everything he moved. His own rage at coming home to find his house seemingly disrespected was fresh in his mind—no sense inflaming Awapuhi's followers outside.

Stevens worked his way out to the backyard, finding nothing of interest, and finally faced the yard. It was a big square lot with a locked steel storage unit in back and several spreading *kukui* nut trees, casting pools of shade over a small Hawaiian-style *hale*. The barbeque on a cement pad near the porch was still smoldering. He turned it off, checking inside the compartment underneath.

Nothing there.

He had a pair of bolt cutters in his crime kit and took them out as he approached the steel shed, favoring his wrenched ankle. He wasn't quite ready to put Esther Ka`awai's psychic moment to the test by checking around the *kukui* nut trees. Instead he cut the lock off the shed door. There was no lighting inside, and evening tangled the shadows of trees into patterns of darkness. Inside the shed was as black as lava. He flicked on his light and shone it around.

A table, piled high with various folded flags, a megaphone, and equipment that looked like Awapuhi used it for his rallies with the Hui. One side of the shed appeared to be filled with yard tools.

Nothing of interest.

Stevens turned toward the three kukui trees, planted in a rough triangle. The grass was undisturbed around the bases. But in the middle was the small *hale* built in a rough A-frame shape on a wooden platform, covered with palm thatch, as was traditional. It was big enough for several people to sit inside. Stevens imagined Awapuhi using it to talk to his inner circle, or for chant and hula practice, as the lawn was smooth as a golf green.

He flicked on the light as he reached the *hale* and

shone it around inside. Nothing. A woven palm frond mat covered the floor. He lifted the mat and flipped it to the side. All along the edge, he checked the boards of the platform, and in the middle, three of them were loose.

He went back to the shed, picked up a shovel, and used the edge to pry the boards up.

Pono came to the back porch. "What've you got out there?"

"I'm not sure." Stevens didn't look up, instead wrenching up a board with a screech. Shining his light underneath, he could see that the earth looked freshly disturbed. "Come see."

With Pono's help, he brought up the other two boards, and Stevens used the shovel to dig into the dirt below. Only a few strokes down yielded a *thunk*, and he and Pono used their hands to uncover a black plastic bag.

It was extremely heavy.

Stevens felt his heart thudding with exertion and excitement as they hauled the bag up onto the undamaged boards of the hale and ripped it open.

Sure enough, the great smooth stone shaped like an egg that Okapa had described was inside, along with two smaller pieces of stone, rough and raw-edged, about the size of dinner plates.

Stevens was glad he had his gloves on as he picked up one of the rock slices, turned it over, and exposed the deep but delicate tracery of a petroglyph of a dancer under a three-arch rainbow shape.

"Beautiful," Pono said, rubbing his mustache, a frown between his brows.

"A very interesting development," Stevens said. "Why would the man who swears he's all about protecting the *heiaus* have the looted artifacts hidden at his house?"

"Guess we'll have plenty of questions for him down at the station," Pono said.

It took two of the officers who'd been guarding the front of the house and Pono to wrestle the plastic bag they'd uncovered back to Stevens's Bronco. Even though they'd closed the bag so that the contents weren't visible, the crowd looking on got to murmuring.

"Coconut wireless is going to be buzzing about this," Pono said, getting in the front seat beside Stevens. He was referring to the local gossip grapevine.

"Can't be helped."

The radio crackled to life. It was Gerry Bunuelos reporting in. "No sign of either of the suspects we're looking for at their residences."

"Post a general APB, and fax their photos to the airport," Stevens said, as they pulled into the station.

Pono had a dolly brought and wheeled the artifacts to the evidence room as Stevens limped into the building, headed for Omura's office. When he got there, Omura stopped him with a hand. "Shut the door."

"Thought we were in a hurry to interview Awapuhi?"

"Yes, but he's lawyered up, so no hurry at the moment. Let them sweat a bit. I might even turn off the AC." She almost winked, and Stevens smiled, collapsing into one of the chairs in front of her desk and tearing off his perspiration-soaked Kevlar vest.

"We found something big at Awapuhi's house. A game changer."

"What?"

"The artifacts." Stevens described the search. "According to my source, Councilman Muapu is behind all these thefts."

"Let's contact Oahu right now. See if they can pick him up. Is your witness credible?"

"Absolutely," Stevens said, hoping Esther wouldn't say anything about exactly how she'd known where the petroglyphs were hidden. "She's a Hawaiiana expert, so high up she was asked to be one of his Council of Five that are guarding the museum Muapu is planning to create with the artifacts."

They called Marcus Kamuela and, through a snowy Skype connection, filled him in. Stevens sent him pictures of the recovered artifacts. "Awapuhi is implicated by a different witness in the murder of the art thief. We're going in to interview him now. See if you can move fast to arrest Muapu."

"Will do. Glad we're finally getting a break in this case, though I'd almost rather the artifacts were being smuggled out of the country than to find our own people were stealing them," Marcus said, frowning.

"There are a lot of missing pieces here," Omura said. "Just bring the man in and try to crack him. Let him know one of his Council is willing to testify."

Marcus nodded and cut the connection.

Omura looked back at Stevens. Sighed. Steepled her fingers. "I have bad news for you. Of a personal nature."

Stevens stiffened. "Anchara's case?"

"Nothing I can discuss with you on that. No, it's Lei's aunt, Rosario Texeira. She died today. She was found deceased, covered by one of those shrouds."

Stevens shot to his feet. "Is Lei all right?"

"She's fine. Her aunt's death appears to have been painless."

"Lei tried to call me, but I was in the middle of the raid." Stevens ran his hands through his hair in agitation.

"The police officers that responded to Lei's call in San Rafael were the ones to tell me Rosario Texeira had died and to fill me in on the situation. They wanted to check her creds, position, and the shroud case Pono opened for you guys. Your wife could probably use some emotional support right now, but I need you here and fully present with your game face on for this interview. I almost told you all this afterward, but I thought you'd never forgive me for sitting on it."

Stevens glanced up. He saw worry in the captain's eyes.

"You're right. I wouldn't have forgiven you. But if you're worried I can't focus on bringing down Awapuhi, you're wrong there. Just give me five minutes to call Lei."

"Five minutes. Meet you at Interview Room Two." Omura got up, picked up her file and pen, and glided smoothly out of the room.

Stevens speed-dialed Lei's number.

"Michael." Her voice was hoarse, and he heard the clog of tears in it.

"Omura told me. I'm so sorry," he said, and pressed his fingers into his eyes, trying to hold back his own tears at the memory of Lei on their last visit, snuggled in bed with her beloved aunty. "Did she suffer?"

"No." Lei blew her nose. "In fact, the ME thinks she died of natural causes." Lei told him how the nurse had come and she'd thought the woman injected her with something. "He won't know until the autopsy. And then, there was the bomb."

"The what?" Stevens's blood pressure soared as Lei filled him in on the block of C-4 set on Aunty Rosario's body, and Lei's deactivation of it.

"And there's still one shroud unaccounted for. Who is doing this to us?" He heard his voice rising and struggled to control it. "We have to get some traction on this."

"I know." A small silence. Their breathing fell into sync.

"I love you," he said. "I'm glad you knew how to deal with that bomb."

"Good."

He wanted to chuckle but couldn't. "I have some more news. We're closing in on the end of the *heiau* case." He told her about picking up Awapuhi and recovering the artifacts. "Your friend Esther was the big break."

"Glad she called you right away. I want to come home. Work my case. But I have to stay here until Aunty's funeral."

"Well, when my case wraps up, I'll join you. I wouldn't miss it."

"Call me when things settle down."

"I am still waiting for that. Gotta go. Interviewing Awapuhi."

"I need you."

"You got me. Talk soon." Stevens cut the connection

and stood. His ankle reminded him of its injury. With a grimace of pain, he hobbled as quickly as he could down the hall toward Interview Room Two.

Chapter 27

L ei set her phone down. It was dark in California, three hours later than in Hawaii, and in the kitchen she could hear her father splashing around. He seemed to calm himself by cleaning, and he hadn't stopped since that afternoon when he arrived back at the house with Momi.

Lei settled back on the double bed in the room she'd painted the blue of Hawaii skies the year she'd moved in with Aunty. Her aunt had taken down her teenaged posters of action heroes and rock stars, but otherwise the simple space was unchanged.

What would happen to the house now? She pillowed her hands beneath her head, thinking through the situation. It would take at least a week for Aunty's body to be autopsied and released for burial. Aunty had told Wayne and Momi she wanted to be cremated and her ashes scattered on San Francisco Bay, and some of them taken back to her beloved Hawaii.

Rosario had come to be embedded in her adopted home of San Rafael. Lei knew her memorial was going to be huge, and a big deal to plan, but Lei just wanted get on a plane and go home.

Home to Stevens's arms, to her familiar bed, to Keiki. To work, where she had a job to do and could keep her mind off her grief. Home, to try to find a murderer who seemed to be pulling puppet strings all around them.

"It has to be Terence Chang," Lei murmured, staring at the ceiling. That reminded Lei she hadn't checked in with Marcella about her friend's reopening of Chang's case, and now there was a lot to update her on.

She phoned Marcella, and when her friend didn't pick up, left a message that it was urgent they speak regarding new developments.

She got up and went into the kitchen. Wayne looked up from scrubbing the sink. His face seemed to have aged in the hours since Lei had called him about Rosario's death; his cheeks were sunken and eyes hooded. His dark visage reminded her of her first glimpse of him in prison orange, and how things had changed so much since then. She walked to her father and opened her arms. He dropped the scrubber into the sink and embraced her.

"I keep thinking of doing something for Rosario," Wayne said into Lei's hair. "Bringing her something to eat. Checking her blood pressure. I've walked to her door a dozen times, and I don't remember she's gone until I get there."

Lei couldn't speak, just tightened her arms, and then finally let go.

"I've been thinking while I've been cleaning." Her dad turned to the fridge, took out a couple of Heinekens, popped the tops, and handed her one. "Sit down. I have an idea I want to run by you."

"I'm listening." She took a sip of the beer.

"Rosario left her half of the restaurant to me and the house to you. I'd been planning to ask you if I could stay on here and do some volunteer ministry while working at the Hawaiian Food Place—but now I'm thinking of something different."

"She left me the house?" Lei frowned. The beer tasted yeasty and strong, and she remembered she was pregnant and pushed it aside. "She never said anything to me."

"Yes. We talked it all over because we had time to. She wanted to give you and Stevens something to get started in life, and prices are almost as high in Marin County as Hawaii. You should be able to sell this house for enough to buy something similar on Maui if you want. The house is paid off."

"That's incredible. I can't believe she was so generous. I thought she'd leave it to you—it makes sense for you to keep living here."

"She left me income, in the form of my half of the restaurant. So I was thinking. Now that you are bringing home this baby, and having another one, you're going to need help. Child care. And I'm going to need something to do with myself besides bus tables and wipe counters at a restaurant." Wayne pushed a hand through his long, silver-streaked curls. His eyes, when they met hers, were vulnerable, dark circles beneath them. "I always wanted to make up for those years we lost, but we still haven't had the chance. What do you think about selling this house and buying something big enough on Maui that I could live with you and Stevens? As your nanny. Or, as I've heard them called, 'manny.'"

Lei's mouth quirked. "You, a 'manny?'" Her eyes trailed over his muscled, tattooed arms, picturing him changing a baby. She could see it. His intimidating appearance was all a front. She'd never seen him be anything but gentle—but he'd guard their house as fiercely as Keiki would.

"I was very good with you when you were little. But of course you don't remember that," Wayne said. "And you know I can cook and clean."

Lei's chest ached with the feeling of her heart melting. "I can't think of anything I'd like more. Keiki will be beside herself."

Wayne had stayed at Lei's little cottage on Kaua'i during one of her postings for a while, and the big Rottweiler had become almost as attached to Wayne as she was to Lei.

Her father turned away, and Lei could tell by the way his shoulders were hunched that he was trying to hide his emotion. "Well, there are a lot of things to settle, but I hope you will ask your husband. Talk it over."

"He's going to love the idea as much as I do." Lei got up and embraced her father from behind, resting her cheek against his shoulder. "Losing Aunty has taught me something. We can't take anything for granted. We have to be with our *ohana* while we can. Knowing you'll be home to take care of the house and baby Kiet is a huge relief to me. And you couldn't possibly be any worse at child care than me and Stevens. We don't have a clue. We'll be Googling everything."

Just then Lei's phone vibrated in her pocket. She took it out, saw Marcella's number. "Dad, I have to take this."

"I'll make us something to eat." Their talk seemed to have energized him, and he turned toward the refrigerator.

Lei went back to her bedroom.

"Lei. What's going on?"

Lei shut her door and threw herself on her bed. "So much." She told Marcella about Aunty's death, enduring her friend's exclamations of shock and grief. Marcella had become attached to Aunty as well. Knowing Rosario had been terminally ill didn't mitigate the shock of her sudden, suspicious death. "So now, more than ever, I need someone tracking everything Terence Chang is doing."

"I have Hilo PD on him like white on rice, and I've got Sophie monitoring his online activity. So far, we haven't found anything, but this guy has major computer skills. He could be orchestrating all this from his back bedroom just like he did on that other case."

"I know. And here I am in California, having to sit on my hands while that nurse who killed Aunty is roaming around with her briefcase, free as a bird. I just want to go home and work, where I can do something. Speaking of, there have been developments on that. I'm sure Marcus knows already." Lei filled her friend in on the breaks happening in the *heiau* case. "But we still need to find the killer of the Norwegian art thief. It may or may not be Awapuhi. The two thugs that held the Norwegian are still in the wind. I wish I could go home and work, be with Stevens. I have nothing to do here but be reminded Aunty's gone."

"You should go. I'm sure Omura needs your help with all that going on."

"I need to stay. Help my dad with my aunt's funeral. Oh, and I'm pregnant."

"What!"

"Yeah. Like you said, what's one more? Anyway, I hope you're right about that—and about giving us a date night sometime."

They talked more and Marcella said, "Keep me posted. Believe me, if we had any probable cause on Chang, we'd be bringing him in."

"Okay. I guess I have to let that be enough."

"Oh, and on a personal note—Marcus asked me to marry him." Marcella's voice quavered.

"I was waiting for that," Lei said. "Congratulations! Because you said yes, right?"

"I told him I needed to think about it."

"Holy crap, don't do what I did!" Lei exclaimed. "He adores you, and you guys couldn't be better together! For God's sake, if you learned nothing from what I did and what happened with Anchara—please, marry the man!"

A long pause. "You might be right," Marcella said. "I just have to be sure. I mean, the rest of my life is a long time, and I worry I'll let him down."

"Seriously, you have it so much more together with him than I ever did with Stevens, and I love being married more than I ever imagined. I don't know what I was so scared of."

"Even though Stevens is messed up by Anchara's death? Like you told me about?"

"More so, because of it. We're there for each other in ways you can't imagine until you make that commitment." Lei pressed her fingers against her lips and shut her eyes, remembering their passionate lovemaking.

"Well, grist for the mill. Gotta run!" Marcella said, and cut the connection.

Lei went back into the kitchen. Her father had reheated more of the beef stew.

"I think you should go home," he said without preamble, setting the bowls on the table as she came in. "It's going to take a while for them to release your aunty's body and to plan the memorial. You should go back to work. I know it helps you deal with things."

Lei sat down. The stew smelled delicious, and her dicey stomach turned on and said yes. She picked up her spoon. "I want to stay and help you pack up her things. Plan the memorial. It's the right thing to do."

"Sweets." He put a hand on hers, made eye contact. "I can take care of all of that. What I can't handle is you pacing around like a caged lion, frustrated because you can't work this case, needing your husband and your dog."

Lei laughed, a sudden upwelling of mirth, and he laughed, too. "Now you see the real me. Still want to come live with us?"

"More than ever. The hope of doing that has given me a real second wind. But, of course, I respect what you and Stevens decide."

"Well, I'll just have to hop on a plane and get home to talk with him about it," Lei said. "Thanks, Dad. I think you might be right about how I cope. But we'll come back for her memorial, for sure."

"With any luck at all, you'll be bringing my new grandson with you." Wayne dug into his stew.

"Now, there's something to worry about. Stevens didn't say anything about that investigation, but hopefully something's happening there. Something that doesn't involve us as suspects."

"You'll just have to fly home to find out."

Chapter 28

Stevens and Omura stood outside Interview Room Two. "I'll take the lead," Omura said. "Let's hold back the part about the artifacts until the right moment."

"Sounds good." Stevens glanced into the glass insert in the door. Awapuhi was an intimidating presence, even cuffed to the table. His lawyer, a slender young Hawaiian man dressed in business casual, leaned in close to talk with him.

Omura fluffed her hair, flicked a nonexistent speck off her sleeve, squared her shoulders, and led the way into the room.

Stevens limped over and turned on the recording equipment on the wall. Omura recited the date, time, and the names of the people present, pausing for the young lawyer to provide his name. "Keiran Moniz."

Once they were settled, Moniz started in. "My client tells me you failed to identify yourself as police personnel when you came to the door, hence his defensive actions."

Stevens drew his eyebrows together and made eye contact with Awapuhi. "I stood on your step and rang your bell, Mr. Awapuhi. You opened the door and tried to blow me away. I didn't have time to identify myself. Good thing I wasn't there selling Girl Scout cookies." He felt the stress of those moments color his voice with sarcasm as his ankle throbbed, reminding him the leap to safety hadn't been without a price. "You fired on me. That's ten years of hard time for felony assault with intent to do deadly harm to a law enforcement officer."

Charles Awapuhi glowered. The lawyer shuffled a few papers. "Not identifying yourself was a critical oversight, Lieutenant Stevens," Moniz said.

"'Maui Police Department' were the first words out of my mouth after I yelled 'gun,'" Stevens said. "Glad I had lungs left to say anything at all."

Omura smiled, placating. "It's too bad things got off to that start, Mr. Awapuhi, because Maui Police Department has only ever wanted to support the *heiau* investigation and protect the artifacts in their sites. The officers who came to your house just wanted to run a few things by you. Discharging a weapon at a police officer is a very serious action we need to address. But we have another matter we're concerned with. What do you know about the killing of Norm Jorgenson, a visitor from Norway?"

"I don't know notting," Awapuhi growled. "I never killed nobody."

Stevens remembered noticing before how the Hui

leader thickened his pidgin and hid behind it.

"Were you aware Jorgenson is linked to the artifact thefts here on Maui? We haven't been able to compare trace yet, but he could be linked to all the *heiau* burglaries," Omura said.

"No, I nevah knew dat."

"With your connections in Maui Police Department, I'm surprised that you nevah knew dat," Stevens said, deliberately imitating Awapuhi.

"I said, I never knew notting about this Norwegian." Awapuhi gave Stevens stink eye at the implied collusion.

"Are you called 'the Man' within the Heiau Hui? 'Kane'? As a respectful nickname?" Omura asked.

"Sometimes." Awapuhi looked down at his hands, and Stevens could see that they carried the marks of hard work. "But I'm not the only one they call that."

"Who else is called that?" Stevens asked. Awapuhi just glared.

Stevens glanced at Omura—this line of questioning wasn't going anywhere. She gave him the tiniest head nod.

"Mr. Awapuhi, can you explain how the artifacts that were stolen from the Haiku *heiau* were found in your backyard?" Stevens asked.

Awapuhi's head lifted and eyes narrowed. "You had

no right to go into my home!"

"On the contrary." Omura slid the search warrant across the table to the lawyer, whose youth showed in his consternation as he took the documents. "Sorry we weren't able to hand you these things in person, what with the gun battle going on."

The lawyer scanned both the arrest and the search warrant. "These appear in order. I am counseling my client not to answer any more questions."

"Mr. Awapuhi." Stevens caught the other man's eye and put all his disillusionment into his voice, each word dripping with contempt. "You claim to care about your people's heritage so much, and yet you're the one stealing the artifacts. You're 'the Man,' all right."

Awapuhi smacked his fist down on the table, pride and anger overriding his lawyer's advice. "There is a bigger picture here. We must protect these precious relics of our culture; keep them safe in a place where they can be preserved forever. Not have just anyone trampling through our sacred places, destroying them."

"So this was doing a good deed? Chiseling them out of the stones your ancestors carved them into and mounting them on a wall somewhere? Whose great idea was this?"

At that, Awapuhi folded his lips shut and shook his head. He sat back and folded his arms. "I'm done talking."

They continued the questioning for several more minutes, to no avail. Stevens was satisfied—Awapuhi had admitted he knew about the artifacts and even given a hint as to why they'd been taken. It was as much as they could hope for with no further bargaining leverage.

"Your client will be remanded to Maui County Correctional Center until his arraignment. Please explain the process to him," Omura said.

They got up and left as Awapuhi began bellowing abuse at his lawyer, pounding the table some more. Outside in the hallway, Stevens leaned on the wall to take the weight off his ankle. Omura frowned.

"Did you get that looked at?"

"No time. It's just a sprain."

"Get it looked at. File your workplace injury report." She looked down at her file and made a note.

"Yes, sir." He felt stung by her abrupt tone. "Did you hear anything on the radio? My earbud was dead in there."

"No. They haven't contacted us. When you've had your ankle checked, I'll get back to you, but you can go home now. Good job getting 'the Man' to admit he knew about the artifacts. It wasn't much, but it was something."

"Thanks." He followed more slowly, limping, as Omura pep-stepped down the hall to her office. The aftermath of adrenaline overload and the stresses of the day caught up with him suddenly, his body sagging with exhaustion. Going to the emergency room felt like a personal nightmare. He decided tomorrow was soon enough, though he filled out the workplace injury form and left it with the watch officer.

Stevens swung by Pono and Bunuelos's cubicle, missing Lei with a sudden hungry fierceness. This spot was where he used to find her when he came by Kahului Station. Now she was placed with Torufu in another cubicle, but he imagined he could still spot her curly head just visible at the top of the padded wall. A lonely night filled with the possibility of bad dreams awaited him at home, and he dreaded it.

Pono looked up with a quick grin. "Nice job getting Awapuhi to admit he knew about the relics."

"I had to shake something loose. Hey, have you heard anything about Anchara's case?"

"No. Been too busy to try to pick up anything from McGregor and Chun. They've been really closemouthed on the whole thing."

"Well, Omura told me they were following some other leads, so I guess that's good," Stevens said. "Want to get a beer?" He knew Keiki would be at home waiting for him, and for dinner—but so were those nightmares.

"Sure. Let me just close up a few things."

"What's up with your ankle?" Gerry Bunuelos looked at the leg Stevens was favoring. "I imagine the captain wants you to get it checked out."

"Just a sprain, and I'm too tired to go to the emergency room and deal with all that."

"Let me have a look. I was a paramedic before I switched to police work."

"Great. It'll save me a trip. And while you're at it— what's happening with chasing down those suspects? Toaman and Guinamo?"

"Sit on this box over here and take your shoe off," Gerry directed. "I always keep an extra-stocked medical kit in case I come across a situation on the job." Bunuelos reached under his desk for a large white plastic box marked with a red cross.

Stevens's respect for the short, wiry detective went up another notch as he sat down on a box of computer paper and undid his shoe, prying it off the swollen foot with a grunt of pain. Gerry knelt in front of him, rolling his pant leg up and peeling the sock off to expose the ankle, swollen and purple with bruising. He snapped on a pair of rubber gloves.

"Nasty," Pono commented from his work station.

"I'm going to palpate this, try to see if it's broken. If it is, you need X-rays and all that. I need to see how much mobility you have. This is gonna hurt a bit."

Stevens gasped as Gerry palpated the swollen ankle, moving in a systematic way from the calf down to his toes. "As to your suspects, Torufu and I ran down their addresses. No one home. Interviewed neighbors and roommates." He held the foot firmly but gently, flexed it up and down. "How's that?"

Stevens gritted his teeth. "Sore, but I don't feel anything worse than when you were touching it."

"No one has seen the suspects since the day of Mahoe's attack," Pono said. "My guess is, after Guinamo planted his story at the hospital, the two of them got out of town. Now, where they went? No idea, but this is an island. They can't get off without taking a boat or a plane, and we've got the Coast Guard on alert for those and their pictures at the airport. Contrary to what people say, the security checks at the airport have been amazingly good at catching fleeing suspects."

"It would make it a lot easier to crack Awapuhi with them in custody," Stevens said.

"Agree." Bunuelos tore open a tightly wrapped Ace bandage. "I don't think the ankle's broken. It's too late to make a whole lot of difference right now, but you should take a few days off and ice this and keep it elevated."

"Don't see that happening, but thanks for the look-see," Stevens said as Bunuelos wrapped the ankle securely.

"This will help stabilize it. But seriously, if you were seeing a real doc, they'd put you on rest and crutches for a few days at least. These things can become chronic if they aren't allowed to heal."

"That's why it's a good thing I happened to be passing by," Omura said from the doorway. Sometimes Stevens thought she rolled around on wheels, she was so good at sneaking up on the men unnoticed. "Two days of mandatory sick leave."

Stevens groaned. "Not now, Captain. We're just breaking the case."

"And nothing more is happening until we bring those other two suspects in and can use their testimony to leverage Awapuhi. We just need to see what Oahu does with Councilman Muapu and if that goes anywhere. I called Kaua`i and am having them bring in and interview Esther Ka`awai, get her testimony recorded. So there's nothing critical for a couple of days. Sick leave. That's an order." Omura pointed a finger at him, cocking it like a gun. She turned on a shiny heel and motored off.

"Sorry, man," Bunuelos said, fastening the bandage.

"I'm just dreading going home and rattling around the empty house without Lei. I guess I can keep working on the baby's room." Stevens ran his hands through his hair.

Gerry rolled Stevens's sock back on. "I'll put the boot on with no laces." He carefully fitted the lightweight hiking boot over the bandaged foot.

Pono had powered down his computer and picked up his jacket. "Just texted Tiare, and she gave me the go-ahead to take you to get some food and drink at the Ale House. Gerry, come with us and round up that Tongan. Let's make it a bro night on the town, help Stevens drown his sorrows."

Chapter 29

Stevens leaned on Pono's shoulder. His friend had driven him home after a couple of beers at the Ale House had turned into a pitcher or two and driving became out of the question. They'd had to unlock the gate, get Keiki settled, unlock the house, and disable the alarm.

"Thanks, man. I owe you for this," Stevens said, clapping Pono unsteadily on the back as the big Hawaiian sat him on the side of the bed and pulled his boots off his feet, careful of the injured ankle.

Pono lifted Stevens's feet onto the bed. "Not sure you're going to thank me in the morning, buddy."

Stevens fell back, already asleep.

Morning brought the buzzing of the phone in Stevens's pocket, a disorienting feeling as it shrilled and brought him up from a black sleep. Stevens fumbled around and dug the phone out, put it to his ear.

"Michael?" Lei's voice.

"Lei." He hoisted himself upright and groaned, clutching his head. Keiki looked up from the end of the bed at this sign of life.

"You okay?"

"Not so much." He swung his feet to the floor and the sprained ankle hit, sending an electric bolt of pain up his leg. "*Youch!* I sprained my ankle yesterday during the raid, and I drank too much at the Ale House with the guys last night. How are you?"

"I'm at the airport. Got the first flight out this morning at five a.m. Can you drive? Come get me."

"You are? That's great." He pushed his hair out of his eyes. "What time is it?"

"Eleven a.m. Hawaii time. Want me to get a cab?"

"Hell no. I just need fifteen minutes to get in the shower and get on the road. On my way." He closed the phone and pushed himself upright. He staggered to the shower and remembered the bandage on his ankle, unwound it before he got in. He was dismayed to see the florid bruising around the swelling.

It ended up taking more than fifteen minutes to shower, swill aspirin and cold coffee from the day before, feed Keiki, and let her out, and get outside onto the front porch. One of the guys must have driven his truck home for him because it was inside the gate, and his keys sat on the porch rail under a note: *Drink lots of water and take anti-inflammatories today. Gerry.* He crumpled the note with a smile in spite of the pain pulsing at him from various points. The guys had been the perfect distraction last night.

He rolled the gate open, blinking without seeing in the overly bright sunshine, and unlocked his truck with the key fob. He lifted the Bronco's door handle, his back to the gate, and something hit him hard on the back of the head.

Stars exploded in his vision as he staggered forward, collapsing against the truck, dimly aware that he'd just turned his head to open the car door and that had probably saved his life.

Stevens used the truck for leverage, shoving back from it with all his strength into his attacker. He heard a grunt, but what he felt was liquid fire in his right side. He'd just been stabbed, his brain told him, pain waking him up into full alert. He felt the knife skitter off his ribs, unable to sink in with his forceful movement and turning body.

Tucking his head, Stevens spun toward his attacker, ignoring a bolt of pain from the bad ankle, bringing up his left fist to connect with the man's body—but his attacker had moved out of the way, leaping backward out of range, a knife held in his right hand.

Stevens hunched over the wound in his side, his back against the truck, assessing. An Asian man, dressed all in black with golden-brown skin and a slender build, five foot ten in height and moving with easy grace, took a martial arts stance in front of him. He held a wicked six-inch combat blade in his right hand.

The man leaped forward with athleticism Stevens had already noticed. Stevens heaved to the left, bringing his right fist around to smack the man's head as he got into range—being taller was his one advantage, but he was barely able to connect a glancing blow before the man was gone again.

There was no sound but their panting breaths, and Stevens felt his stomach hollow out with fear. This guy was well-trained. Fresh and uninjured, he moved like a ninja. Stevens felt like an ox headed for slaughter: huge, slow, unarmed, crippled by a hangover and a sprained ankle.

The man made another leap, knife extended, and Stevens used his arm to deflect the blow upward—but felt an instant, searing burn on the outside of his forearm.

He'd been cut again.

This time, as the man retreated, he yelled.

"Anchara, my wife!" The man struck his chest, eyes glaring. "I kill her! I kill you!" He paced back and forth with catlike grace, eyes narrowed. Bared lips showed a chilling smile as he took in Stevens's level of impairment. He paused, gaze intent on Stevens, and lifted the knife. He drew a finger along it and licked off Stevens's blood, taunting him.

He was enjoying this.

"Sick bastard!" Stevens said, his arm tight over his wound, hunched against the truck. "I never knew she had a husband, but I can see why she ran from you."

In Stevens's wildest imaginings, he'd never thought the "Asian man" who'd bought the shrouds was the abusive man Anchara said she fled Thailand to get away from. She'd left out the minor detail that she was married to that man.

Stevens considered his options. Try to get into the car. Dive underneath. Run into the house for his gun. Nothing appealed because everything left him exposed to a killing strike, and he didn't have the speed or mobility right now to go after the guy with his bare hands.

"Keiki!" he bellowed, remembering the Rottie was in the backyard. She usually went out, did her business, and took a nap back inside the house.

Seconds later the big Rottweiler came barreling around the side of the house, huge and deadly as a missile. A rumbling growl in her deep chest powered blistering speed as Keiki launched herself from at least six feet away onto Stevens's attacker.

He saw the dog fly through the air, heard the man's startled scream.

Saw the blade flash as the man went down, hard.

He heard Keiki's fierce growls as she got her teeth into him, and they tussled back and forth on the ground.

Stevens hobbled as fast as he could into the house, his right arm clamped against the stream of blood running down his side. He clomped at top speed to the bedroom, grabbed his Glock, and ran back out the front door.

Keiki was standing on the body of her enemy, jaws locked around his throat. Still growling. The man wasn't moving.

"Keiki. Come." Stevens's short-circuited brain couldn't remember the word Lei had told him would unlock Keiki in attack mode, but the dog let go. She backed off the body and turned toward Stevens—and now he saw the man's knife protruding from her side.

She took a couple of steps toward him, whimpered, and collapsed onto the ground.

He crashed down the steps, fumbling his phone out of his pocket. "Need an ambulance! Now! Three victims down!"

He spat out the details of his badge number and location as he tore off his shirt and ran to the dog's side. She was breathing in little pants, her eyes still open. Blood oozed around the hilt of the blade. It wasn't all the way in, and he couldn't see any bubbles, which was good. He wrapped the shirt around the entrance wound and held it in place with pressure—it was never good to remove a knife from a wound in the field. Hopefully, the blade had missed her lungs and vital organs.

"Just rest," he whispered. "Good job, Keiki. You saved me, girl."

He'd begun shaking with shock. He gritted his teeth to keep them from chattering as he leaned on the dog. Kneeling, pressing on the dog's wound, he looked over at Anchara's husband, wondered if he was alive. He couldn't bring himself to care.

He lay down very slowly beside Keiki, his arm tight to his side to keep pressure on the bleeding, eyes on his attacker.

He and Keiki couldn't die now. Lei and Kiet needed them.

He shut his eyes a moment, trying to imagine how Lei would deal with losing her aunt, her dog, and him all at once, while trying to raise Kiet. It was so alarming an idea his eyes popped back open.

The ninja was sitting slowly up, his hands over his throat, his eyes so wide white showed all around brown irises. Blood oozed between his fingers, but only a trickle. Keiki must have pinched his carotid artery until he passed out. Stevens, one hand on the dog's side and the other holding the Glock, brought the gun up, just enough to aim at the man's midsection.

"Lie down." Stevens's voice was raspy. Instead, the man looked wildly around and began to get to his feet.

Stevens fired the Glock. Keiki made a convulsive

movement under his hand at the loud report, and he pushed her down as hard as he could, eliciting a yelp.

The ninja collapsed back onto the ground. Stevens had fired to miss, but he wouldn't miss next time. The wail of sirens was a relief, but he didn't lower his weapon until Ferreira, in one of the responding squad cars, leaped out and restrained the man.

"This dog needs skilled first aid," Stevens said when the paramedics tried to help him. "Don't worry about me. Take care of her." He refused treatment until an emergency vet had been called and one of the technicians sat with Keiki, keeping pressure on her wound and administering oxygen. Finally, Stevens collapsed, feeling weak and dizzy. They took his vitals and loaded him onto a gurney.

Ferreira came over. "I called the captain. She said she was dispatching McGregor and Chun to take your statement about what happened here. I gather this is the guy they've been looking for in connection to your ex's murder."

"Would have been nice to have a heads-up about that," Stevens said, watching the paramedics from a second unit finish bandaging the man's throat. Other than minor cuts from Keiki's attack, he appeared unharmed.

Stevens suppressed an urge to lift his weapon and plug the man in the chest. Instead he handed his Glock to Ferreira. "Discharged this once. He must have been waiting outside our yard for me to open the gate. Caught me unawares and unprepared. If Keiki hadn't saved the day, I wouldn't be talking to you right now."

He lay back, and they loaded him into the ambulance, inserting an IV. "Don't let anyone leave until Keiki is taken care of!" he yelled back at Ferreira.

The doors shut and the siren turned on as the ambulance pulled out.

Stevens remembered that Lei was waiting for him at the airport. He insisted they dig the phone out of his pocket.

"Where are you?" She sounded irritated. "It's been a really long fifteen minutes." He opened his mouth to answer. Instead, his vision narrowed to a tiny black dot and winked out.

Chapter 30

Lei frowned at the phone, buzzing static at her. "Hello? Hello?" Stevens's number had appeared when she answered, but it seemed like he'd been cut off. She tried the number back, but voicemail came on.

Lei paced back and forth at the curb beside her suitcase, a route she'd already walked multiple times. Something was wrong. It had been an hour. Even with a hangover, it wasn't like him to delay. She'd been so eager to surprise him. She frowned and bit her lip, the restless Maui wind tossing her curls into disarray as she called her oldest friend, Pono.

"Pono, I'm here on the island, at the airport," she said. "Stevens was supposed to pick me up, and I can't reach him."

"Lei, dammit. There's something going down. I heard a distress call going out to your address. I'm trying to find out what's going on."

"Come get me!"

"I'll know what's up by the time I'm there. See you in fifteen."

Lei hung up and yanked her suitcase over to the cement surround, lifting it up. She unzipped it and took out the molded-plastic gun case holding her weapon. Popped the clasps and took it out.

She heard a shriek. "She has a gun!" Lei took her badge out of the case where it rested with her weapon, held it up.

"Maui Police Department. I'm preparing to respond to an emergency—not at this location."

Airport security came rushing over, weapons drawn, and Lei rolled her eyes, putting the Glock back into its molded foam carrier. "MPD," she said, holding up her hands and her badge. "Call in my number, please. My partner's on his way."

The drama of getting her weapon out at the airport was just settling down as Pono pulled up beside the curb in his lifted purple truck, the cop light on his dashboard strobing. Lei carried her bag and weapon case over. He hoisted them into the truck bed and Lei climbed into the cab and buckled on her shoulder holster, sliding her weapon into it. "Pono. What's happening?"

He peeled the truck away from the curb. "Stevens was attacked when he opened the gate to leave the house. Asian man, apparently Anchara's husband from Thailand. The suspect McGregor and Chun have been looking for."

"She was already married?" Lei knew she shouldn't

be focusing on that irrelevant detail, but she couldn't seem to help it. "What?"

"The perp was armed with a knife. Stevens and Keiki are alive, but injured."

Lei's eyes went so wide that they felt strained. She turned to her ex-partner. "Both of them?"

"According to Ferreira, who was at the scene, Keiki saved Stevens's life. He was already injured from yesterday's raid, had a hangover, a sprained ankle, and was unarmed. A sitting duck."

"Is he okay?"

"Don't know. About either of them."

"Oh God," Lei said, and felt a return of the nausea that had plagued her on and off throughout the flight. "I'm gonna barf."

Pono didn't slow down. Instead he handed her a McDonald's bag, an empty fries carton still in the bottom. "Here."

She put her face in the bag, sucked some breaths until the nausea passed. The smell of French fries was oily and thick.

How quickly things can change, she thought. *Nothing is for certain, especially when someone wants you dead.*

They pulled into the emergency area of Maui Memorial, and the truck had barely stopped moving when Lei leaped down and ran inside to the intake booth, shoving people aside and banging her badge against the window. "Lieutenant Stevens. Where is he?"

The startled receptionist rattled her keyboard, searching, and looked back up. "He's in surgery. Third floor. You can wait outside."

Lei was standing in front of the elevator, tapping her toe, when Pono arrived. He threw a meaty arm over her shoulder. "He's going to be okay. Ferreira says his wounds were bleeding a lot, but he didn't think it was terminal."

Lei shook her head. "And Keiki?"

"She was taken to Kahului Animal Hospital."

"I'll call."

Looking up the number and calling gave Lei something to do as the elevator arrived and took them to the third floor. Lei was able to find out that Keiki was also in surgery, having the knife removed from her side. They had no further report on the dog's progress.

Lei's clothes felt too tight, her shoes pinching, her heart pounding. The doors opened on the third floor, a barren square of chairs and a stack of battered *National Geographic* and *People* magazines marking the waiting area. No one was at the nurse's desk behind a glass window.

"We just have to wait," Pono said, squeezing her

shoulder. "Sit. Breathe."

Lei sat and breathed, putting her head down between her knees, her mind racing. There was so much she didn't know. There was nothing she could do right now but pray. She folded her hands and rested her forehead on them, murmuring the Lord's Prayer over and over.

Pono worked his phone on the other side of the room, finally coming back. "I've got news for you."

"What?"

"Gerry and Torufu tracked down the two suspects we've been trying to nail for the Norwegian's murder. Guess where they were?"

"No idea."

"Hiding out at Manuel Okapa's house. Apparently, the three of them did the Norwegian."

"Talk about misdirected anger." Lei frowned. "Now they'll spend the rest of their lives in prison. How is Stevens's recruit, Mahoe, doing?"

"He's recovering. Gonna be okay." Pono sat down beside her. "Things seem to be wrapping up on the *heiau* case. Marcus Kamuela brought in Councilman Muapu, who is denying everything, of course. But Esther Ka`awai has also given her testimony, and she even knew the location of the artifacts on Oahu. The team went and found them all. So he doesn't have much of a leg to stand on."

"Good," Lei said, pressing her fingers into her eye sockets. "God, let them be okay, please." She knew her father would want to support her, but she lacked the energy to call him and tell him this latest development—it was too hard to even speak the words.

Swinging doors opened and a doctor came through, holding a chart. "Leilani Texeira?"

"Yes?" She sprang to her feet and almost keeled over, spots circling in her vision. Pono steadied her as the doctor approached.

"Michael Stevens is your husband?"

"Yes."

"I'm Dr. Salvato. Your husband's going to be okay. I had to order a transfusion because he'd lost a lot of blood, but the knife wound was shallow. It cut along his ribs under his arm, about six inches in length, but didn't penetrate any organs. His arm was also cut, but no permanent damage."

"Oh, thank God." Lei had to sit down again.

The doctor frowned. "You all right?"

"Yeah, just relieved."

"He's going to have a few more scars to add to his collection, is all. We strapped up his sprained ankle, too."

"When can I see him?"

"Now. He's still sedated, but comfortable."

Lei followed the doctor, but glanced back at Pono. Her former partner made a shooing motion with his fingers, telling her to go on.

The first thing she noticed was how pale Stevens was. His tan lay over his skin like a layer of paint. His cheeks were hollow, his dark hair mussed, and his long frame barely fit on the bed. She felt a surge of love so powerful it made her gasp.

The doctor hung the chart on the wall and nodded that she could approach. She took one of the molded-plastic chairs, dragged it over next to Stevens, and picked up his hand—the one with the wedding ring on it, still shiny and new.

He opened his eyes. "Lei?"

"I'm here." Her throat closed over the words, and she cleared it. "You sure took your time picking me up from the airport."

His mouth quirked up on one side. "Got held up by a ninja."

"I heard you're adding to the scar collection."

"Glad that's all it is. If it weren't for Keiki, you'd likely be a widow right now."

She lifted his hand and lay it against her cheek for a long moment. She pressed a kiss into his palm. "I love you."

He curled his hand away, lifted it to stroke her hair.

"Missed you. Come here and kiss me."

She stood from the chair, and leaned down to give him a peck on the lips. "There."

His hand, still tangled in her hair, tightened. His arm flexed, pulling her down onto him. She lost her balance, sprawling across him, and he gave a hiss of pain—but now his hand used the grip on her hair to turn her head, and his mouth met hers with hungry intent. Their kiss felt as necessary as CPR, and as life giving. Lei's body went slack and her eyes closed in surrender, even as she smelled the sweat of near-death on him—and maybe because of it.

"Ahem." A throat-clearing from the doorway.

Lei scrambled off of her husband and turned to face McGregor, his florid face impassive. Chun, his silent shadow, was the one to look a little embarrassed.

"We need to interview your husband regarding the attack," McGregor said.

Lei sat back down on the chair and picked up Stevens's hand again. "Interview away."

They fetched more chairs. Stevens worked his bed control to sit up straighter, and Lei gave him some water.

"When were you planning to tell me Anchara already had a husband and that he was the one who'd killed her?" Stevens asked. Even with the anesthesia, Lei felt the tension in him, the anger. She squeezed his hand in both of hers.

"We didn't know that," McGregor said. "We did know that a man matching the description of your attacker was the one to accompany her into the motel. We tracked the shroud and knew that he'd purchased the one that was found under her body—and two more. We've been looking for him ever since."

Lei said, "I know where another of those shrouds turned up—draped over my aunt's body in California. That leaves one shroud still unaccounted for."

"We heard about your aunt from Captain Omura," McGregor said. He made eye contact with her, and it seemed sincere. "Very sorry for your loss."

"Thank you," Lei said. Stevens's hand tightened on hers in support.

"Getting back to the attack. Tell us a blow-by-blow of what happened."

Stevens went through the harrowing moments in detail. Lei looked down at his hand, a strong, pleasing shape that she never tired of looking at. She concentrated on the tiny hairs on the back of it, the long fingers, the raised map of veins over muscle and bone. She thought of all that hand could do and shut her eyes on imagining it cold and dead, never touching or loving her again.

Focusing on Stevens's hand helped screen out how close she'd come to losing him and her beloved Keiki to a jealous maniac with knife skills.

Lei frowned, tuning in to catch the part of Stevens's story where the man had identified himself as Anchara's husband. "Michael. This means you and Anchara were never legally married. Didn't you check that out?" she asked.

"She told me she was being sold in marriage against her will to a man who was a known abuser in her village. That's why she fled and took the cruise ship job, which turned out to be a sex slavery ring. She said she'd never been married before, and I believed her. There was no way to check any of it."

"Doesn't change anything, I guess," Lei said, but somehow it did. Stevens was hers. Hers alone, and always had been.

"Back to the suspect. We have him down at the station, and we're looking for an interpreter, because he speaks limited English. What we want to know is how he knew where to find Anchara and how he knew where your home was. Could he be the one behind the shroud threats? Or do you think there's someone else involved?"

Lei told them about Terence Chang and the longstanding feud with the Chang family. "There's an open FBI case on Chang. I just checked with Special Agent Marcella Scott, who's working it. She said they haven't been able to pick anything up. He hasn't left the Big Island, and they even have surveillance on his Internet activities, without anything new. He's my best guess at who has the means, motive, and opportunity to go against us this way. He could have found this man, bankrolled his trip, fed him all the information he needed to kill Stevens and Anchara, paid for the nurse who planted the bomb at my aunt's house—all from the comfort of his back bedroom."

McGregor and Chun looked at each other. "We'll check out the rest of this and let you know what we get from Mookjai with an interpreter," McGregor said. "But he's lawyered up already, and he's a foreign citizen, so we're not hopeful. We agree someone else fed him information to help him navigate a strange country this well. He had a burner phone on him, and only a few numbers on that. We're running them down, but so far they're just other burners."

"So I'm guessing he gets deported and nothing happens to him," Stevens said.

"We're going to fight to keep him here and prosecute him for Anchara Mookjai's murder, but the evidence tying him to that crime scene is circumstantial. We can get him on attempted murder in your case."

"On a positive note, you're cleared of all suspicion," Chun said. "I thought that might brighten your day. You two will be parents soon."

"Yeah," Stevens said. "I guess so." He tightened his grip on Lei's hand.

They left, and Stevens gave her hand a tug. "Come back over here."

"Shouldn't we talk about the case? I'm not sure we're out of danger with another shroud floating around out there. And Anchara! She was already married!"

"I'm a bigamist," Stevens said, grinning. Lei gave him a little punch. The whole thing was terrible and tragic, but somehow Lei could tell Stevens felt as she did—their vows were only to each other now. "I know why she did what she did—she was desperate. But I never would have married her if I'd known she was already married to Mookjai."

"I know." Lei let him pull her in for another kiss, filled with promises of what they'd be doing when they were able. Finally, she sat back down on the chair. "I need to go check on Keiki."

"Go. I'm feeling it now, anyway. This old man needs a nap."

"I'll get some backup to make sure you're safe." She gave him one last kiss and went to the door, getting her phone out to make some calls.

She had to blink back tears at the sight of Pono, sitting on a chair outside, already on guard. "Got people lined up to keep an eye on him until he's discharged," her friend said. "Go check on your dog."

She didn't need any more encouragement.

Keiki was out of surgery by the time she got to the modest little animal hospital, and the technicians let her go back into the recovery room, where the big Rottweiler was still sedated to keep her wound stabilized.

"She's going to recover fine, if there's no infection," the vet told Lei. "I was able to remove the knife and repair the internal damage. Your husband made the right call leaving the blade in place."

Lei sat with the big dog for a long time, stroking her square head and playing with her silky ears. There with Keiki, alone in the antiseptic-, doggy-smelling room, Lei put her head down against her dog's warm side and cried all the tears she needed to, releasing the stress and grief of the last few weeks.

Chapter 31

S tevens and Lei sat on the couch the next evening as the news recapped the *heiau* case. Wendy Watanabe, bright in a turquoise suit, described the "bizarre plot" headed by Councilman Muapu to gather a secret museum of Hawaii's sacred artifacts to keep them from being lost to the elements or "the disrespect of outsiders." A clip of Muapu's square brown face, eyes glittering with conviction, was played.

"In the next hundred years, our most sacred places and the objects that represent our culture are going to be lost—to development, to the elements, to graffiti by kids who no longer remember how sacred they are. The museum was meant to protect that, to safeguard our history and preserve it for those of our blood to see and experience."

Watanabe came back on. "Mr. Muapu denies having any knowledge of the murder of one of the thieves he employed to steal the artifacts. In his statement to the press, he asks forgiveness for taking this action without bringing it before people for a vote."

"Wow," Lei said. She leaned against Stevens's good side as they ate chili and cornbread. "Seems like Muapu's not backing down. Going to try to spin this that he was doing it for everyone. I bet he even runs for reelection."

Stevens set his empty bowl down on the arm of the couch, but not where Keiki, lying on her dog bed with a cone around her neck, could reach it. He couldn't resist putting an arm around Lei, bringing her in against his good side. He couldn't get enough of being physically close to her. It had been only a day since he got out of the hospital, and he wasn't done thanking God that he was still alive. They'd spent most of the time he'd been home in bed, sleeping—and when he felt up to it, doing other things.

Lei's phone rang and she got up and answered it, picking up their bowls and taking them to the kitchen. He heard her greet her father.

He refocused on the news. They'd moved on to recap the arrest and capture of Red Toaman, Mana Guinamo, and Manuel Okapa in the slaying of the Norwegian art thief.

"Officials involved in the case tell us these men tracked the art thief and killed him on their own. Leaders in the Heiau Hui movement have denied any involvement in the brutal slaying."

A clip ran of Charles Awapuhi being interviewed. "I had nothing to do with that man's murder," he said, his diction perfect and face concerned. "I apologize publicly for holding the artifacts at my house on their way to the

museum, but I believed Muapu when he said he was
doing this to protect the culture."

"Wasn't it contradictory to be a part of stealing the
artifacts and also to be organizing a movement to protect
them—from yourself?" Watanabe inserted a microphone
back into his face.

"I see now that it was misguided," Awapuhi said. "But
I do believe that the sites must be guarded, so that our
heritage can be preserved."

Watanabe came back on. "In a positive turn of events
in all this, preservation experts from the Bishop Museum
in Honolulu are helping to reinstall the petroglyphs and
other artifacts to the *heiaus*, and a statewide law has been
drawn up declaring *heiaus* and sites with petroglyphs
to be historically significant and not to be developed.
Literature profiting from disclosing their locations is also
banned by the new state law, which will go forward for a
vote in the next session."

Stevens looked over into the kitchen, where Lei was
washing the dishes. "Did you hear that, Sweets?"

"What?" She came out, drying her hands. She was
wearing that peach silk robe he'd bought before their
wedding, and he liked the way it wrapped her like she was
a present he'd never get tired of opening.

"The state's banning mention of the sites in books like
Maui's Secrets and declaring the *heiaus* protected."

Someone rang the bell on the outer gate. Lei had increased the security measures at their little house, installing an exterior camera, intercom, and remote gate lock before Stevens got out of the hospital.

They both looked at the monitor near the kitchen door. A man with a truck was standing outside the gate, holding a clipboard. "Wonder who that is." Lei depressed the button to speak to the man. "Hi. What's your business?"

"Delivery of baby furniture from Anchara Mookjai," the man said.

Lei gave Stevens a quick glance, then replied into the intercom. "I'll be right out to help you." To Stevens she said, "I know what this is about. Just rest. I'll handle this."

He frowned at the mention of his ex's name, especially in connection with baby furniture, wondering what was going on. He snapped his fingers, and Keiki came over, moving stiffly, and sat at his feet. He put a hand on her collar to keep her from going any farther toward the door.

The news dragged his attention back as Watanabe wrapped up the story and moved on. "Following up with another brutal murder on Maui, a suspect in the murder of pregnant woman Anchara Mookjai has been identified. Danan Mookjai was the pregnant woman's husband, and a foreign national. He is being held indefinitely without bail until agreements can be made about his extradition, or if he will face charges in the United States for Mookjai's murder and the attempted murder of a police officer. This case draws attention to the ongoing problem with domestic violence here in Hawaii, and worldwide."

The front door opened, and Lei backed in, carrying one end of a heavy-looking, hand-carved cradle, the delivery man the other. They carried the cradle into the baby's room, and Stevens's hand curled around his Glock as he tracked the movements of the deliveryman, still worried that, even with Mookjai in custody, some new threat would come against them.

One shroud was still unaccounted for.

"Let's just put the rest on the porch," Lei directed the deliveryman. "We have to find space and room for it all."

Once the man had left and the gate was locked again, Lei came back and flopped down beside him. Stevens narrowed his eyes at her. "What's all this?"

"Anchara's baby furniture for Kiet. I broke into her place when I was looking for his name. She'd prepared so beautifully for him that it broke my heart when the landlord said it was all going to Goodwill. So I told him we'd find a family with a new baby that could use it. He called me, and I gave him some money and told him to have it delivered here at the end of the month. Figured baby Kiet should know how much his mama loved him."

Stevens reached over, played with one of her curls, moved by her gesture. "I love you for doing that." He turned to look over his shoulder. "But we already have a lot of baby stuff. We can return some of it, I guess."

"We might need it all," she said. Her eyes were flecked with shades of brown from umber to burnt sienna, and they'd never looked so vulnerable to him. She took his hand gently and placed it on her belly. "We're going to need a lot of baby stuff."

His mouth went dry and his throat tightened. "What are you telling me?"

"I'm pregnant. Yeah, I know. Terrible timing. But I'm pretty sure it happened before we knew about Kiet." She looked away, and he saw her lips tremble. "Anyway, it's too late now."

He brought his hand up and turned her face to his. Tears hung on her lower lashes like tiny pearls as he breathed words into her mouth. "You've made me the happiest man in the world."

She threw herself on him, and he grunted with pain but took her in his arms anyway, where he knew she needed to be. He submitted to a rain of kisses, sniffles, and inarticulate explanations about how she'd been feeling strange ever since that "really special night," a pregnancy test she'd done in California, and her father moving in with them to a bigger house.

He sat up at that. "What?"

"Aunty left me her house, and Dad wants us to sell it

and buy a bigger place here. He'll come live with us and be our 'manny.' He can take care of the kids while we work."

Stevens felt a slow grin pulling up his cheeks. "That's the second best thing I've heard all day. It's so crazy, it could work. Your dad plus Keiki equals some pretty good child care plus security."

"I'm so glad you like the idea." They kissed some more. He fiddled with the ribbed tank shirt she'd thrown on to move the furniture.

"I liked you better in the robe."

"I have some more news. Dad called to tell me Aunty's memorial is next week, and the ME's office has declared Aunty's death to be natural causes." Straddling his lap, she snuggled up against him. He could tell she was being careful not to put weight on his injury. "Heart failure is what they're saying, related to her cancer. I have a feeling Aunty just let herself go after she told me what she told me."

"What did she tell you?"

"That she and my grandmother Yumi hired the contract hit on Kwon."

Stevens's arms tightened involuntarily around her. "That's right, she told you that. Your family is something else."

"My family is your family now."

"I guess so. A scary thought."

"I know."

"Speaking of family, my bro, Jared, called me in the hospital. He's transferring in a few months to a job with Kahului Station."

"Good. It'll be fun to have him here. The more, the better. I guess I better make some reservations for the memorial."

"Why don't we go get Kiet on the way back from the memorial?"

She went still in his arms. "I'm scared."

"Of a baby?" He smiled, dropping a kiss into her hair. "Guess you better get over that."

"No. Scared I won't—love him. Be a good mom to him. Same old shit." Agitated, she climbed off Stevens to pace. "I'm weirded out about being pregnant, too. But I'm even more worried I won't have the right feelings for Kiet."

Stevens shut his eyes, remembering the tidal wave of emotion that had overtaken him in the hospital, holding his son in his arms. Kiet was hard not to love. "I have a feeling it's going to be fine."

Chapter 32

Lei held Stevens's hand too tight on the porch of the foster home on Oahu. She knew she was doing that, but she couldn't loosen her grip. The social worker had finally finished with her verifications yesterday and had given them permission to take Kiet home. She looked around, at the late-afternoon sun slanting across a bright bougainvillea hedge around the modest house. She smelled the rich sweetness of the plumeria blossoms on the tree beside the porch as Stevens pushed the doorbell.

Lei felt wrung out by the stress of the memorial. Hearing there was no progress in tracking the mysterious nurse who'd left her aunt dead, planted with a bomb and a shroud, hadn't helped. She and Stevens had stayed in California an extra few days, helping Wayne pack the house and clean it up to put on the market, and that had also taken a toll. Lei was both emotionally and physically drained.

Not the best time to meet her new stepson.

A woman with a kind, freckled face and fading red hair unraveling from a ponytail came to the door. Round blue eyes blinked at them.

"Welcome." She swung the door wide. "We've been expecting you. I'm Sally Goodwin, and this is my husband, Burt."

Burt was large and on the upside of fifty, and the baby tucked into the crook of his arm looked ridiculously tiny, though Lei knew he was now three weeks old.

"Glad you two could make it. We're sorry to see the little guy go, but happy he's going to be with family."

"Thanks for your kind words and for your kindness to our son," Stevens said, a tremor in his voice. "Can I hold him?"

"Of course." Burt handed the child over to Stevens. Lei had never seen the expression that came over her husband's face before: "dreamy" was the word to describe it. He took the swaddled baby, tucking him against his good side tenderly. Lei felt her throat close at what a beautiful sight it was.

Sally tapped Lei on the shoulder. "I have his things all packed up. He doesn't have much. Do you have a car seat for the ride to the airport and for the plane?"

"Uh, no. We have one on Maui, but I guess we didn't realize..." Lei felt inadequate and clumsy as the woman handed her a plastic seat shaped roughly like a scoop with a handle and a cloth shopping bag filled with diapers and other accouterments.

"I made him an extra bottle for the trip, but I hope you

have a diaper bag at home."

"Yes, we do," Lei said. "Thanks for all of this. For keeping him."

"Well, this part is difficult for us. We get attached to the babies, you know, and he's such a happy, easy baby, we're having a hard time saying goodbye. So it's better if you two just get on the road." Lei saw that Sally was fighting tears as she thrust the items into Lei's arms. "Travel safe. Send us a picture now and again."

Lei and Stevens got back into the taxi. Lei felt stunned as the Goodwins shut their door. Stevens put the baby into the car seat and fumbled with the buckles until the taxi driver got out and showed him how to strap the seat in, facing backward.

"We have some extra time before the plane," Lei said. "Let's go visit my grandfather Soga. Introduce them." Stevens nodded, Lei gave the driver the address, and they finally got on the road. Lei sat on one side of the baby seat and Stevens on the other. They both looked down at Kiet.

He'd lifted a fist to his mouth and was gnawing on it, and his blue-gray-brown eyes were trained on Lei's face. She gazed back at him and reached over to brush the thick tuft of upright black hair. "He looks like a little cockatiel or a punk rocker, with this mohawk."

"His eyes still haven't changed color," Stevens said. "They said this color could be brown, or green, or something in between."

Kiet hadn't taken his strangely compelling eyes off Lei's face. There was nothing uncomfortable in his gaze, just a steady acceptance and mild curiosity, as if he'd look at her all day and that would be enough. She brushed his cheek with her finger, feeling how peachy-soft it was, and he turned his face, mouthing for her finger.

"I know what that is," Stevens said. "Rooting reflex. Helps the baby find the nipple when he's nursing."

"Oh," Lei said, and she could swear she felt her own nipples prickling, as if bearing witness to what he said. Impulsively, she leaned forward, put her face close to the baby's, into the space between his neck and shoulder. She inhaled the scent, some potent baby perfume that she couldn't get enough of. She felt that melting sensation around her heart—it was his smell that won her over. "I want to hold him."

Stevens grinned. "He has that effect on people."

Kiet just blinked his eyes at them and sucked his fist.

They pulled up at Lei's grandfather Soga Matsumoto's modest home near Punchbowl. Lei unbuckled the baby from his straps and hefted him up, supporting his head, against her shoulder. That wonderful baby smell filled her nostrils as his light, springy, soft weight settled in her arms.

Getting out of the taxi, one foot still in the car and

one on the sidewalk, Lei realized this baby boy was hers. As much hers as he was Stevens's. She was the only mama he'd ever have, ever know, ever remember. For the first time, that felt good to her. "Thanks, Anchara," she whispered, wishing every good feeling these days wasn't chased by tears.

Lei walked up the cement path, leaving Stevens to pay the taxi driver and deal with the car seat and belongings. She put her finger on the doorbell, and a gentle chime sounded inside. She stroked the incredibly soft back of the baby's head as she waited, one arm tucked under his protruding rump. Holding Kiet made her feel something totally new—peaceful but strong at the same time. She turned her head to breathe in the smell of his tender neck. "Delicious," she whispered.

Lei heard her grandfather's shuffling steps. The door opened, and the stern visage brightened at the sight of her. "Surprised me, Lei. I wasn't expecting you. Whose baby is this?"

"Your new great-grandson," Lei said.

Soga broke into a huge grin and gestured her and Stevens, loaded with baby stuff, inside. "How is this possible?" Soga asked. "But give him to me while you tell me."

So they told him the story, and that another baby was on the way, and he served them tea and wiped his eyes over the news. They fed Kiet and explored the mysteries of bottles and diaper changing.

Eventually, Soga drove them to the airport. Kiet fell asleep in the carrier and caused comment and interest wherever they went. On the plane, with the baby sleeping in his seat between them, Lei looked over at Stevens. "I have a feeling God is breaking us in gently. Are all babies this good?"

"I don't think so." Stevens reached across the sleeping infant and took her hand. "Are you still worried? About loving Kiet?"

"I didn't know there was this much love in the world," Lei said. "It changes everything."

And it did.

Acknowledgments:

Thanks to my awesome team: Noelle Pierce, Bonny
Ponting, and Holly Robinson, faithful beta readers,
retired Captain David Spicer, who helped me with police
procedure, Penina Lopez, my copyeditor, and of course,
my Facebook friend readers, who gave me the idea for the
heiau desecrations!

I also beg forgiveness that poor Keiki had to get hurt
again. Recently Nalu, our faithful Chihuahua terrier and
the model for Keiki, was injured in a pit bull attack. As
we were weeping over her, I was reminded again of the
powerful bond between people and their pets. This book
was an emotional book to write, filled with the "dark
lava" of our most powerful emotions, and I hope you'll
stick around for the ride as we move on to *Fire Beach*, Lei
Crime #8. Excerpt follows!

With much aloha,

Toby Neal

Sign up for Book Lovers Club and news of
upcoming books at **http://www.tobyneal.net/.**

Watch for these titles:

Lei Crime Series:
Blood Orchids   (book 1)
Torch Ginger   (book 2)
Black Jasmine   (book 3)
Broken Ferns   (book 4)
Twisted Vine   (book 5)
Shattered Palms   (book 6)
Dark Lava   (book 7)
Fire Beach   (book 8) coming Fall 2014
Companion Series:
Stolen in Paradise:
        a Lei Crime Companion Novel (Marcella Scott)
Unsound
        A novel (Dr. Caprice Wilson)
Wired in Paradise
        A Lei Crime Companion Novel
        (Sophie Ang coming soon)
Middle Grade/Young Adult
Island Fire (coming soon)
Wallflower Diaries
        Case of the Missing Girl
        (currently on submission with agent)
Contemporary Fiction/Romance:
Somewhere on Maui
        An Accidental Matchmaker Novel
Nonfiction:
Under an Open Sky
        Essays on Nature (coming soon)
Children of Paradise
        A Memoir of Growing Up in Hawaii
        (coming soon)

Sign up for Book Lovers Club and news of upcoming
books at **http://www.tobyneal.net/**

Fire Beach Sample

Lei Crime #8

By Toby Neal

Fire was poetry. Flame was destiny. The Fireman smiled to himself as he said the words out loud, tasting the way they sounded.

Heading for an ignition site brought that poetic side out in him. Next to him, on the floor of the battered old truck, a rusty gas can rattled as he drove down the deserted sugarcane hauling road. Harsh red dust rose from the potholed dirt as Maui's strong trade winds kicked up already.

He'd chosen a cane field they'd be burning in a week or two, yellowing since the company stopped watering, fifteen-foot flowering tassels of mature sugarcane waving like mares' tails. But if he burned it first, the cane company would lose their harvest, two years of work and thousands of dollars. That was part of his agenda. But only part of it.

He pulled the dust-covered truck over at one of the points of origin he'd chosen. He splashed the area with a mix of diesel to cling to the sugarcane, plus gas for ignitability, and tossed a match. He jumped back into the truck with that kick of adrenaline, and floored it to the next ignition site where he repeated the process. And a third time.

The Fireman looked back down the road into the wall of rising flames. It was catching faster than he'd planned. Maybe this one would jump the highway, really put a thrill into the Road to Hana for the tourists.

He stood there and savored a feeling of power as crackling energy released all around him. The sweet-smelling, burnt-sugary smoke soared into the higher elevations and hit colder air, coalescing into mushroom-cloud shapes. White cattle egrets flew in, landing in the road to feast on fleeing insects. A familiar roaring filled his ears as the heat fanned his cheeks.

The fire was a creature of beauty. He extended a hand to the flames, enjoying the multi-sensory experience he'd unleashed—and a back swirl of wind blew a tongue of embers to sear that hand like the lash of a whip. He gave a cry, and hurled the gas can he was still holding into the oncoming inferno before it could explode.

He leaped into the truck, threw it into gear and peeled away. He couldn't help ducking as the gas can exploded behind him, metal shrapnel hitting the vehicle like terrible burning hail. He floored it and pulled away toward safety, bouncing crazily down the potholed dirt road toward the highway. He lifted his hand, seared across the back in a stripe that looked like raw steak.

He licked the burn, tasting ash and his own blood.

"Bitch. How I love you."

Behind his racing truck, the wall of flame swept forward into the field with a crackling howl like a thousand demons in chorus. Insects, birds, mongeese, rodents and one lone man fled uselessly before it.

Lieutenant Michael Stevens picked up a call at his office in Haiku. "Bro, it's Jared." His little brother's voice sounded amped up and hoarse. "I thought I'd better call you. You know that cane fire this morning?"

Jared was a firefighter with Kahului Station, recently transferred to Maui to get away from the holocaust of summer fires in LA—but from what Stevens could tell, Maui hadn't been the mellow posting Jared was hoping for.

"Yeah, I saw the smoke. Smelled it too. Thought they were just doing a scheduled burn." Maui was one of the last places in the United States still growing and harvesting sugar. The plantation operated at an annual loss in part because of the vast amount of water and resources it took to produce even a single pound of "white gold." The harvesting process was also pollution-heavy. It began with burning fields to get rid of excess leaves, leaving the stalks behind, heavy with syrup, to be processed.

"No, we think it's an arson burn." Jared coughed. Must have inhaled some smoke, Stevens thought. "We've almost got it contained. Remember, I told you there have been at least three of these arson cane fires in the last month. Anyway, there's a fatality from this one. Some guy was sleeping in the field. Tourists found him on the side of the road, crispy as a chicken wing."

Stevens winced inwardly, trying not to imagine what "crispy as a chicken wing" looked like in human form. Likely he'd get to see firsthand. He stood, reaching for the shoulder holster hung on the wall to strap into. "So it's a homicide, if that was an arson fire."

"Right. I thought you'd better know since it's in your district."

As if on cue, his radio crackled with the call to respond. "Thanks for the heads-up, Jared. If I don't see you at the scene, I'll see you at dinner tonight. Still coming, right?"

"Right. I'll bring dessert." Jared had begun making weekly visits to have dinner with Stevens, his wife Lei, their son Kiet, and Lei's dad Wayne who lived with them and provided child care.

Stevens hung up and stuck his head outside his office to holler to his veteran detective. "Ferreira! Oh-four on Hana Highway!"

They got on the road in Stevens's brown Bronco, cop light strobing on the dash. Ferreira, a middle-aged man of portly build and grizzled visage, worked the radio getting as much information as he could. "Ambulance is there. Too late, but at least they can keep the lookie-loos away."

"How far is the vic from the fire?"

"On the edge of the highway. Fire burned up to the road, like they usually do. Fire department is working on keeping it from spreading."

"This will add more tension to the whole no-burn movement," Stevens said thoughtfully, rubbing the tiny purple heart tattoo in the crook of his elbow with a thumb as he drove. A vocal faction on the island had begun protesting the traditional method of harvest, citing asthma and a host of other environmental concerns.

"I don't see how this has anything to do with that," Ferreira said, frowning. "These burns are just some misguided kids making trouble. Don't see how arson that's just killed a man has anything to do with the controlled burns the cane company does for harvest— something they've been doing for a hundred years."

"Okay. I hope you're right." Stevens knew Ferreira was from a big family that had come over to Hawaii in one of the original immigration waves, working their way up from the "cane camp" shantytowns to powerful positions in local government and solid occupation of the middle class. He'd heard Ferreira lament the demise of sugarcane agriculture in Maui often enough not to argue with the man. He also knew proponents of the change to machine harvesters would make the argument that the drying fields in preparation for controlled burning provided tempting targets for arson.

They sped down the winding two lane highway that followed the windswept coastline. Even responding to a call and driving at top speed, Stevens sneaked a few looks out his window at the ocean, a tapestry of blues from cobalt to the palest turquoise at the foam-flecked shore. Surfers, windsurfers, and kiteboarders all played along this coastline, and the colorful sails leaping over the waves reminded him of darting butterflies.

The fire was still burning in the charred field as they came around a corner to where barricades had been set up, diverting traffic along an old road that connected above the beach town of Paia. Stevens pulled up and parked the Bronco, snapping on gloves and picking up his crime kit as Ferreira did the same. "Booties would be good," Ferreira said, slipping on a pair of elastic-edged blue material shoe covers.

"Good idea. Though I'm not sure how well these are going to hold up on this ground," Stevens said, looking at the still-smoking rubble that lined the road.

Just as Jared had told him, the fire had burnt up to the highway, eating everything in its path down to the black ribbon of road. Fortunately it hadn't jumped the highway. The fire zone was very close to the oceanfront community of Kuau, a cluster of residences along the coast. Stevens had spent the last year at a little apartment in Kuau and had an affection for the ragtag collection of older plantation-style homes interspersed with oceanfront mansions.

They walked on the road and approached the body, draped in a white cloth that was turning red in patches from body fluids.

The medical examiner, Dr. Gregory, had beaten them to the scene. Squatted beside the body, he was wearing an aloha shirt decorated with cartoon menehunes, his attention fixed on the grisly sight before him.

There was an unpleasant, oily quality to the smoked-barbeque odor of the body as Stevens inadvertently sniffed the air. He was glad Lei hadn't had to go out on this call. Four months pregnant, his wife's worst symptom seemed to be oversensitivity to smells. This one would definitely have had her running for the nearest toilet.

"Ah, Lieutenant," Dr. Gregory said, looking up. Magnifying glasses made him look like a bug until he pushed the optics up onto his reddened forehead. "Got a few interesting things about this body."

Stevens gave a nod to Ferreira to go find the fire investigator. They'd be relying heavily on the fire department's assessment of the evidence found at the burn site. He squatted beside Dr. Gregory as the man uncovered the body further. Bits of clothing and skin clung to the sheet. "I wish they wouldn't have covered the body with this," the ME fussed. "Losing trace here."

"So this is what human barbeque looks like," Stevens said. "Not pretty." He'd seen burn victims before, but not since he moved to Hawaii five years ago. "Jared told me that's what he looked like."

"Not pretty at all. Look at the feet."

Stevens looked. The toes were burned off, the feet curled as tendons retracted. "No shoes?"

"Exactly. I wonder if that's significant. Maybe that's why he got so close to the road and yet still couldn't outrun the fire."

Stevens looked around the corpse, didn't see anything beside him, no marks on the ground. "Guess he collapsed here from the smoke and then the fire got him."

"I think he was running, and on fire," Gregory said. "His feet are more burned than his hands, and the back of his clothing is completely gone."

Stevens tried not to imagine the man's terrible death, instead focusing on next steps. "Did you check for ID in his pockets?"

"I need to go over the whole body at the lab," Gregory said. "The cloth that's left is burnt right onto his skin. Anything still on him will be degrees of melted. I need to keep it all clean and preserved. Anything else you need here? Because I'd like to bag him."

"Are the fire investigators done?"

"We should check." Gregory radioed, and a young

man, moving with athletic grace in spite of heavy fire-retardant gear, broke away from a knot of firefighters and came their way.

"Tim Owen. Fire investigator for the county of Maui." He introduced himself, and Stevens shook his gauntleted hand.

"Lieutenant Stevens. You already know Dr. Gregory."

"Yes."

"I want to bag the body, Tim," Gregory said. "Need anything more?"

"No. I'm still determining the point of origin, though the directionality of the char pattern makes me think it started somewhere on the cane haul road. This guy was somewhere in this field when it went up. Maybe a homeless guy, sleeping in the cane. No shoes makes me think so."

"So what did the body tell you?" Dr. Gregory, the ME, asked. Stevens thought he might be testing the fire investigator's assessment.

"Wasn't trapped in the flames for an extended period—see, the arms are in fairly good shape." Owen pointed out the folded, crabbed arms. "His face is even recognizable. The feet are worked over, but they were exposed, maybe he ran across some burning area with bare feet. Beneath the body, he's got fabric intact. So my take is, the fire woke him up but he was probably dazed from smoke. These cane fires move fast, and he wasn't moving fast enough. He collapsed, here, and the fire flashed over him. Burned awhile in this spot, enough to cook his feet pretty good."

Gregory nodded. "Good."

"We don't get many vagrants or homeless sleeping in the cane." Stevens said. "Lots of spiders in there." The cane spiders were famous in Hawaii. Hairy and brown, with long slender legs, they grew six to eight inches in diameter and dominated their home in the sugarcane. "The cane is sharp. Not much camping in there between the spiders and leaves sharp enough to cut you."

"Seems like that's a good thing. I'm new here, so just getting the 'lay of the land' so to speak, but I'm already concerned with so many of these arson burns happening. Makes me think someone's targeting the sugarcane company," Owen said.

"Could be," Stevens said. "Do you have any inspections or interviews set up with them?"

"Matter of fact, I do. Tomorrow morning, talking with upper management at the Puunene Mill, seeing if they have any idea about who might have it in for them." Owen wiped his sweating face with a bandanna, and Stevens could see how young he was, and new to the island, he might not get that far talking to the locals without support.

"Well, now that this is a homicide case, how about Ferreira and I tag along?"

"That would be great." Stevens didn't think he was imagining the note of relief in the young man's voice. "Can't understand the pidgin when people get going."

Ferreira stepped up, stuck out his hand. "Joshua Ferreira. Know a lot of people at the company. I can help."

"Excellent."

They exchanged details for the next morning's meeting while Dr. Gregory and Tanaka, his assistant, got the body bagged with the help of the EMTs who had come out on the call. Stevens was relieved when the body, still reeking even in the bag, was on the way to the morgue.

Human barbeque wasn't something he ever wanted to see again. A bad feeling clung to him, along with the smell.

Lei Texeira drove up the winding two-lane road through rural Haiku on Maui's north shore. Tall eucalyptus trees, giant tree ferns, wandering vines, and bright sprays of ginger and heliconia bordered the road. It was a mellow thirty-minute drive from her workplace, Maui Police Station in downtown Kahului, to the home she and Stevens had bought in the countryside area. Her flagging energy lifted as she turned up the graveled driveway. Coming home always did that for her, especially now that her father, Wayne, had moved to Maui and was taking care of baby Kiet during the day.

Their new house was set back from the road behind an automatic gate. She hit the buttons and retracted it. The fence around the property was ten feet high, made of cedar, and provided both protection and privacy. Keiki, her battle-scarred Rottweiler, greeted the truck with happy barks and ran alongside as she drew up to the house.

"New" wasn't actually the right word for the house. It was forty years old, surrounded by fruit-bearing trees, and built in the sprawling plantation-style she and Stevens loved. It had been added onto so the original square had multiplied. Still, the size and acreage would have made it an impossible investment for a young couple just starting out if Lei's Aunty Rosario hadn't left Lei her bungalow in California as an inheritance. Wayne had helped them sell it after Aunty's recent death to buy the house, and now they carried a small, manageable mortgage. The property even had a small *"ohana"* cottage, where Wayne lived.

She pulled into the open garage, beeped the truck locked, and went up the steps to the security door. "Hey Dad," she called, unlocking the steel-grilled door. Even out here in the country, they weren't safe. An unknown enemy they'd taken to calling the 'shroud killer' was still at large, and until he was found, they needed to take every precaution.

"Hey, Sweets," her dad called from the kitchen. "He's

excited to see you." Lei heard the baby yell, "Ba-ba-ba!"

"I'm coming!" Lei exclaimed, slipping her shoes off onto the rack beside the front door. "Let me just drop off my weapon." She padded quickly to the bedroom, draped the shoulder holster over the headboard of the king-sized bed, emptying her badge and accouterments into a basket on the side table. She and Stevens were going to have to start locking up their weapons soon, but they had a few months more until Kiet began crawling around and getting into everything.

Lei was eager to get a shower, but Kiet was waiting. She hurried across the polished wood floor of the living room to the kitchen, and broke into a smile at the sight of her stepson in his chair seat on the table, waving his hands, one tooth shining like a pearl in the big grin he gave her.

"Who's my handsome boy?" She smiled into Kiet's jade-dark, smoky green eyes. His shock of black hair always stood on end, and it quivered like a rooster's tail as she unstrapped him from the bouncy chair. The baby immediately grabbed her curls with both hands, giggling as she lifted him, blowing on his tummy. He kicked his legs and giggled some more, and she hugged him close, turning to her father. "He's in a good mood, Dad."

Wayne was checking something on the stove. By the smell, she guessed it was teriyaki chicken. "He's had a great day. Now that tooth is out, he's back to being our happy boy."

Lei put the baby on her hip, and took one of his chubby hands in hers and pretended to waltz around the kitchen. Kiet yelled with excitement.

"Don't get him too riled up before dinner, or he'll throw the food. Remember what happened last time," Wayne said.

"Oh yeah." Lei snuggled her face into Kiet's neck and blew, and he giggled again. "He'll calm down. I have to go shower anyway, in a minute."

"He's not going to want to let you out of his sight."

"Is that so?" Lei swung Kiet around in front of her, and he laughed again.

"I'll give him his bath in the sink. That'll distract him," Wayne turned on the water.

"Until Daddy gets home," Lei said. Stevens had a different way with Kiet than she did, but the baby seemed to enjoy being with his dad just as much.

Wayne ran the sink full of warm water and Lei undressed the baby, stripping off his onesie and diaper. Wayne, his smile indulgent, checked the water temperature with his wrist, and gestured for Lei to bring him over.

"Come on in, the water's fine, little man," he said, taking his grandchild, but the minute Kiet's feet touched the water, the baby drew them up against his body, squinching his face. "Oh, not warm enough?" Wayne added more hot water, holding the baby close.

Lei left them sorting that out and went back to the bathroom off the master bedroom. She showered, and as she did these days, checked in with the changes in her body. Her breasts were a size larger and tender, and her belly had a fullness to it that had tightened the waistband of her jeans. Another thing no one had told her about pregnancy—how taut her uterus was, like she was growing a coconut in there. Other than occasional nausea and an acute reaction to smells, Lei felt great.

It was a strange feeling that her body knew what to do all on its own. She still felt surprised that this was the direction her life had gone—marriage, motherhood, living in a house with her dad as the 'manny'—but she couldn't imagine another life, now. The grief that she wasn't sharing this with her beloved aunt still came over her in waves, and this time she shut her eyes and turned her face into the flow of water from the shower, letting the sorrow move through her.

She was out of the shower and playing with Kiet out on the porch when Stevens drove up in his Bronco. Sitting in the old porch rocking chair, she turned Kiet outward as Stevens got out of the truck. The baby flexed his legs, hopping and reaching toward his father. "Ba-ba-ba!"

"Hey, little man." Stevens came up on the porch, leaning down to kiss the baby. Lei drew back, sniffing, before he could kiss her.

"Yuck. Shower first. Been near a fire?"

"Yeah. You saw the smoke earlier?"

"Sure did. Another cane fire. It was out by the time I passed it."

"Fire caught a body this time. I'll tell you when I'm out of the shower and you'll let me kiss you." He winked as he went inside. Kiet bounced and strained after his father as Stevens disappeared into the house.

Lei spun the baby around. "He'll be back. In the meantime, you'll have to make do with me."

Kiet grinned, grabbing a handful of her hair and putting it in his mouth. She was still detaching it as she made her way back to the kitchen. "Can I help you with anything, Dad?"

"Nope. Tell that husband of yours dinner's ready in fifteen minutes." Wayne was tossing a salad. He'd learned kitchen skills in prison, and been on kitchen duty for a year, he'd told her one day. He prepared healthy meals for the family five nights a week, kept the house picked up, and took care of the baby during the day. Lei insisted on paying him a small salary and he had his own cottage. So far, the arrangement seemed to be working out. As far as Lei was concerned, it was close to perfect, and the busyness seemed to be helping Wayne stay distracted from the loss of his sister.

"I'll go tell Stevens," Lei said. She tried to put the baby in his bouncy seat, but he grunted and writhed and arched his back, so she toted him back into the bathroom, opening the shower to say to Stevens, "Dinner in fifteen. Is your brother still coming?"

"Said he was," Stevens said, not turning around, and she took a minute to enjoy the view of his long, muscular back as he rinsed his hair under the flow of water. Then Kiet pulled her hair again, and Lei sighed as she turned away. Chances to join Stevens in that oversized shower were few and far between nowadays, with the baby to keep entertained and her father always around.

She heard the beep-beep-beep on the control panel by the front door that told her someone had punched in the code and activated the gate—probably Jared. Only a handful of friends had the code. Lei felt her spirits lift— she enjoyed Jared's company, and his presence at their family dinners livened things up.

She walked out onto the porch as Jared drove up in the lifted tan Tacoma he drove, pipe racks on the truck stacked with his 'toys'—a couple of surfboards, a stand-up paddleboard, and a single-man canoe.

"Hey bro," Lei called as he got out of the vehicle. She held up Kiet's hand and waved it at him. Jared grinned, walking toward her with the swift grace he shared with Stevens. He had similar height and blue eyes, but more regular and chiseled features, a leanness that looked

whipcord strong, and as a firefighter he spent time
working out that Stevens didn't put in. When he wasn't at
the station he was out enjoying the ocean sports of Maui.
All of that added up to spectacular.

"Hey sis. Hope you weren't the one cooking," Jared
said, with that wicked grin that Lei knew had kicked a lot
of hearts into overdrive. She pretended to punch him in
the rock-hard midsection and he folded comically, making
Kiet laugh.

"You know better than that," Lei said. "Take your
nephew, please. He's eating my hair again."

"He has good taste," Jared said. "Hey, buddy." He
pried Kiet's hands out of Lei's hair and lifted him up.
"How's my favorite future firefighter?"

"He's going into something safe. Like accounting,"
Stevens called from inside the house. "Stop that evil talk."

Jared grinned again, heading into the house with the
baby, and Lei racked her brain for who she could set
him up with. Sophie Ang? Her friend was still single,
though it had seemed like there might have been some
sparks with Alika Wolcott, Ang's MMA fighting coach...
Lei tried to imagine her serious tech-agent friend with
daredevil, fun-loving Jared. They were so different, it just
might work.

She followed Jared into the house and helped set the
table while Jared and Stevens discussed the fire and the

"human chicken wing" found on the side of the road. "What do you think of the new fire investigator? Tim Owen?" Stevens asked.

"Seems to know his stuff. I've taken him out stand-up paddling. Since we're both new to the island, we've been getting out on the ocean together."

"I envy your schedule," Stevens said. It wasn't the first time he'd said that, Lei thought. Maybe the time had come for the two of them to just work the hours they were supposed to—but she doubted they would be able to stick with those kinds of resolutions the next time a big case came along.

"Thanks for making dinner, Dad," Lei said, kissing her father's leathery cheek quickly as she took a large casserole dish swimming with teriyaki chicken from him. "This looks so good."

"Easy stuff," Wayne said. "Hard to go wrong with good ingredients."

"Hey, Mr. Texeira, this looks great!" Jared said. He'd handed Kiet off to Stevens and took a pot of rice from Wayne. "Thanks so much for having me."

"Always room and food for family," Wayne said. "It's past time you started calling me Wayne, already. Hope you brought that dessert you promised me last week."

"Oh yeah, thanks for reminding me. I left it in the truck."

Jared took off, and Lei quirked a brow at her father. "What's he bringing?"

"Surprise. Let's go to the table while the food's hot."

They sat down around the picnic table on the covered back deck, mercifully screened from mosquitoes, and Stevens was able to get Kiet into his bouncy seat. The baby still needed too much support to sit in the high chair, so he was positioned on the seat on the bench.

"My turn to feed you, tonight," Stevens said to Kiet, tying on the boy's bib. Lei loved how they traded everything off with the baby.

"His rice cereal's in the microwave," Wayne said, carrying a big wooden bowl of salad past Lei to set on the table as she fetched the baby's bowl of cereal. Jared returned, with something in a brown paper bag that he stowed in the freezer.

They ate, sharing snippets about the day. Jared told them about the rash of arson cane fires. "There've been four of these, as you guys must have seen in the news. But now that there's been a homicide, it takes things up a notch. With you guys working with Tim, hopefully we'll get the arsonist sooner rather than later."

Wayne shook his silver-shot, curly head. "Homeless guy had to be pretty desperate, sleeping in a cane field."

"Just what I said," Stevens replied. "It'll be interesting to see if there's more to it than that." Lei watched him feed Kiet a mouthful of rice cereal with the soft plastic baby spoon. Kiet smacked his thighs in excitement, then tried to grab the spoon. "Catch it with your mouth, little man," Stevens said, smiling as he got another bite into the baby.

Lei put her hand on Stevens's thigh, kneading the muscles there. His patience and tenderness with Kiet made her love him in new ways. But happy scenes like this always reminded her of Anchara, Kiet's murdered mother, Stevens's ex-wife. The baby's presence with them was wholly due to tragedy. Her killer had been caught, but Lei still thought there was more to the picture than the man had ever confessed.

But, maybe he *had* been the shroud killer. After he was taken into custody, things had gone quiet. In four months, there had been nothing further after an escalating series of events. Lei took a bite of salad, wondering if she could get away to her computer after dinner. She had a secret she was working on, and there would be hell to pay if Stevens found out about it.

To Be Continued, Fall 2014.

Sign up for Book Lovers Club and news of upcoming books at http://www.tobyneal.net/